He turned. "You have words for me, ma'am?" His brown eyes flashed warning behind his little glasses.

"You have broke into my shop! I shall call the constable!"

"Your door stood open. I found it so, as it was this morning. See to it, ma'am, if you wish to prevent unwanted visitors. As to the constable, call him if you please. I am taking this boy."

"You shall not. He is mine."

"Show me his indentures."

"Why, I…"

"The boy has no papers with you. He is not a slave to be oppressed and beaten, and he is not yours."

"You cannot take him!"

"I shall. Indeed, I do you a favor in saving you the trouble of caring for him." He tipped his hat. "However, if you have cause for complaint, seek out Mr. Benjamin Franklin of Philadelphia. Come, Nick." And with that he drew the boy into the dark night, to a waiting carriage which hastened off along the London cobbles.…

RAVE REVIEWS FOR *BENJAMIN FRANKLIN AND A CASE OF CHRISTMAS MURDER:*

"A very entertaining book...A good deal of exceptional dialogue in the syntax of the times, a fair smattering of social history, and some excellent Christmas lore...and a terrific ending, with a great deal of danger on the ice of the frozen Thames."
—*Mystery News*

"A tale as delicious as a Christmas pudding...Hall surrounds his famous historical personage with diverse and lively characters, puts them in an exotic setting, and produces a plot that boils merrily along."
—*Publishers Weekly*

"A breezy mystery...A flawless combination of setting, characterization, dialogue, and plot...These novels inspire in the American reader a sense of our shared heritage."
—*Booklist*

"Robert Lee Hall has given us a Ben Franklin displaying all the qualities for which he is legendary. Mr. Hall's choice of subjects and his extensive research makes these books more than just entertaining, they are enlightening as well."
—*Mostly Murder*

"Captivating...Rich in atmosphere." —*Boston Herald-American*

BENJAMIN FRANKLIN TAKES THE CASE

The American Agent Investigates Murder
in the
Dark Byways of London

ROBERT LEE HALL

ST. MARTIN'S PAPERBACKS

BENJAMIN FRANKLIN TAKES THE CASE

Copyright © 1988 by Robert Lee Hall.

Cover illustration by Jeff Walker.

All rights reserved. No part of this book may be used or reproduced in any manner whatsoever without written permission except in the case of brief quotations embodied in critical articles or reviews. For information address St. Martin's Press, 175 Fifth Avenue, New York, N.Y. 10010.

Library of Congress Catalog Card Number: 88-1855

ISBN: 0-312-95047-0

Printed in the United States of America

St. Martin's Press hardcover edition published 1988
St. Martin's Paperbacks edition/March 1993

10 9 8 7 6 5 4 3 2 1

For my son, Brian

❧ *PREFACE* ❧

THIS story came to light because my secretary fell off the back of a truck—actually a secretary-bookcase, American, circa 1780, a tall, sturdy fellow, walnut veneered, with sash doors, a drop-front, and six deep drawers, three on either side of a shallow knee hole.

Behind the knee hole hid a secret compartment; in it, a stack of yellowed foolscap paper covered with handwriting.

This hiding place was unknown to me as I skidded to a stop on Interstate 76 a dozen miles outside Philadelphia on a cloudy Tuesday afternoon and ran back to survey the damage, a wrack of splintered wood on the gravel shoulder. I had just started my return trip to California with my booty: armoires and highboys and settees crammed in a rented U-Haul. They were my spinster aunt Ivy Goodale's legacy—her money had gone to the A.S.P.C.A., but, stray cats and dogs having no need of dining room chairs or antique secretary-bookcases, her furniture had come to me.

Thank God, Aunt Ivy loved me!

I saw the papers at once, in long grass poking out of an old-fashioned leather pouch, which had tumbled free when a large chunk of the back of the secretary was sheared off by its violent skid. I glanced back; the rear doors of the truck, which I had neglected to latch, hung open accusingly. I groaned. An appraiser had told me the secretary was the most valuable piece of furniture of all, worth thousands. Now it looked a total loss.

Yet the pouch held value beyond money.

Since then I have learned that many eighteenth-century desks contained secret compartments. Opening the musty-smelling pouch, I glanced at the first words in a kind of angry distraction, as willing to fling them to the wind as save them. Yet in spite of idiosyncratic handwriting and antique spellings (which I have modernized for this printing) I could hardly stop reading, finishing the pages four hours later in a truck stop outside Harrisburg.

Because my father often showed me the budding branches of our genealogy, I have known since I was young that I trace my lineage to a man named Nicolas Handy, who came to America in 1762. This Nicolas Handy was my great-great-great-great-great-great grandfather. I also knew the family legend (unsubstantiated until now) that he had had a close association with a famous founder of our nation.

In my hands I held proof that the family legend was true.

Why was the manuscript hidden? I do not know. A father wrote it for his son who secreted it for his son—but, through some accident (perhaps a sudden death), the hiding place was forgotten. In any case the story belongs to a larger history than mine; I am pleased to offer it to the world.

October 12, 1795

My Dear Son,

  On this day in the year of our Lord, 1795, I have attained the age of fifty. At that same age a certain man, of whom you know, for he was used to dandle you on his knee when you were young, first met me and took me under his wing.

  Since your birth I have oftentimes pondered whether I ought to impart to you certain facts about my relations with this gentleman which I have kept hidden.

  This happy natal day in the bosom of my family has decided me: a father should keep nothing from his son.

  And so as shadows fall I mount the stairs to my study, candle in hand. Seating myself at my old desk, where I have writ much—but nothing so important as this—I light my lamp and take up my pen.

  At last, my son, you may know the truth.

Your loving father,
NICOLAS HANDY

❧ 1 ❧

*IN WHICH a dog barks, a man dies—and I
meet the remarkable Mr. Franklin . . .*

BELOW the attic window of the shabby, tilting house on
Fish Lane the wooden sign creaked on its hinges: INCH,
PRINTER, in peeling letters, though no one saw it, for it was
night—morning, rather, about five A.M. I judged from my narrow
bed under the thin comforter that gave little comfort and less
warmth. I sat up, rubbing my eyes. What had waked me? Some
sound? More likely the knowledge that if I were not soon down
and about, scurrying to my chores, Mrs. Inch or Buck Duffin
would give me a drubbing. The crying of the watch floated up
from the London cobbles like the wail of a ghost.

Thus, with no hint of new light, began that October day, 1757,
which was to change my life.

Heedless of waking Buck, who slept in the warmest corner of
the attic under not one but two eiderdowns which Mrs. Inch
herself had sewed for him, I rose in the bruising cold and
stumbled to the tiny, cracked window overlooking Moorfields,
hard by the London Wall. Once this had been a respectable
quarter, but time had tarnished it, though it still huddled like a
cringing beggar near the skirts of fashion. Far below, a single lamp
fought the darkness of the crooked street. By its feeble glow I
could just glimpse our watchman scuttling like a beetle to earn his
pittance. I smiled wryly at this folly—his quavering hue and cry

1

would save no man from robbery or murder. My gaze rose. Did a light flicker briefly at Mrs. Couch's across the way? Above her house the London rooftops were a jumble of black angles under a smoky lid of night. Southwest the dome of St. Paul's loomed, and though I could not see the Thames I felt her near, flowing tirelessly under London Bridge and past the Tower where, a hundred years before, King Charles had lost his kingdom and his head.

Was dead King Charles happier than I, Nick Handy, condemned to death-in-life at twelve years old? Despair welled up, and for an instant I thought of flinging myself to the cobbles below but hardened my heart. Hope still flickered in my breast; I would fight free!

But that must be tomorrow—or some tomorrow to come. For now: the grinding life of a boy of work. The attic was black as printer's ink, but my clothes were where I always dropped them before tumbling wearily into bed; so in the gravelike dark I struggled into leather breeches and the coarse, ragged shirt Mrs. Inch never mended ("—plenty good enough fer the likes o' you!"). Next: stockings and the scuffed, buckled shoes that were hand-me-downs from Buck. Last, and quickly, for I was quaking with cold, the greasy woolen jacket and scarf that barely kept off the chill until I should light fires in the grates below, from which only then might I be allowed to steal a half-minute of warmth before being whipped on like some beast of burden.

Tears started to my eyes at the injustice, but as always I sought comfort in the memory of my mother, stroking my hair in a fine big house. Had that house ever been real? Had she?

Yet in the midst of groping towards the door I stopped short, remembering last night, when Mr. Inch had caught me on the steep wooden ladder as I trudged up with my candle. In my mind I heard again his brittle voice, calling with chilling stealth: "Nicolas! Hsst! Young Nick!" and I pictured him slipping to my side, clutching my arm, peering close out of gin-bleared eyes—so odd a moment, so frightful, as if we were highwaymen met on some lonely midnight road.

2

"Y-yes, sir?" I had said.

His words hissed in my ear. "You needn't do your early chores tomorrow, Nick. Indeed, make certain you do not, for I shall see to 'em."

"But, why, sir?"

His lids narrowed slyly. "Truth to tell, there is a partic'lar person I am meeting, and I should prefer to greet this partic'lar person alone." A floorboard creaked, causing him to start and peer suspiciously. Then a spark of triumph leapt in his eyes, as if he had at last wrested some prize from life. He waved a crumpled paper beneath my nose. "You may come down at seven, Nick; that is time enough, but not afore. 'Til then, sleep. I shall see to things." And he groped away.

Now in the black, chill morning I shivered to recall it. For reasons which I could not name I feared for Ebenezer Inch. Indeed I loved the man. He was brought low by gin and beer, ground down under his heartless wife's thumb, yet he treated me kindly, though he suffered her wrath for it ("Yer a fool to spend tuppence on the worthless boy!"). Secretly he gave me books, which he knew I loved, books that showed a world that might sometimes be harsh but which opened a high road against the crooked little path I was bound to day by day.

Yet the morning proved out of the ordinary in more than one way, for I sensed that Buck Duffin was not abed. There came no rough tossing, no ragged snore from the far corner of the attic. Cautiously I crept into the blackness. Yes, the two thick eiderdowns were tossed aside, and Buck was gone.

Where?

I cared not. Eagerly lighting my poor stub of candle, I felt under the ticking of my bed for the precious book: *The History of Tom Jones, a Foundling*, by Mr. Henry Fielding. Finger to lips, Mr. Inch had entrusted me with this first quarto, with the promise of the other five to come. I opened the book. "A Foundling"—how those words wrung my heart! And how Squire Allworthy's kindness in taking in the unknown babe touched me! I ran my fingers along the good, strong binding, riffled the pages, smelled

3

the ink. Words bound in leather! I might hate Inch, Printer, yet I loved the printer's craft. My eyes flew over the sturdy, well-set lines, tracing Tom's adventures, but a bone-weary exhaustion numbed me. The little candle guttered. My lids drooped and shortly the book fell upon my chest.

The last I heard before sinking into sleep once more was the strange wild cry of a dog.

A rough blow flung me from bed to the floor.

Through a ringing in my head I heard a cock crow. Feeble light leaked through the little window, and my eyes focused on a black, looming shape.

Buck Duffin stood over me.

"You," snarled he, "still abed? Mrs. Inch'll skin yer hide, and I'll laugh to see it!"

I scrambled to my feet. "Don't you lay another hand on me!"

Buck thrust his big paws on his hips. "Who'll stop me?"

"I will."

"You'll do no such. Never 'ave, never will." He lunged, but I darted into a corner and drew up my fists.

"Stand back!"

He guffawed. He was seventeen years old, more than a foot taller than I and broad-shouldered and hard as iron from working the presses. He had coarse reddish skin. From under his shock of black hair his little eyes glinted. They were not stupid eyes, but they were cruel, and it did not help to know that Mrs. Dora Inch's spoiling had made him that way.

Then he was at me, my fists batted aside as if they were feathers, and I found myself pulled up under his nose by my collar. His hot breath hit my face. "Now. Dressed but not gone down? Wot's the meanin'?"

"M-Mr. Inch s-said I could sleep 'til seven."

"Haw! It's wot the Missus sez that counts. The truth—yer just a lazy cur, ain'tcha?"

I was choking. Spots swam before my eyes. "M-Mr. Inch said . . ."

Buck flung me aside. "Never you mind. Mrs. Inch'll be s'prised at you, very s'prised indeed." He chortled as if he had made some jest which only he understood, before his face blackened like a thundercloud. "Now, git down and light them fires!"

"I'll see to you one day!" I flung out by the door, but he did not answer. Fully dressed, he turned away, hands opening and closing at his sides as he gazed down at his rumpled bed so I could no longer see his face.

In spite of my brave show my heart pounded with terror as I crept down the ladder to the second story, where the Inches and their daughter Matilda kept their rooms. The house was frigid; Mr. Inch had not done as he had said. The gin had spoken for him last night—oh, why had I not seen it?—and he was snoring still, unaware that his wife's elbow waited to jab him downstairs to his living.

Could I make up for my wasted two hours?

Then I heard a rustling and, glancing along the second-story hallway, saw Matilda Inch just going in her door. This startled me, for she nearly always lazed abed till ten. Further, she had surely been out, for she was dressed in a full skirt and little fur-trimmed jacket over which she wore a long, dark cloak, and her cheeks were rosy with cold. Her manner was sneaking. Had more than the October morn lent her cheeks that glow?

Glimpsing me, she rushed over to shake her finger under my nose. "You haven't seen a thing, hear?" she squeaked in her high little voice. "And you are to keep your mouth shut, you you—" Her blue eyes fairly crossed thinking how to upbraid me.

"Yes'm," said I. Tilda was twenty, with straw-colored hair and a broad flat face. "O, pretty!" her mother crowed. As pretty as a stout pewter jug, thought I, it being plain the daughter's path lay where her mother had trod; she would weigh twelve stone before she was thirty.

Tilda sniffed haughtily. "Why is this house so cold? Mama will box your ears!" She flounced into her room.

With no time to guess what had called her out, I crept downstairs.

5

Dawn was just sweeping away the night, glimmering through the small glass panes of the little shop fronting Fish Lane where we sold slates and pencils, parchment, chapman's books, pen nibs, inkhorns. Behind that was the large print shop, with its two presses and fonts of type and strings where the printed sheets were hung to dry like clothes on a line. I inhaled the inky smell. There seemed another smell, one I did not quite know—but I had no time to puzzle over it as I hurried to the kitchen below, where the first fire must be laid, in the big brick oven. Hoping every moment that Mrs. Inch's beefy hand would not suddenly slap me to an accounting, I set tinder aflame under the black hanging pots, then scurried back up to the printing room to lay a second fire, after which I must sweep up and tidy before brewing up a kettle of thick, syrupy ink in the small rear yard.

"Well, young sir," came a voice.

I started. A stout, balding man stood just inside the printing room door rocking on his heels and gazing about with a broad, pleased smile. His clothes were plain worsted stuff, and he had no wig but wore his fringe of straight brown hair tied back with a ribbon. Squarish little eyeglasses perched on his nose. He held his tricorn hat in one hand and in the other a bamboo stick with which he rapped the wooden floor.

"How did you get in?" said I.

"O, by my two legs. Mr. Gout let me. Mr. Gout is my great enemy these days, but he sometimes suffers me to venture abroad. You are too young to be acquainted with him, I perceive. Indeed, for your sake I hope you never meet him." A step forward. "But I see you mean otherwise. I entered by the door of your shop." Gesturing behind him, he cocked his head. "It lay open. Should I not have come in?"

"Open?" I had not heard the bell.

"To the world."

Silently I cursed Tilda. Or had it been Buck who, neglecting the lock, had allowed this stranger to pester me when I must hurry to 'scape beating? "Our shop is shut," I flung at him. "You must come back some other time."

"A pity," sighed he, "when I have traveled so far." But he made no move to depart. "You are a printer, I perceive."

My fists clenched in desperation. "I am a common drudge, can you not see that? And I must be at my labors!" At once my cheeks flamed, less with shame than fear. What if he brought some valuable custom, and I insulted him?

But the gentleman only raised his brows. "Are you not an apprentice?"

"No."

His broad forehead wrinkled. "Pray, why not?"

"I have no one to pay my fees. O, please, sir," begged I, "let me be at my chores, so Mrs. Inch does not beat me."

He stiffened. "Mrs. Inch beats you? Yet you set type for the shop."

"Why . . . how do you know that?"

"The evidence of my eyes." Setting aside hat and bamboo, he grasped my hands. "Observe this callus on the left thumb. And this flattening of the right forefinger. You use the composing stick frequently. You use it well too, do I hit the mark?"

It was as if he saw into my soul, for I took fierce pride in my skill—though I would brag to no stranger. My gaze rose, and I saw that the brown eyes behind the square-lensed glasses were not so obstinately foolish as I had at first thought, but were sharp beneath their seeming vagueness. Yet they smiled, and I was stung; I wanted no kindness from this interfering man.

"As for doing my job well," muttered I, jerking back my hand, "that is not for me to say. It is for Mrs. Inch, and—"

"O, Mrs. Inch," he peered close, "—but what of Mr. Inch, eh?"

"Mrs. Inch rules here, I tell you, and she will beat me if I am not about my chores. Will you not leave?"

"I should much rather help."

"Help?"

He gazed about. "Your master's shop sorely needs setting

aright. Disgraceful!" He tugged at the folio pages on the lines. "These sheets need stacking by the bindery, and the tympans and friskets of both your presses need cleaning if you are to turn out work that is not smudged. In short, there are chores enough for two, and since many hands make light work I should like to lend mine. What do you say, young . . . what is your name?"

"Nick," I gave him.

His eyes narrowed. "And your surname?"

"Handy."

He gazed solemnly at me as the lonely echo of coach wheels sounded from Fish Lane. "Handy." He pulled at his lower lip. "The name tells much, for I believe you may be handy indeed, though you be insolent too. Yet you show spirit, and I am happy to know you, Nick." He thrust out his hand.

I stared at it. Never before had any man—or boy—made such a frank tender of friendship, and for this gentleman to do so softened my anger which had been so provoked by his kindness. With much show of reluctance I put out my hand. He clasped it heartily, and I thought it a good thing to shake as firmly and honestly as he. I made nothing of it, however—nor did he. Whisking off his coat, the gentleman beamed about. "In truth, I love a printer's shop!" And without further ado, leather shoes creaking, voice merrily humming, he began smartly pulling down the dried pages and removing them to the bindery.

I stared after him only a moment. I did not know what Mrs. Inch would do or say if she found some stout gentleman helping her boy of work to finish what he ought already to have done, but there was clearly no abridging him; besides, in my straits I ought to be grateful and I was soon at work beside him, so that shortly we had done all which would have taken me thrice the time alone, and it was done much better in company.

I lit the fire. As I was blowing up the coals the gentleman's tongue clucked, and I turned to find him gazing down with a great frown. "Alas, it is a poor thing," said he, shaking his head.

"What, sir?"

"Your stove. A thing ought to be made for use, and what use be

8

a fire in a house but to warm its inhabitants? Yet the warmth of that flies mostly up the flue. I have invented one far better; it goes by my name: the Franklin stove, they call it."

"You are Mr. Franklin?"

"Mr. Benjamin Franklin," said he.

The name meant nothing; indeed I hardly paid notice, for I had begun to wonder why no one had yet come down, not Mr. Inch nor Mrs. Inch nor Buck. Yet, save for the stewing up of the ink, my chores were done, and I had Mr. Franklin to thank. I opened my mouth to ask him his business—I was ashamed of my former rudeness—when with the look of a cat licking cream he beckoned me to the fonts of type.

"Show me your work, young Nick."

"Sir?"

Plumping me down upon a stool, he thrust a composing stick into my hand, sat, and took up one himself. "We shall have a contest. Set what you like as fast as you can; the words make no matter. I shall do the same." His eyes twinkled. "Let us say three minutes?" With no more ado, he placed his sturdy silver watch beside us and before I could say yea or nay cried, "Begin!"

In truth I kindled at the idea, for no one save Mr. Inch ever praised my skill, and, though I could not have said why, I wanted Mr. Franklin to see how swift I could go. So, hardly thinking, I began setting a favorite passage from *Tom Jones.* My fingers flew, snatching the metal letters and setting the little wooden shims, but I was aware that Mr. Franklin's fingers moved swiftly too. Faster than mine? Yet they seemed at leisure, easy, as if they set mere air. Still I drove myself as never before, harder even than under the lash of Dora Inch's tongue.

At last the hands of the watch swept away the third minute, and we placed our sticks before us, but I was dismayed to see that Mr. Franklin had done half again as many words as I. "John Locke," said he. "The social contract. And you have chosen Henry Fielding, I see. Excellent, Nick!" I was filled with dismay at being bested, but he thumped my arm in a manly way. "Come, young sir, no rainy looks! Though you be not an apprentice you

9

work better than most—better even than some fellows who have their own shops and call themselves printers, for you go smart and neat, with no errata." He gazed at his own lines. "I am rusty, I confess, for, though I kept a shop in America twenty years and printed everything from pamphlets to the King's good money, I have not practiced the craft in years. You are worth much to your master, Nick—but no indentures? Surely they promise you something."

I stared down at my shabby shoes. "They suffer me to eat at their table," said I.

"Ah, Nick!" A great sigh.

Clenching my fists, I glared at him, as if he were the cause of all my ill fortune. "And I may shiver in their attic at night if the chattering of my teeth be not too loud!"

At this Mr. Franklin gazed so pityingly that I could not bear his eyes, and I looked down again and twisted my hands, hating the lump that swelled my throat. "You are put upon indeed," said he softly as the cry of a knife-grinder hallooed from the street, "—yet you wear gold at your neck."

Seeing that my chain and locket had slipped free, I thrust it beneath my ragged shirt. "That is none of your business!" cried I, leaping up so fast I knocked over my stool.

He watched me a long, heavy moment, with a look so deep I could not fathom it. "As you wish," said he at last, softly and, rising, he put on his coat and strode to the bindery, where he took up one of the pages he had piled there and began perusing it with his back turned as if I had vanished from the earth.

I felt sick at this, abandoned, though I knew I had driven him to it and hated myself sorely. I was about to beg pardon—when along came new torment: Buck Duffin thumping downstairs waving a book. "Wot's this I find on the young marster's bed?" roared he.

The book was *Tom Jones*.

"Give me that," cried I, grabbing for it.

Grinning, he held it out of reach. "Wastin' yer time with

10

readin', is't? That's why you can't git down to work? Well, I'll fix that!" And, before I could move, his huge paws had ripped the pages from their binding.

I gaped in dismay. It was as if he had torn my heart. "Mr. Inch gave me that!"

His eyes danced. "Do tell. And, do the missus know? Well, I'll show 'em both wot you does to books." And, flinging the binding aside, he tore the pages through. I pulled at his arms, but it was no use. He tore the pages again and again, scattering the scraps like snow. At last he brushed his hands as if at a job well done. "Clean that up, young marster."

The room seemed filled with a seething red. I flew at him once more, but he felled me with a ringing blow to the head, then came after me, his leg cocked to kick me hard where I lay against one of the presses clutching my temples.

Mr. Franklin stood between us.

Through my pain I saw him. How he had got across the room so quickly I knew not, nor how his bamboo had come into his hand, but it was held firmly and raised, its tip quivering in the air.

Clearly Buck had not noticed him in the far corner. "Wot?" cried he.

Mr. Franklin was red of face, and a shine of perspiration glossed his lip. I thought he would strike Buck, and I knew not what should happen then, for Buck was young and strong and the stout gentleman plainly near fifty. They stared a moment, eye to eye. Then Mr. Franklin's stick slowly lowered until he stood with it by his side. "I am Mr. Franklin, come on business with your master," said he, each word hard and distinct. "Is there no one here who may see to me?"

Buck pulled his forelock. "O, I beg pardon, sir, for the need to discipline this lazy boy. I am apprentice here—mayn't I help you? No? Then I shall fetch master at once." Buck pulled me to my feet. "Clean up, boy!" And he thumped upstairs.

Once again I could not meet Mr. Franklin's eyes, and I knew if he gave me the least kindness I should burst into tears, so I only

11

stood trembling, with my hands clutching my aching head as if to hide from the world.

The gentleman's voice came soft but firm: "You want to knock the wind out of him, lad."

"S-sir?"

"Just here." He poked me under the ribs with his stick, gently. "That's the spot. A fist. An elbow will do as well, provided it's sharp and quick. O, a boot will answer too. You'll find him sitting on the floor. You may reason with him then."

I took my hands from my head. "Reason?"

"Even a bully must be given opportunity to show sense."

"B-but, sir . . ."

"If reason fails?" A sigh. "Then stronger measures, Nick. There is always the other place; kick him there, that's sure to give him pause. But light measures at the outset; always hold something in reserve—steal his wind to begin; time enough then to see if more is called for."

"Yes, sir," said I, forgetting the ache in my head.

Pulling forth a white handkerchief, Mr. Franklin blew his nose. "Gout and distemper too! London is unkind to visitors." He looked hard at me. "I do not like to see you wronged, Nick, for I am a mortal enemy to arbitrary government and unlimited power, where'er I find 'em." Then, smiling, he clasped my shoulder. "You have ink to brew, I believe. When I was your age many's the batch I stirred in back of my brother's Boston shop! See to it, shall you, while I gather the pieces of your book? Perhaps they may be repaired."

I was loath to leave him to that task, but the ink must be done. "Thank you, sir," said I, just as Mrs. Peevy, our cook and maid of all work, bustled in from the cold. Thin and sharp-featured, she hardly glanced at us as she descended to the kitchen. Following, I was shortly in the back yard, an ugly rectangle hedged round by leaning old brick buildings grimed with London smoke, where dawn barely reached. Frost rimed the weeds. My breath plumed whitely, and I pulled my jacket tight about my throat.

A bundle of rags lay by the ink kettle. Frowning, I approached

12

it. Some old linen which Mrs. Inch had flung there for the paper-makers?

But it proved not to be rags.

My breath caught in my throat as I saw the dreadful truth: Mr. Inch sprawled on his back, head bloody, his staring eyes piteously proclaiming that he was dead.

❧ 2 ❧

IN WHICH Mr. Franklin steals many things—including one small boy . . .

I knew not what to say or do but stood benumbed, my head whirling. Then I was on my knees and tugging at him—"O, Mr. Inch!"—though I knew it would do no good. I had seen corpses slipped from houses by the men in black, husbands and wives, children too (for death came easy and often to Moorfields), but their faces were always covered and they were always ferreted away on creaking wheels in such a kind of quick, shameful stealth that I had never met death close on. Now it stared right at me with sightless eyes, Mr. Inch, who alone of all humanity had cared for me!

At last I rose and peered about. How had it happened? My frantic gaze could find no clue.

Then I saw that my hands were covered in blood.

I had known Mr. Franklin but an hour, yet it was only he who seemed capable of saving me from I knew not what. I ran in to seek him—but it was Mrs. Dora Inch I found; I struck her huge, hard belly just inside the kitchen door.

I backed from her.

She gaped down at me. "You!" she lashed out with her harsh tongue; then: "*You?*"

"O, it's him right enow, Missus," sniffed Mrs. Peevy from among

14

her pots and pans, flinging pepper into the hot-water gruel. "The little wretch was just alarkin' in the shop when I comes in."

But Mrs. Inch seemed not to hear. Her tiny, squinting eyes never left me, though they were as large as ever I saw them, and she appeared unable to get her breath. For a moment, as she swayed over me like an old Moorfields shanty about to tumble into the street, I forgot poor Mr. Inch in terror that the formidable woman should strike me, though I could not say if it was fear or fury that made her tremble.

Then I knew what she gaped at: the blood on my hands.

"What . . . ?" cried she. Her eyes found the door through which I had just run, and she pushed past me out into the yard. "Eben, not Eben!" I heard her wail and watched her fling herself onto the frost-rimed weeds beside him. I turned to fetch Mr. Franklin—but found him already at my side, very grim. He glanced once at Mrs. Peevy, once about the kitchen, his eyes seeming to take in all. He saw the blood on my hands. "Wash, Nick," said he somberly and without more ado stepped into the yard.

I stared down at the dreadful red smears and felt myself go pale. The warm kitchen spun about me, and I thought I should vomit but made myself stumble to the bucket by the stove and plunge in my hands. "'Ere now!" Mrs. Peevy snapped, but I paid her no mind. The blood sank away, the cold water revived me, and though my heart was down I stood on my feet with a clear mind.

Amidst my grief I saw my future: life worth not a groat lacking Mr. Inch.

At that moment Buck Duffin huffed and puffed into the kitchen. "The master ain't to be found," growled he. "Where's the gen'leman was askin' after 'im?" He glanced towards the open back door. "Wot's the to-do?"

Mrs. Peevy said nothing, for she had seen the blood and only made silent gulping mouths like a bird that had lost its peep, while Mrs. Inch sent more wails from the yard: "Not Eben! Not he!" With a wickedly merry glance—was I at fault? would he be

15

allowed to wield the switch?—Buck eagerly hurried out to find the source of these laments.

I followed, nearly running into Buck, who stopped short.

"The devil!" croaked he as he saw Mrs. Inch in the weeds beside Mr. Inch, tugging his shirt.

My gaze went to Mr. Franklin. He stood near her, very still. Behind his little square glasses his eyes seemed lost in bewilderment, but I had learnt to look close and saw that he glanced quickly, slyly everywhere, up at the high neighboring windows, which began to show faces drawn by Mrs. Inch's cries, into the corners of the yard, at the drab brown weeds spattered with old ink. At last he moved, in a deliberate way, grasping Mrs. Inch's heaving shoulders. With some struggle he drew her to her feet. "He is gone, poor man, nothing any of us can do. Pray, come into the house and calm yourself."

She looked at him, and turned paler than ever, and I thought she would shriek. She shook free his hands and stood fat and quivering in her morning smock, moaning piteously. I was amazed, for she had shown little enough affection for her husband alive, cursing and belittling him at every chance. Had she loved him in spite of all? In any case she made a great show of sorrow. Buck too, who had often sneered at his master's drunkenness, looked stunned and white as a clout under his coal-black hair.

And I? I was heartsick. All was overturned.

Mrs. Peevy was by this time whimpering in the kitchen door, clutching her breast. Mr. Franklin stepped to her. "Fetch a blanket to cover the poor man," said he softly, at which she blinked, bobbed her head, and scurried off.

He turned to Buck. "We shall need a constable, young sir."

"Constable?" Buck seemed hardly to know the word. "O, aye, sir, a constable," and he backed into the house.

Mr. Franklin came to me. "Courage, Nick. I need paper and pen. At once."

"Yes, sir," said I. As I turned to go I thought Mrs. Inch gave us a sharp, mean stare but could not be sure, for her laments burst out

16

anew. I brought paper, pen, and ink, and using a little slate for desk Mr. Franklin scribbled a note. Blowing on the words, he folded it and handed me twopence. "This is for Dr. John Fothergill." He wrote the address on the outside. "Find a runner, a fast one. Quick, now."

I knew the apothecary's boy next door should be very glad of twopence. In a wink I was pounding at his door.

It was half-past eight o'clock.

I was back in less than three minutes. As I hurried into Inch, Printer, I frowned for not hearing the bell. Glancing up, I saw that indeed Mr. Franklin had spoke right, for the brass tongue that licked the bell and made it tinkle was bent. How came it so? There was no time to wonder; stretching on tiptoe, I straightened the little curl of metal before returning to the yard, where I found Mrs. Inch and Mr. Franklin in a kind of grim truce, neither quite looking at the other, she still huffing but with less conviction than before, while he gazed down at his black buckled shoes in frowning thought, like a parishioner waiting out the drone of a parson's saws. Mrs. Peevy shivered forlornly in one corner. She had brought a blanket, under which poor Mr. Inch lay mercifully covered.

Suddenly Mrs. Inch's finger leapt out at me. "You! You killed my Eben!"

I blanched. "I did not, ma'am."

But she had already given way to one of her spites, which was like a runaway horse carrying reason madly astray. Her face burned red; her lids squinted to accusing slits. "Blood on yer hands! I saw it. Peevy saw it too, and we'll have you took off and hauled up before the magistrate for what you are, a wicked, murd'ring boy, and you'll be locked up in Newgate and hung on Tyburn tree for all to see, as an example of a perfidious scoundrel! O, you . . . !" She came for me and would surely have pummeled me had not Mr. Franklin stepped between us.

"The boy has done no harm," said he. "I will vouch for it."

Her eyes flicked to him. "And who, pray tell, be you?"

"Mr. Benjamin Franklin, from America."

Her face worked in sputtering fury. "Go back to America, then," with great spite. "You have nothing to do with English law."

"English law?" He sighed deeply. "Why do so many on this shore forget that we in America are English too? As for departing England, I may do so only when I have accomplished that for which the good people of Pennsylvania sent me hither. Meantime, should the boy be called up before a justice, I must bear true witness, swearing before God that he has been in my presence this past hour and more and had no blood on his hands 'til he stepped into the yard. Mrs. Peevy must say so too, as must your apprentice." He looked my way. "I do not deny the general truth of what you say—the boy may be very wicked indeed—yet as to particulars, when he was with me he showed no signs of guilt but went about his chores unblushing. This too must I swear." He made a small bow. "Begging your pardon, good woman, but you would surely waste much time in pressing charges which have no chance of being proved."

His tone was calm and unprovoking, which only stung Mrs. Inch the more, she being unused to being crossed. It was clear she still longed to fly out at me, yet her greatest care was ever to preserve her own advantage (I was well used to watching her mind calculate behind her tiny eyes). Thus, though she spat in the weeds and screwed up her face and whined in her throat—she did not come for me. "I'll leave be for now," muttered she, "—though for all I know the boy may've done it earlier and be brazening it out."

"Why, so may anyone in this house," observed Mr. Franklin quietly.

Mrs. Inch blinked. There followed a great silence, save for the murmur of London, wakening. In the windows of neighboring houses many faces stared down as if at a play in a playhouse. I watched Mr. Franklin but discovered naught but his mild gaze upon Mrs. Inch, who for her part hung her head and began to quaver and shortly fell on her knees beside her husband in more dire show of woe.

At this Mr. Franklin glanced at me—a wink, or was it only a glint of light in his glasses?

At that moment came the constable, Buck Duffin puffing at his heels.

"Constable Nittle," said this gentleman to Mr. Franklin in a rumbling voice. He was tall and imposing in his black greatcoat and flat little hat. Hamlike fists protruded from his sleeves, and his long shiny jaw looked to've been shaved within an inch of its life. "Murder, is't?"

"So it seems," said Mr. Franklin, "—unless Mr. Inch slipped on the dew and struck his head on the fire grate or ink kettle." Constable Nittle nodded darkly but made no move, and there followed some awkward shuffling of feet amongst us. Mr. Franklin made an encouraging gesture. "Naturally, sir, you will wish to examine . . . ?"

The constable scowled. "Was about to do so. Shall do so now." Stomping heavily, he peered close at grate and kettle. "No blood."

"Truly murder, then?" inquired Mr. Franklin after more silence.

"Murder!" pronounced the constable.

There came a further uneasy shifting of feet. "Sir . . . ?" Mr. Franklin gestured toward the body.

"Must view the victim!" rumbled the constable.

Mrs. Inch rose noisily from her dead husband's side, and with great drama Constable Nittle flung away the blanket. I near cried out at seeing Mr. Inch once more, pitifully destroyed. His mouth was open in what seemed a plea. If I could but have answered it! The constable briefly turned the body, so we could all see the terrible gash upon the back of the neck, to which he pointed in great triumph. "Cause of death!" And, standing, he glowered suspiciously from face to face.

"Should you wish to have our names?" inquired Mr. Franklin softly.

As upon each preceding hint Constable Nittle swooped upon this like an owl upon a mole, drawing forth a chewed stub of pencil and fiercely grinding each of our names into a dog-eared little book, along with our reasons for being present. Mr. Franklin gave his last: "I came to see to some printing," said he, to which Mrs. Inch snorted skeptically, as if she thought he had come solely to strike down her husband.

At that moment Tilda Inch pushed her way amongst us, stared at her father, and at once set up a shrieking and windmilling of arms. Her mother enfolded her, and together they made a clenched, heaving mass, Mrs. Inch stroking her daughter's straw-colored hair, while Tilda wailed, "Who shall care for us now? Who shall pay for my dresses?"

Constable Nittle added Tilda's name to his list. "So!" pronounced he, glaring round in his long black coat and rising and falling on his heels, thrusting out his great, shiny jaw meaningly as if we must now confess which of us had murdered the victim or be struck by lightning.

Mr. Franklin continued to act with mild deference. "Naturally the constable will wish to interview the watch?" offered he.

The constable's eyes flashed. "The watch! Find!" roared he at Buck, who started and bolted like a rabbit. While we waited, Mr. Franklin spread the blanket back over Mr. Inch. As he did so I saw him look sharp about the body before standing aside in deep, sober meditation, pulling at his lower lip. What thoughts crossed his mind? There followed a quarter of an hour of great unease, during which the constable paced among us with many darting glances into each face, as if to catch us at our guilt. Mr. Franklin watched the man's heavy boots with distress. The reason was clear: if the murderer had left traces, the constable's boots must efface them.

At last Buck returned with a wiry old man. "Found 'im at th' Twelve Bells, yer honor," announced he. The new arrival was a wizened fellow whose shabby suit fitted his bones as tight as sausage casing. This was Mr. Barking, whom I had glimpsed making his rounds four hours ago. He had sunken cheeks and a grizzled chin, and—the Twelve Bells being a favorite haunt of watchmen after their cold night's work—he reeked of a powerful decoction of beer. Yet though Mr. Barking might have lifted some jolly bumpers with his cronies he peered at us with sharp, lively eyes.

20

"Murder's been done, ye say?" he addressed Constable Nittle while he chortled among his whiskers.

"Victim," pronounced the constable, pointing at the mound under the blanket.

Lifting the blanket, Mr. Barking only chortled louder. "The printer, is't? Aye," he emitted a high cackle, "we'll all go his way soon enow!"

"Indeed we may," put in Mr. Franklin soberly, "yet I believe the constable wishes to discover why this poor man went so soon. Pray, tell us what you saw on your watch."

Constable Nittle ponderously poised his pencil over his book.

Mr. Barking rubbed his grizzled jaw. "As to wot I saw, it were nothink," said he.

"Nothing?" Constable Nittle grumbled.

"Didn't I say so? No one in the streets these past many hours. O, there was a gen'leman's fine coach at p'rhaps five o'clock, which drew up into the lane and stopped and then moved on."

"Coach," pronounced Constable Nittle as he wrote in his book.

"Did you see the occupant of this coach?" inquired Mr. Franklin.

"Nay. It were many yards distant."

"A pity—though there was perhaps a family crest?"

"May've been, but t'was not for me to look for it. The coach departed quick enow, and nary a soul did I see otherwise."

At this I blinked—had I been mistaken in believing that both Tilda Inch and Buck Duffin were out?—yet I kept silent, though Mr. Franklin saw me start, and a tiny frown marked his brow.

"But mightn't some person come into Fish Lane without your knowing?" asked he.

Mr. Barking scowled. "I makes my rounds and I sees all!" He shook a finger under Mr. Franklin's nose. "Not a mouse stirs in the narrowest lane hereabouts but wot I knows it."

"Are your ears as apt as your eyes? Did you hear nothing either?"

"Naught more than th' usual moans and sobs—save the yelp of a dog."

"Did you see this dog?"

21

"Nay."

Mr. Franklin only nodded, while Constable Nittle pressed more words into his book: "Heard nothing."

Ten minutes later Mr. Franklin and I stood in the yard, alone save for Mr. Inch under his blanket beside the ink kettle. No sun yet found its way to us, and I shivered looking up at the few faces remaining in the neighbors' windows, mostly small children's, smudged and curious. At Mr. Franklin's soft urging, Constable Nittle had entered in his book what each of us said we were about these few hours past, but there proved little enlightenment, for no one had seen or heard anything, it seemed, all claiming to have been fast asleep, Mrs. Inch pleading that she knew not when her "dear Eben," as she called him, had risen and come down. Though I had seen Buck's empty bed, had seen Tilda, too, returned from some errand, when the constable came to tower over me like some monstrous soot-blackened chimney, I dared not say so for the threatening looks these two darted. I only stammered that I too had slept soundly. This act much shamed me, for I saw that behind his little glasses Mr. Franklin looked askance at my stammering, and I flushed to think he might read my thoughts.

Shortly after, he had murmured that the constable might wish to pry about indoors, the wisdom of which Constable Nittle had gruffly seized upon. Buck and Tilda and Mrs. Inch and Mrs. Peevy had dutifully followed his heavy bootsteps—though Mr. Franklin hung back, showing with a small motion of one hand that I was to stay too. A lone sparrow settled upon a stark, twisted mulberry by a grimy wall as the gentleman peered at the high box of bricks that surrounded us. "No way in or out, eh, young Nick? Save through the house?"

"No, sir," said I.

"Unless the murderer lowered himself from the window of a neighbor house, then climbed back to it. Do you think it possible?"

"It is possible, sir."

22

"But not likely?"

"I know not, sir."

Sighing, he squeezed the flesh between his eyes. "Ah, it is a black business! Poor Mr. Inch. Had he enemies, Nick?"

"His wife," blurted I.

He only pursed his lips. "Well, we must hasten, before they return. Help me, lad, though it be a sad piece of work." I followed to Mr. Inch's side, where we pulled back the blanket. Again I was appalled to see my master laid low. He had been short of stature, and looked even smaller in his bloody, ruined state. "He had a full, thick head of hair, had he not?" murmured Mr. Franklin.

"Aye, sir," agreed I dismally.

"It is a wonder such a wife did not cause it to fall out. And nary a streak of gray. Did he dye it, Nick?"

"Why . . . not to my knowing, sir."

"Did he ever wear a wig?"

"Never, sir."

"Mm. A plain man. A kind man." His eyes flicked to me. "Was he kind to you, lad?"

At this I held back sobs with trembling lips. Mr. Inch!

"No need to speak. Your feeling answers my question." Kneeling, Mr. Franklin wrinkled his nose. "I smell spirits. Ah, they are the ruin of the age! Did he tipple, Nick?"

"Yes, sir."

"Immoderately?"

I clenched my fists. "I will fault him for nothing!"

Mr. Franklin only nodded. "You are loyal in that. Yet I thought I smelled another smell, in your shop. Do you eat licorice?"

"I receive no such treats from Mrs. Inch."

"But perhaps Buck? Or Tilda?"

"I have never seen licorice at Inch, Printer."

"I see." Mr. Inch wore knee breeches and a sleeveless worsted waistcoat over a white cotton shirt, his leather printer's apron over that. I was taken aback when Mr. Franklin began to pry into his pockets, though he assuaged my dismay: "We must help where help is wanted. I mean no disrespect to your dead master, but this must not be left to the likes of Constable Nittle. I shall reveal to the law what I find, if anything, if't appear right and necessary. Did you note how very curious Mrs. Inch was about her husband's pockets?"

"Curious?"

"How she tugged at him! A fine show of grief—in which her fingers deftly explored every fold. Was she a cutpurse once, lad? Indeed she would've made a fine one, yet methinks she ended empty-handed, and perhaps there was nothing to be . . . oho, what's this?" He drew a crumpled scrap of paper from a waistcoat pocket. Glancing sharply at the house to see he was not observed, he tucked it away in his clothes. "And now, though I hate to do it, the poor man's hands . . ." Both were clenched tight. Mr. Franklin prised open the left, which proved empty—but the right revealed a large brass button. He held it by the edges, his warm brown eyes dancing behind his glasses, and I could hear his agitated breathing. He hid the button with the paper. "And here is best of all." With my help he lifted the right hip—to reveal a carving knife on the crushed weeds beneath. "The tip of the handle has been plain as day all along. I feared it would be discovered, but the grieving wife knelt on the other side of the body, so did not note it. As for our brave constable, I need not have worried, for he barely sees the tip of his nose. Do you recognize it, lad?"

It was very fine, polished steel with an ebon handle—and bloodstained. "It is none of ours," said I.

"No?" Using a handkerchief to pick up the knife, he hid it about him with the rest of his booty, then stood with some creaking of bones. Yet almost at once his eyes narrowed, and with surprising agility he dropped down again beside the body, his nose very low as he brushed his hand along the ground, ending with some flakes of white in his palm. I was startled to see that they were tiny seashells, broken along one edge. "But, how . . . ?" said he, peering at the wound to the back of my dead master's neck. "Could't be . . . ?" Replacing the blanket, standing, he wore a distant, clouded expression, very grim, that made me shudder.

There was a sound from the kitchen, and quick as a wink the shells vanished into the handkerchief, with which the stout man dabbed his brow as if that were all the reason he held the cloth— yet the sound proved to be only Mrs. Peevy showing a lean, sturdy gentleman in a gray powdered wig into the yard.

Mr. Franklin's face lit. "John!" cried he, wringing the man's hand. He turned to me. "This is my good friend, Dr. John Fothergill. And this bright young lad is Nicolas Handy."

"Nicolas," said the gentleman, by the sound of him a Scot. Mrs. Peevy withdrew.

Dr. Fothergill gazed about with squarish, piercing eyes. He was a gentleman indeed, in black velvet breeches, oyster-gray waist-coat, and long blue velvet coat. He pointed his fine ash stick at the blanket. "The unfortunate deceased?"

"It is, John," said Mr. Franklin solemnly. "Can you say when he died?"

"I may, but . . ." The doctor gave his friend a sharp glance, as if to ask why he had been called to such a place as Moorfields, where life went so cheap, but this was brief, and with a little shrug he went to the body, knelt, and began his work.

"Fothergill was the first to describe diphtheria," said Mr. Franklin. "Many's the letters on scientific matters which we exchanged across the Atlantic. Indeed it was he who prepared my electrical essays for publication on this shore."

I knew not what "electrical" meant, so only nodded while the doctor prodded Mr. Inch's abdomen, peered into his staring eyes, felt his limbs. Last he turned the body a bit, the better to view the wound to the back of the neck, then rose as cool as if he just got up from supper. "Felled by a blow to the head," said he, pulling a white linen cloth from his sleeve. "Whether that killed him or no I cannot say, but there is a dreadful bruise and crushing of flesh. I should guess it rendered him unconscious. Then came the awful hacking at the back of his neck. To what purpose? Who did this, Ben?"

"I too should like answer to that."

The doctor wiped his hands on the cloth. "As for the time of death, taking into account the degree of rigor in the lower limbs and the chill October morn, I should guess about four hours ago."

"Near five o'clock, then." Mr. Franklin thoughtfully adjusted his glasses. He appeared about to say more when a commotion arose in the house. "What . . . ?" said he and led us rapidly into the kitchen and upstairs past the printing room to the shop in front. There we found Constable Nittle, Buck, Tilda, and Mrs. Inch in an uproar. All was in order—the wooden shelves displaying lamp-black, sealing wax, reams of paper, and the like—save for Mrs. Inch's little cubbyhole and desk tucked almost out of sight to the right of the entrance. This was in disarray, drawers pulled open, papers scattered about, an ink pot spilt on the floor.

"Robbery, that's what it was!" cried she as we came in. "The vile miscreants were after my . . . our . . . money!"

Constable Nittle's look flashed lightning. "And killed your husband when he caught 'em at it!" pronounced he.

"Why, so it must be!" gasped Mrs. Inch as if he were the cleverest soul in Christendom. "They broke in last week, didn't they Buck?"

Buck nodded. I, too, recalled the shattered pane and signs of search just seven days past, things tossed about, though nothing had been taken that I knew.

"And did you keep money there?" put in Mr. Franklin.

She snapped her face his way. "Indeed I did!"

"Pray, how did these thieves know where to search for it?"

She looked taken aback. "Why . . . they snooped first, o' course—come in pretendin' to want work done and saw me put it here, in my metal box, and come back but landed upon poor Eben."

"Snooped, saw, landed!" Constable Nittle entered triumphantly in his book.

"So it was mere accident he was killed?" said Mr. Franklin. "Ill luck, indeed. And did they take your money?"

She peered into the metal box. "Thank God naught is missing."

"That at least is fortunate." He turned to his friend. "Well, John, we must depart this sad scene, for I have much business to attend to." He stepped into the print shop to retrieve his hat, which he had left next to the fonts of type. Standing near the shop door, I alone glimpsed what followed: he scooped a handful of metal letters into his black felt tricorn before fitting it tight onto his head, at which I was much bewildered.

Returning, he bowed as innocent as you please. "Come, John," said he and with not a glance back drew his friend with him out the door.

I felt abandoned to a terrible fate. Constable Nittle harumphed and reiterated his certainty that Mr. Inch had been murdered by robbers whom he surprised at their stealing, thus dismissing Mr. Barking's equal certainty that he had seen no person enter or leave Fish Lane. Mrs. Inch again fulsomely flattered the constable's keenness, at which he seemed to wish to smile, though his jaw would not let his mouth do it.

At last, making some final black marks in his book, he strode off to convey his findings to the Justice.

Mrs. Inch at once turned on me. "Clean up that spilt ink, you upstart boy!" shrieked she, cuffing my ear, all her show of woe vanishing into a grumbling fury that rattled the house like a bowl rattling ninepins. "Eben!" cried she in a new tone that said, "How dare you be murdered?" Tilda stood near a box of quills whimpering and biting her nails, but Mrs. Inch only grabbed her by the ear—"Shut up, you silly girl!"—and dragged her squealing upstairs. Buck grinned meanly under his black hair as he bumped past me into the printing room. I am master now! his pleased look crowed.

My heart sank further in my breast, and I gave over to sobs as I scrubbed on my knees.

O, Mr. Inch, is't only I who mourn you?

About noon the undertaker strode in and solemnly measured Mr. Inch for his box. Shortly the men in black came with their cart and bore my master away on creaking wheels, and I had to

27

hide in the kitchen for fear I might show what I felt to the heartless people of the house, though to give her credit Mrs. Peevy sprinkled a tear or two into the copper kettle where she boiled bedclothes in a great cloud of steam.

Hoping no one should pay mind to me, I spent most of the day in a corner of the print shop repairing the errors which Buck had made in setting type, for he spelled very poorly and was hasty as well, wanting to bully his way through everything.

But at last like an undertaker's black cloak night fell over Inch, Printer, and I could hide no more.

Mrs. Inch had always suffered me to eat at table with them, but at the far end so the serving dishes came to me last, with often little more than picked bones and scraps, though Mr. Inch had used to slip me choice morsels afterward. Mrs. Inch liked to belittle me. "You'll marry a fine gentleman one day, my dear Tilda," cooed she often to her daughter, "while you, Nick Handy, shall marry the workhouse if you don't mind your manners!" Buck would guffaw while she urged him to eat more boiled beef. Mr. Inch had always stood as a buffer between me and his wife, for she never let fly her full wrath when he was about, no matter how sunk in his cups he was—but this gloomy night my master was no more, and almost at once Mrs. Inch began to sharpen her claws.

I slid as far down in my chair as I was able, but we were hardly seated at the long plank table before one of her coarse, red hands flew up. "O, no, Buck, hold back that platter! No mutton for Nicolas." She thrust her pointed chin at me. "You told the robbers where to find my money, did you not, you spying slyboots? You'll not swallow a morsel in this house 'til you confess!"

"I know no robbers," protested I. "I know nothing of your money."

"No? Liar! You've been thieving all along! A penny here, a penny there. I've missed 'em, and it was you filched 'em, I know it was!"

"No, ma'am," said I.

"Not a bite, then," roared she, her white housewife's cap flapping.

This suited me. Mr. Inch's death had stolen my appetite, and I was content to sink down even farther, hoping she would leave me be.

But my acquiescence only served to set her aboil, and she began to rail against the day she had taken me in: "Nothing but trouble, you snooping boy . . . you never earn half what you eat." At this Tilda nodded vigorously, and Buck too was quick to lend support: "Just so, ma'am, give 'im what for!"

This stung, for I always did more work than Buck, and better too, and I well knew their printing would suffer without my labors. So, folding my arms, I determined to starve if need be, to spite them all!

Mrs. Inch huffed and puffed. My silence so enraged her that by the time the currant pudding came round she was as hot as coals and trembling like a teakettle. Flinging the pudding against the wall, she leapt to her feet. "The switch, Buck!" demanded she. "We'll teach this boy!"

Tilda looked quite gay and clapped her hands to have such entertainment, but I had no mind to give in easily.

"You'll teach me nothing!" cried I, jumping from my chair.

"No?" said she, her little eyes glinting. "We'll see."

I dashed upstairs to the front door and near escaped, having flung it open to the dark London lane, when Buck caught me and dragged me squirming into the printing shop. I kicked his shins hard, and he cried out and threw me to the floor. Panting, I scrambled into the corner next to the fonts of type and stared about like some poor trapped beast. Mrs. Inch and Tilda were by this time upstairs too, Tilda laughing gaily, her straw hair dancing, while Mrs. Inch smiled, though there was no gaiety to her look but only brutal glee. Her beefy hands were on her hips, her right toe tapped eagerly. She licked her lips.

Buck presented the willow switch.

"Hold him," said she as she snatched it, her smile broadening. "Hold him a good long time."

"Stay away!" I warned Buck, but he only yawped as if I were a bedbug that protested crushing.

29

He reached for me.

It was then that I remembered what Mr. Franklin had said: take his wind. My eyes fixed on the spot just under his ribs, my fingers tightened into a fist, and as his big hands brushed my shirt I struck.

I heard his grunt, saw the round-eyed start of surprise. Then came a grimace of pain—and indeed he sat on the floor just as Mr. Franklin had said, and he rolled about clutching his belly, spitting outraged cries for vengeance: "Murder 'im, murder 'im!"

"That I shall," keened Mrs. Inch coming for me, switch raised. "O, your mother was a bad 'un, and you're that much worse than she!"

I saw red. "You shan't speak ill of my mother!" cried I—but what was I to do? I could not strike a woman, and besides her switch was long and would find me whether Buck held me or no, in no matter what corner I hid. There was nothing for it but to face her fury, suffering it with all the bravery I might muster.

Her arm drew back, and I braced myself for the first strong blow.

Yet that blow never came, for a hand snatched the switch from her grasp.

"What . . . ?" gasped she.

It was Mr. Franklin once more.

He threw the switch across the room. "Come, Nick," said he, brushing past the gaping woman, clutching my hand and drawing me stumbling to the shop door.

"Here, now!" cried Mrs. Inch.

He turned. "You have words for me, ma'am?" His brown eyes flashed warning behind his little glasses.

"You have broke into my shop! I shall call the constable!"

"Your door stood open. I found it so, as it was this morning. See to it, ma'am, if you wish to prevent unwanted visitors. As to the constable, call him if you please. I am taking this boy."

"You shall not. He is mine."

"Show me his indentures."

"Why, I . . ."

"The boy has no papers with you. He is not a slave to be oppressed and beaten, and he is not yours."

"You cannot take him!"

"I shall, for clearly you do not want him. Indeed I do you a favor in saving you the trouble of caring for him." He tipped his hat. "However if you have cause for complaint seek out Mr. Benjamin Franklin, of Philadelphia. Come, Nick." And with that he drew me into the dark night, to a waiting carriage which hastened off along the London cobbles, I knew not where.

❧ 3 ❧

*IN WHICH I discover kindness, and a
desperate woman applies for aid . . .*

MY mother's sweet voice cried out for me in a huge, dark
house. I fought toward her through a maze of cob-
webbed corridors but could not reach her. "Mother!"
called I in desperation. Then her voice abruptly ceased, and a
shadowy figure with no face came for me with a knife that
dripped blood. "What have you done with my mother?" cried I
over and over until I sat straight up clutching the bedclothes and
shaking. Five A.M.! I must hurry down to light the fires!

But I was not at Inch, Printer. A soft mattress caressed me.
Fresh-washed sheets surrounded me. A comforter smelling sweetly of cedar billowed about my knees.

Was this the place to which Mr. Franklin had conveyed me?
Was I safe?

Trembling, I burrowed back beneath the sheets, dreading to fall
asleep for fear that when I woke my escape would prove a dream.

Yet sleep shut over me as firmly as the covers of a book.

"Still abed," I heard a woman's whisper, then the soft shutting of
a door. Heart leaping, I sat upright fearful I had once more
neglected my morning chores. But this was still not Inch, Printer.
Instead I gazed in amazement at a small, scrubbed room with a
polished mahogany wardrobe and a stand with a gleaming

32

porcelain basin and ewer beside the bed which held me. Sunlight poured through the white curtains of a casement window. Sliding onto bare feet, I listened in a bewildered trembling to stirrings beyond the walls: the rustle of garments, the creak of floorboards, the distant clatter of pots and pans.

What was this place?

Tiptoeing to the window, I parted the curtains. The room proved to be at the back of some house, on the second story. Below, far different from the Inch's raw plot of land, lay a pleasant yard where borders of flowers shed the last of their petals next what appeared to be a small stables.

Violin music played somewhere.

I could recall last night only in a blur: the London streets twisting this way and that, Mr. Franklin beside me, his arm protectively round my shoulders. Then a house and a bustling, rosy-cheeked woman who made much of me—and a younger woman too. But I also recalled a bone-deep weariness from murder and sorrow and abuse, so that I felt raddled and weak and could barely remember how these gentlefolk used me, though they seemed kind to an undeserving boy.

I wore a striped cotton nightshirt. Where were my clothes? Peering in the wardrobe, I discovered only women's dresses and bonnets. I began to be anxious, wishing to be about, to make myself useful, to give thanks, especially to ask what might come next. Cracking open the door, I spied a landing with another door opposite, under some stairs, but no one in sight. The violin sounds grew louder. Creeping across the way I knocked twice and, receiving no answer, made bold to enter. I knew not what to make of what greeted my eyes: some pocked wooden tables with various instruments upon them, and glassware—jars and vials— and wires and tools and many odd bits and pieces the use of which I did not know. The room seemed a sort of small manufactory—but for what? It too was deserted. I backed out and turned right, past the stairs.

There were two more doors on this floor, at the front of the landing, opposite one another. The right-hand door was shut, but the left showed a crack, the music flowing from there. I knocked but was not heard, so called out "Please?" and opened the door.

A naked man stood by an open window playing a violin.

He turned. It was Mr. Franklin.

He greeted me with no shame, setting his instrument on a large featherbed and briskly stepping round it to clap my shoulders. "Up and about, Nick? Excellent!" He tapped his brow. "He that rises late must trot all day. O, I love the dawn!" He sneezed so violently that his steel-rimmed spectacles nearly flew to the floor. "Damn me, Fothergill will belabor me for so provoking Nature." He shut the window. "And how do you find yourself after yesterday's sad events?"

"I am well, I believe, sir." I could not help staring at his frank nakedness. Though stout, he was not fat but firm and solidly built, like a good strong keg.

He suffered my examination blithely. "Air baths, Nick. I take one whene're I can. They season the body. I am fifty, would you credit it?" He chuckled warmly. "Aye, I believe you would. In any case I look for fifty more years to bless me, if gout and distemper will give me leave."

"Yes, sir," said I, still in amazement. I gazed about the room. There were shelves with many books, and a handsome walnut desk with pens and ink and paper, and a comfortable chair by the unlit fire, where I could imagine the gentleman sitting with his *London Chronicle*, which lay open on a small table beside it.

Mr. Franklin began vigorously bending at the knee, down then up then down, with great gusts of breath. This he did twenty times or so. "For the blood, Nick," said he, "—and the brain." He saw me glance at two small painted portraits on his chest of drawers, a plain-looking young woman and a pretty, curly-haired child. "My daughter, Sally," said he, "still in America with my good wife, Deborah; and my second son, Franky, who was stolen by smallpox at four." His bald head furrowed. "Dear Franky, now dead twenty-one years, whom I have seldom since seen equaled in everything, and whom to this day I cannot think of without a sigh." He gazed long at me—it was one of the moments I came to know well, in which he pondered much but revealed little. At last he drew a long maroon dressing gown about himself. "Have you an appetite, lad?"

"Indeed I am very hungry, sir."

His eyes crinkled. "Then let us down to breakfast. Porridge? Rashers of bacon? Good, hot bread?" He rubbed his hands. "Mrs. Stevenson bakes excellent bread!"

Breakfast was served in a cheery room on the ground floor, in back, looking onto the yard I had seen from above. Before going down Mr. Franklin fitted me out in slippers and breeches and shirt much too large. "My son William's," said he, dressing himself, "but they must do for now, for Mrs. Stevenson threw your pitiful, ragged things in the dustbin." Then he led me downstairs. On the way I glimpsed two negro men, one in yellow livery, one in plain worsted stuff. "My servants, Peter and King, whom I brought from America," informed he as we passed a front parlor looking out on a street I did not know. Down another stairs, and Mr. Franklin was greeted with great affectionate respect by the woman I remembered from last night. She was plump in a large rustling blue dress with a frilled white apron, a little lace cap bobbing about her face. A great red mole nestled by the side of her nose.

This was Mrs. Margaret Stevenson, who gazed at me as if at a baby chick. "O, poor orphan!" She smothered me in a hug that smelled of berries and spice, though her nose wrinkled as she held me away from her. "He wants good food," averred she, "—and a good bath."

Mr. Franklin and I sat at a round table spread with a white linen cloth. Shelves of knickknacks surrounded us—little figurines and pitchers. Sunlight flattered the room, as if, unlike the warped, sullen walls of Inch, Printer, this house were sunny by nature. Shortly the pretty young woman whom I had met last night joined us, flying in and pecking Mr. Franklin on the cheek. She was slender, with pink cheeks and honey-colored hair. "I have

35

been reading Mr. Bacon, as you encouraged," trilled she (I later learned this was Sir Francis Bacon), "and you are quite right, he demands much but rewards more."

"Excellent. You recall Mary, Mrs. Stevenson's daughter, Nick?" I jumped to my feet, and she laughed and curtsyed as if I were a gentleman. "We call her Polly," added Mr. Franklin, patting her small white hand with fatherly affection.

Mrs. Stevenson arrived with bread and bacon and porridge and a pitcher of cream, and everything tasted better than food had ever tasted before. I learnt that Mr. Stevenson was dead some years and that Mr. Franklin lodged with Mrs. Stevenson while he was in London on business for the American colony of Pennsylvania. This business produced the only ill ease, for Mr. Franklin's look momentarily darkened when he spoke of it, muttering, "Damn the Penns!" under his breath, though both Polly and Mrs. Stevenson were quick to assure him that these "Penns" must surely come round.

Mr. Franklin beamed once more, grasping both women's hands. "O, I am fortunate, Nick, for our friendship has been all clear sunshine, without the least cloud in its hemisphere!"

This ought to have pleased me, but I was stung, for I felt outside their happy sphere, looking on as always, and a mean, withholding devil lurked in my heart. I watched and listened and nodded as polite as I could, but I did not like how each person cast sly, interrogative glances upon me while they kept cautious silence about my past and future, as if I were some odd bit of baggage left on their doorstep. Mr. Franklin had saved me from Mrs. Inch—but what now? My only benefactor had been cruelly murdered. Might my present good fortune likewise be torn from me?

Following breakfast the gentleman took me into the small back parlor and sat me down on a sofa. He took the chair opposite. "To business. Mrs. Inch does not own you, Nick Handy—nor do I," said he, gazing solemnly in my eyes. "You are free to choose. You may leave this house if you wish. Have you, perhaps, some other haven? Some relations?"

I caught at the gold chain at my neck. "I have only myself," said I.

"I thought as much," murmured he.

Seeing his eyes on the chain, I thrust it quickly back under my shirt.

"You may stay here for now, Nick," continued he, "until we determine some further course. Should you like to do so, lad?"

"Yes, sir; very much, sir. But . . . why did you trouble to take me from Fish Lane?"

His fists clenched on his knees. "Because I could not drive your unjust treatment from my thoughts. Clearly you were deeply loyal to your master. You were excellent at setting type as well, a great asset to Inch, Printer. Yet you were forced to labor under cruel treatment. When I returned yesterday eve I meant only to speak to you, to offer my protection, but, chancing to arrive when I did, just as you flung open the door seeking escape, I took the liberty of walking in. Seeing how you were abused, I could not abide leaving you in the hands of that woman. But I make no unwonted claims. You are your own man, Nick."

"O, I should like to stay, sir! But I do not wish to take charity. I am a boy of work; I *can* work, I *shall*, to earn my keep!"

He flinched at my desperate plea, and a great pity swam in his brown eyes. "You may work, lad. Indeed when men are employed they are best contented. But you are not merely a thing to do labor; you are one of Nature's chief creations who may improve the world with mind as well as with back and hands; do not forget that." He smiled. "In the meantime we shall find occupation enough for you. And now," he rose, "I must be about my business, for the people of Pennsylvania have entrusted me with a trying task—I, who thought to have retired long ago to the leisure of my experiments!" He shook his head. Shortly he was gone in a white wig with his liveried servant Peter, and I was left to Mrs. Stevenson.

This good woman at once measured me for shirt and breeches and jacket, after which she set Polly to cutting cloth while with much humming she boiled up a great quantity of water. This she

37

splashed steaming into a wide copper basin in the stone-floored kitchen.

She touched her mole as if it were a relic she made vows on. "You are to scrub up well, child!" She shook a finger beneath my nose. "If I spy a speck of dirt I shall scrub you all over myself!"

I was left alone to the first hot bath of my life.

"I can build fires, ma'am, and sweep and clean," urged I to Mrs. Stevenson when my bath was done and I stood in a great soft towel for her inspection.

"Child, child . . ." was all she said. She led me to the front parlor, a pleasant room looking out upon the street, and while Polly sewed my shirt Mrs. Stevenson sat me on the sofa next to her and searched my hair, "chasing vermin" as she put it, combing and dabbing on a stinging concoction. I stood this silently. She had her scissors too, and trimmed me up, and at last took me once again to the kitchen and soaped and rinsed my hair and dried it and tied it back with a black ribbon as gentlemen often wore it.

"O, very handsome!" exclaimed Polly, clapping her hands, when her mother showed off her work.

At this I flushed.

Both women set to with their needles. They were freer now, as if some ban were lifted, and inquired about my life at Inch, Printer. They clucked their tongues at what I described but said how happy it was that I had had Mr. Inch to befriend me and how dreadful that he was murdered. This caused me to recollect the scrap of paper and button and knife and shells which Mr. Franklin had secreted on his person, and too the bits of type he had hid in his hat, and I made bold to ask about him.

O! vowed they with strong feeling, he was the splendidest gentleman! So kind and jolly! And famous too for his electrical work! "He is a member of the Royal Society," Polly informed, though I knew not what this signified. I gathered that Mr. Franklin encouraged Polly's interest in scientific matters, which Mrs. Stevenson disapproved as useless for a marriageable girl of eighteen; yet the good woman could say nothing against her

38

lodger. Shortly the servant King arrived with a pair of sturdy new black buckled shoes, which fit pretty well, so that by the time Mr. Franklin returned at four o'clock I was fully outfitted.

I presented myself in the entranceway, wishing to please him, but he was short with me. "You look a young gentleman, as you should," grumbled he, thumping past up to his room, sneezing on the way.

Mrs. Stevenson and Polly exchanged a look. "His business does not go well," said the housewife.

"That he should be treated with disrespect!" exclaimed the daughter.

"Too, his distemper worsens. O, the gentleman *will* have his air baths! Tsk, I shall mix some rum and hot water."

Going separate ways, they left me alone on the first floor landing by the front door. Almost at once came the jingling of the bell, followed by a soft insistent rapping. When no one came to answer, I opened the door. "Please, Mrs. Stevenson's residence," said I.

A thin woman with reddish hair stood before me, wringing her hands. "I wish to see Mr. Franklin about the murder of my brother," said she.

"O, stay, Nick, stay," urged Mr. Franklin but a few moments later. I had shown the lady into the front parlor, then gone up to the gentleman's room to see if he might speak to her. "Her brother's murder?" exclaimed he, all weary disgruntlement vanishing. A spark lit his eye, and he rubbed his hands. Shortly he was down, with solicitous greetings. Bidding the woman sit, he took his place in a chair opposite her, and though I made to leave he motioned me to remain on a small wicker stool nearby. "If you do not object," added he to the lady. "This is Master Nicolas Handy. He worked at your brother's shop 'til yesterday, when I removed him from there."

"And right to do't!" replied she smartly. "He would be better anywhere than there, even if't be in hell."

"Indeed? You are a seamstress, are you not?"

39

She started. "You know of me?"

"Not 'til this moment. Yet I have made a study of occupations. Certain indentations about your fingers and a small callus on your right thumb, in addition to some bits of various-colored thread about the hem of your dress, suggested the trade. Have I hit the mark?"

"You have."

"Make nothing of it. The scientific habit causes one to peer closely at things, even trivial ones. So, you are Ebenezer Inch's sister. My sincere regrets and condolences upon his death."

"His murder, you should say."

Mr. Franklin pursed his lips. For my part I looked close at our visitor. Indeed there were some small bits of colored thread clinging to the hem of her black satin dress, though it took a sharp eye to discern them. She wore a taffeta stole and a white muslin bonnet tied with a dark blue ribbon. She was dressed quite as a lady, yet there was an air of penury about her—her shoes were worn and scuffed at the toes and her black knit mittens were much mended. She had a small, jutting chin and sharp cheekbones; I could see Mr. Inch's face in hers. She was determined— her tight-clenched fists said so—yet she remained uneasy and her eyes darted often, like a bird's spying for cats.

"Well, well, I too believe he was murdered," conceded Mr. Franklin, his chair creaking as he bent gently toward her. "But how may I serve you?"

"By finding his murderer," said she with trembling chin.

He tilted his round face ever so slightly. "Surely that is the business of the law."

"Constable Nittle, you mean?" She sniffed. "I have wasted enough time with Constable Nittle—long enough to see he is a fool! Shall I tell over my day? This morning comes a boy from Turvey's Undertaking to say Mr. Inch will be buried at noon in West Churchyard, if I be pleased to attend. Imagine, this is how I learn of my own brother's death! In great anguish and bewilderment, I hurry round to Fish Lane to see if it can be true. There I must beg on my knees to discover how he died, and then it is only

40

their servant Mrs. Peevy who relents to me. As for the wife, she is puffed with pride and tells me she never liked nor trusted me, and how happy she will be never to see me at her shop again. Her shop! But yet it is, for she is his widow. Next I progress to the Justice, where I discover Constable Nittle with his feet up in the antechamber, but he only reads to me from a little book as if it be scripture and will hear no questions to lead the matter further. Has the Justice more sense, more sympathy? No, he is all yawns and dismissals. What am I to do?"

"What indeed?" murmured Mr. Franklin.

For my part, I was struck cold to my soul—Mr. Inch truly gone, buried, and I with no chance to pay my last respects!

"And his grave," added the woman bitterly, "—hardly more than a pauper's plot with a poor stick of wood at its head, when his wife could surely afford better. O, you must help me, Mr. Franklin."

"How do you know of me?"

"The constable told the names of all who were present at Fish Lane yesterday morn. When I heard yours I sought you out."

"And why?"

"Because my brother spoke of you often—'The one good man I know,' said he."

At this I pricked up my ears. Mr. Franklin had known my master?

"Sad indeed to know but one good man," said Mr. Franklin, shaking his head.

"It is the lot of some not to know so many as that," answered she.

"You have led a hard life?"

"Not so hard as some." Her eyes flew bleakly to me. "Care for this boy, sir; give him some chance!"

"I shall do so. But surely it was robbers killed your brother?"

"I cannot believe so."

"Pray, why?"

"I have long believed my brother was fallen into bad hands. His wife, her sneaking friends, the shop—something about it never has been right. Have you seen what my brother was made to print?" Tears started to her eyes. "O, he was weak, but he was not a bad man, and to see him turn his hand to such vile stuff when he was once the best of printers and sought nothing more than plain, honest respectability. How I curse gin and beer!"

"Yet if it was not robbers killed him, who then?"

Her features set rigid as wax. "His wife!"

Mr. Franklin started. "You are certain?"

"She would murder."

"But your proof?"

"Her character."

"You do not love her?"

"I despise her!"

Mr. Franklin sighed. "No magistrate would pronounce against her on those grounds. We must have substance if you seek more than mere revenge. Is't only revenge, Mrs. Clay?"

"Justice," said she with a hard reluctance.

"Then we must admit all possibilities, including Dora Inch's innocence. Pray, why do you hate her so?"

"You met her, sir, a hard, selfish woman! Too, there is her treatment of my brother." Her gaze dropped to her hands in her lap. "I have other reasons, but they be not to be spoke on."

Mr. Franklin looked as if he very much wanted those reasons, but he did not press her. "Tell me your history, if you please," said he.

She drew herself up. "I am Mrs. Martha Clay, widow of John Clay, a tailor under the sign of the scissors in Bradford Street, but my maiden name was Martha Inch, and I am the only sister, indeed the only living relation—save the wife and daughter—of Ebenezer Inch. My brother was four years older than I. Our father was a leather-dresser, of Kent, a respectable man who taught his children to read and write. He apprenticed Eben early to printing, in London; thus at the age of twelve my brother went off, and I did not see him for some years. Shortly after, our mother died and father fell on hard times, and I saw I must work. At sixteen, I found a place in a milliner's in London, near Eben. We were ever fond of one another, and had exchanged many letters while we were parted, though his had grown troubled and fallen off."

"Troubled?"

"There seemed some difficulty with money, and with a man who was pressing him for it—a man he feared, though I never learned his name. At any rate, Eben was pleased to have me near him in London, and in the next months we spent many happy times together though I was heartsick to see him drink so much. Too, his worries over money increased 'til he seemed quite distracted. Yet he had a good heart, and I longed to help him."

"What year was this?" inquired Mr. Franklin.

"Seventeen hundred and twenty-six."

"More than thirty years ago . . ." murmured the gentleman. "Pray, continue."

"After a time there seemed more than money to torment Eben. The man who had pressed him for it wished to draw my brother into some sneaking business."

"Of what sort?"

"I never knew. O, it was anguish to watch poor Eben squirm and wriggle! At last he succumbed—or was on the brink of doing so, when he escaped and left Watt's printing. 'A benefactor has spared me,' said he in our one brief meeting before he fled London, north, to a printing establishment in a small town in the Midlands." Mrs. Clay's face hardened. "Would it had been some other town, for there he met Dora Pulley."

"Who is now Dora Inch?"

"The same."

"And when did you see your brother again?"

"Not for many years. I guessed from his letters that he still drank, but he prospered for a time, even opening his own shop. He wrote to me of the woman named Dora Pulley. 'She has a head for business,' said he, and I was glad for him, though my joy did not last long, for after she had him in marriage she applied her evil influence, and his letters grew less frequent, and I began to wonder sometimes if she did not intercept mine and keep them from him, for I had had bad luck and was very down and strongly wanted money to save me, but he never answered my pleas, not to say yes or no. A woman who is desperate and alone has a hard time of it, Mr. Franklin."

He nodded in sympathy.

Her chin lifted proudly. "Yet I did not do as many in my place might; I was no Moll Flanders. Rather than turn thief or whore I gathered together what I could and hoped for a husband. My father was dead, and there followed many bad years when I did not hear from Eben at all, yet I scraped by and at last found Mr. Clay and was a good wife to him twenty years, though we had no children. He died three years ago. I still keep his shop, which lets me hold up my head."

"And when did your brother return to London?"

"Some dozen years ago, though it was not until after my husband died that I learned quite by chance that he was here. We had a tearful reunion—imagine rediscovering an only brother after so long! Yet I saw all too soon that drink had him by the throat, as did his wife. He was caught between two hard places. I visited him sometimes in Fish Lane, but was so ill met by the woman that I soon gave that up. We took to meeting in my shop or in St. James's Park, where we strolled arm-in-arm remembering better times." She gazed at me. "Before I gave up going to Inch, Printer, I saw this boy there. I pitied him."

At this her brother's gray eyes seemed to shine out from hers, and her words so touched my heart that I fought a lump in my throat.

"Of late Eben seemed afraid," Mrs. Clay went on. "Of what I do not know, but I feel sure it was something relating to this fear which caused him to be struck down yesterday morn. It may not be his wife—but yet it may. O, I know not. I *do* seek justice. I am but a woman, yet you, a man, may do something, mayn't you? I have no claim on you, but I apply nonetheless."

She fixed a look of fierce hope on Mr. Franklin, but he said nothing for some time, seeming lost in a trance, the soft afternoon light glowing in his glasses. The cry of a knife-grinder echoed from the street beyond the tall curtained windows, and I could hear the muffled sounds of Mrs. Stevenson preparing supper belowstairs. "Well, I shall do what I can," said the gentleman at last, "though you must not expect much from a poor agent of a distant colony."

"O, thank you!"

"Have you ever been to America, Mrs. Clay?"

She blinked. "Why . . . no."

"But had your brother?"

"I believe not. He met you here, did he not?"

Another far-off look. "I was indeed in London many years ago." His gaze became sharp. "Do you know aught of the American Indians?"

She started a little. "Near nothing. Why do you ask?"

"Oh . . . seashells," said he abstractedly. "You said your brother had fallen into bad hands. Hands other than his wife's?"

"May be."

"You spoke of her 'sneaking friends.' Who?"

"Before today I had not been in Fish Lane many months, for more than a year. But I used sometimes to see her speaking to persons whose eyes would not meet mine. At these moments she would glower at me as if I were a spy set upon her by some enemy, and would whisk these persons from view. Indeed, she called me spy today."

"Used the very word? These suspicious persons—men and women both?"

"Mostly women, come to think on it."

"Did any drive off in a fine coach?"

She gave a mocking laugh. "They were not the sort."

"And the lad, Buck Duffin—what do you know of him?"

"Mrs. Inch favors him, though why I could not say. He has been corrupted into thinking he is better than he is. There is ambition in that house, Mr. Franklin. Dora Inch hopes to marry her daughter far above her station, though where she will find dowry enough to persuade some squire's impecunious son to take on Tilda I cannot guess."

"O, it may be more than money will do that." He asked one or two more questions, but there seemed little she could add; so, with further kind assurances that he would do his best though all might come to nothing, he saw her to the door.

Returning, he stood gazing speculatively at me. By now the day was shading into dusk and the front parlor swam with shadows. "What do you make of it, Nick?" asked he.

"A question has been puzzling me, sir. If Mr. Inch was murdered because he surprised robbers at Mrs. Inch's money box by the shop door, why did they do him in in the back yard, where neighbors might hear?"

"Why do you think?"

"Please, sir, I believe there were no robbers."

His smile was barely visible in the gloom. "Indeed I believe as you."

Mrs. Stevenson bustled in. "Dear Mr. Franklin!" cried she as the gentleman sputtered a great loud sneeze.

❧ 4 ❧

IN WHICH the investigation begins . . .

WITH much clucking, like a mother hen, Mrs. Stevenson pressed Mr. Franklin to climb up to bed. She touched her mole. "You *shall*, sir! At *once*, sir! Else your distemper will turn to a catarrh and a pleurisy and who knows what may be?"

Indeed his eyes were red, his nose damp, and, noting her finger on the formidable mole, which seemed to signal the last word in dealings with his landlady, he shrugged and relented and shortly was propped up and tucked in soundly in his room, a fire blazing in his hearth, an infusion of inchona bark in wine by his bedside.

"Read to me, Nicolas," commanded he gently.

"Gladly, sir." Following his pointing finger I pulled from his ample shelves a slim red-leather volume.

"The Spirit of Laws," said I, "by—"

"Montesquieu," pronounced he, patting the bed to show I might sit there. "Proceed."

I did so, the fire crackling at my back. The gentleman's brown eyes seemed to drowse, yet they watched me, and I sensed he tested me; thus I was pleased to read tolerably well, so that if unfamiliar words sometimes caused me to falter yet I got my tongue round their sound. In truth I hardly listened to what I spoke, for the interview with Mrs. Clay remained much on my mind. Under what circumstances had Mr. Franklin previously

47

knqwn my dead master? Was it then untrue that he had come to Fish Lane merely on business? This stirred new interest in the scrap of paper, the button, the shells. What had shells to do with Indians? As for the black-handled carving knife, finer than any I had seen at Inch, Printer, was it sure proof that Mr. Inch had not surprised robbers who then killed him? Most puzzling of all, why had Mr. Franklin swept pieces of type into his hat?

"You read well, Nicolas," said the gentleman after a time.

"Thank you, sir," said I.

That afternoon Dr. Fothergill arrived, summoned by Mrs. Stevenson. The Scots gentleman raised a brow to find me at Mr. Franklin's side but said nothing, only thumped Mr. Franklin's chest and peered into his throat and eyes. "Still at air baths, Ben? I hold the morning air pernicious, but will you be advised? Well, well, we may nip this in the bud—though cupping may prove to be called for."

Mr. Franklin waved a dismissing hand. "Bark will suffice. I have found by a good deal of experience that three or four doses taken at the first symptoms will generally put a cold by."

A handsome young gentleman strode in. "Not well, father?" said he with a brisk air of having just got in from some business.

"William!" Mr. Franklin beamed upon him. "Fothergill says I must avoid the air—though I cannot see how that which sustains life may pander to illness."

The doctor sniffed. "At a certain age a man ought to begin to imitate his children, especially one so sensible as your William."

Mr. Franklin chuckled. "Come, Billy, meet the latest addition to our household, young Nicolas Handy. Nick, this is my son William, who accompanied me to London to study law. It is he who has the room opposite mine, though I am sorry to say he is not often there." He winked. "His studies at the Inner Temple keep him much away—as does his gadding about the town."

"I confess that all things esteemed most curious engage my attention," said the young man primly, looking me up and down. I judged him twenty-five or so. He wore clothes very fine, which fit him well, and a small white wig.

"How do you do, sir?" said I.

He examined me through a little glass, which hung from a ribbon. "Is this some stray?"

"Not a bit of it!" assured Mr. Franklin. "He is a boy I found much put upon. I have taken him in."

His son gazed at me skeptically. "Well, as my father insists upon having you, welcome. Yet, be grateful—see you do right by him."

"O, I mean to, sir," said I.

"I heartily hope so."

Humming, William strode off. I thought I should go too, for Mrs. Inch had beaten into me that I must be seen and heard as little as possible, but Mr. Franklin bade me stay. "You may learn something, Nick." Thus I remained while he and the doctor talked of the sun's rays, the cause of dew, waterspouts, musical instruments, electricity, and many other subjects. I marveled at the range and vigor of their discourse; to their minds nothing was given but must be probed and examined. Dr. Fothergill was also a Fellow of the Royal Society, this being a club of scientific investigators, much honor accruing to him who was admitted to it. Day waned to evening. Mr. Franklin was hot in argument of the advantage of "pointed conductors" when Mrs. Stevenson came to say supper was laid and, with a curtsy, that Dr. Fothergill was wished to stay to it.

"I shall fetch up a tray for *you*, sir," said she to Mr. Franklin, but he protested lying abed while we made a jolly company below.

"Never fear, I shall bundle up warmly, dear lady." And he pulled a great fur cap onto his head.

Shortly we were all—his landlady, Polly, Mr. Franklin, William, Dr. Fothergill and I—round the table in the dining room, candle flames leaping, spoons clicking on white bone china amid the aroma of boiled beef. I saw from certain small glances and smiles that Mrs. Stevenson and Mr. Franklin believed some romance might arise between William and Polly; yet the young woman seemed to find Mr. Franklin's son too stiff, often tweaking him with little jibes. Indeed she appeared to favor the father, and I began to see that though he was not handsome—in truth, rather plain—Mr. Franklin was favored by the ladies. There followed much lively conversation, and, though at first silent, I was led by and by to join in the laughter, sometimes even to put in a word or two. It crept upon me that here was truly no Mrs. Inch to glare me down or Buck Duffin to kick me under the table, and I forgot for those two candlelit hours that horrible murder had been done to the one man who had been a father to me.

I slept again in the cozy room at the back of the house.

"Fetch a hackney coach, Peter," commanded Mr. Franklin briskly next morning. "Master Nicolas and I must be off."

I had led a very circumscribed life at Fish Lane, hardly glimpsing the Thames. And as for the finer streets of London, they were as strange to me as the New World. I had seen few men of the African race and now peered close at Peter's black, burnished face hovering in the doorway. He wore yellow livery. "Yes, sir," said he, bobbing his head before smartly going downstairs.

Mr. Franklin saw my eyes follow him. "Peter is a loyal, sturdy fellow, none better. He and King sleep in the attic room above."

"I heartily hope, sir, that it is a warm attic, unlike the one I shivered in at Inch, Printer."

"Ah, Nicolas!" sighed he.

In ten minutes Peter was back with a coach. Mrs. Stevenson produced a coat for me to wear over my new shirt and breeches, and a cap as well, though she protested heartily Mr. Franklin's going out and insisted on winding a long woolen scarf three times about his neck. To this he submitted with a cheerful patience. "You are as good as a wife, dear lady." And he patted her hand, at which her cheeks flushed bright as a berry, and she fluttered off like a bird to her kitchen.

His expression grew gloomy. "My business with the Penns runs very ill. How it galls me to cool my heels in the antechambers of power when my people in Pennsylvania wait on my deeds! Yet that leaves time to see what I may do for Mrs. Clay. I intend to return to Fish Lane, Nick, with you by my side."

My heart sank at this. "If you wish, sir."

"Never fear, Mrs. Inch shall not lay a finger on you. Let us be off."

We stepped out the door onto a little porch. The day was not as fine as yesterday, there being little breeze to carry off the London smoke, so a brown murkiness suffused everything.

Mr. Franklin paused to stretch his arms. I took this opportunity to examine our environs. The street was a pleasant one, with much rattling traffic. Number 7 gleamed in brass at my shoulder, and I saw we were part of a double row of brick terrace houses sloping gently toward a timber yard by the Thames, not fifty yards away, where rowboats and wherries plied the gray-green waters and fishermen cast their nets. "Craven Street," Mr. Franklin pronounced, gesturing, "lately called Spur Alley. We are nearly in the shadow of Northumberland House." He pointed up away from the river. "That way lies the Strand. Many barristers from Gray's Inn reside in Craven Street." He laughed. "There is even a song." In a fine baritone he warbled:

> For the lawyers are just at the top of the street,
> And the barges are just at the bottom;
> Fly, honesty, fly to some safer retreat,
> For there's craft in the river and craft in the street.

A passing vegetable coster with a great hooked nose peered at the gentleman singing on the stoop, but Mr. Franklin merely smiled and made a little bow and a surprising little caper, and I had to laugh both at that and the wit of his song.

Shortly we were in a hackney with Peter at the reins.

I had but one other time ridden so fine, and that was when Mr. Franklin brought me to Craven Street. But that had been at night, I in a stunned, crumpled state due to Mr. Inch's murder. Now the morning air filled my nostrils, and I longed to see all. Seeming to sense this, Mr. Franklin directed Peter to drive about so I might view London. Indeed it was the first time I had seen much of the great city, and I gazed at everything with keen interest: St. James's Park, the grand houses along Pall Mall, the bustling commercial streets, the great squares, Covent Garden Market, and the surging throngs everywhere, gentlemen and ladies in finery and women and children begging in rags. Again I felt Mr. Franklin's brown eyes watching me. What passed through his mind? He seemed to wish me to be pleased—he took delight in my delight—but a growing affection made me fear to lose him, as I had lost my mother and Mr. Inch.

My anxiety must have shown, for he patted my shoulder. "Banish fear, Nicolas. You have found a home and shall never leave it but you choose to do so."

"I hope so, sir."

At last we approached Moorfields, the ways growing narrower, the houses overhanging and seeming to beetle and frown, and I could not suppress a shudder. Yet I put my trust in Mr. Franklin. He ordered Peter to stop some distance from Inch, Printer. "We shall walk, lad, for I wish to learn the lay of the land. Faugh!" He leaned heavily on his bamboo as he got down. "I may one day soon keep my own coach, for these hackneys are wretched things! Indeed this one has roused Mr. Gout to terrible spite." Yet such was his keenness that he was soon striding along as if his legs were as free from pain as mine, I scurrying by his side as he poked his nose everywhere, like a hound on the scent. "And what is this lane . . . this alley . . . where does this lead . . . how far does that go?" Carts passed us, and we were jostled by people with faces I knew and did not know, but all eyes looked right through me. We made a very circuitous route. "Watchman Barking spoke true when he said he should spy anyone who left or entered Fish Lane," observed Mr. Franklin, "for it is the center of a maze of streets."

At last we came in sight of the words INCH, PRINTER on their peeling wooden sign; above them, the small attic window out which I had gazed like a rat in a cage just two mornings past. I shivered. How much had changed for me! Mr. Franklin halted opposite my former prison, his head cocked, his eyes narrow behind his glasses, his right hand pulling in deep concentration at his lower lip. The lane was little more than a dozen feet wide; there was nothing taking about the view: a three-story house with two steps up to its shop door and an iron railing separating the areaway from the street. Indeed the house at our backs, Mrs. Couch's, was very like it. We stood against her railing.

A stirring caused me to glance behind me, down into her areaway. Two sharp, glittering eyes met my gaze.

"The boy, is't not? Who ran away from Inch's?" came a high squeak of a voice.

"Yes, ma'am," said I.

Mr. Franklin turned to gaze down too. "And who may this gentlewoman be, Nick?"

"Mrs. Couch," said I.

He tipped his hat.

"O, a fine gentleman," said she.

"A plain gentleman, ma'am," said he.

Another squeaking laugh. "Please come in, sirs. I shall be right up to let you." She disappeared into her lower door.

Mr. Franklin's glance asked what we were to make of this. Then his face contorted, his cheeks grew red. He sneezed loudly, twice, and blew his nose.

Two moments later we were seated in Mrs. Couch's front parlor.

Mrs. Couch offered Mr. Franklin sherry. A dark-haired young woman delivered it on a little silver tray. She was very pretty, wearing a dress cut low over a powdered bosom, and she smiled coyly on Mr. Franklin and on me, too, which made me flush. She wore much paint, her lips quite scarlet, yet I guessed she was no more than sixteen. She swished her hips in a provoking way, which made me feel unaccountably sad. No happiness lit her eyes; indeed her smile seemed put on with her paint, and I was brought to mind of my captivity at Inch, Printer.

"Your daughter?" inquired Mr. Franklin when the girl was gone.

"O, I have many daughters," said Mrs. Couch with a wink.

"I see," said Mr. Franklin.

For my part I looked about the room with wide eyes. There was nothing like it at Inch, Printer—come to that, at Number 7, Craven Street, either. It was a crowd of curtains and sofas and cushions, all soft and plush, pink and vermilion, piled high in a kind of warm, luxuriant jumble. The light was very dim. Mrs. Couch reclined on one of her sofas, at my elbow. She must be past forty but was painted too, with a patch on her little jutting chin and one on her cheek. She was as round and plush as one of her cushions and her ample flesh threatened at any moment to tumble from a gown more low-cut even than her serving girl's. She smoked a little pipe which had anise seed mixed in the tobacco; the smell was everywhere. Her eyes were as sharp as a ferret's.

"You are Mr. Franklin?" said she.

"You know my name."

"I have spoke to Mrs. Inch. You have an enemy in her, sir."

"Pray, why?"

"You have stolen her boy."

"She does not own him. Nor do I. I have told Nicolas he may go where he pleases."

Smoke billowed from her lips. "He chooses to remain with you?"

"For the time being."

She laid a beringed hand on my knee. "And where is that, child?"

"In Craven Street, ma'am," replied I.

She withdrew her hand, for which I was very glad, for it had gripped me like the claw of a hawk. Her gaze slid back to Mr. Franklin. "Why should you take interest in an orphan?"

"You say you have many daughters, Mrs. Couch. Are they not orphans too?"

She laughed her squealing laugh. "Some may be. Yet I do not think you give this boy shelter for the reason I offer my girls a home."

"A home, you call it?"

"Aye. For gentlemen, who like it better than their own."

"Gentlemen who arrive in fine coaches?"

54

"All sorts come here. Should you like to make it your home sometimes, sir? I doubt not it would please you."

"O, I think not, Mrs. Couch." He smiled over his sherry. "Your present hospitality is a great sufficiency."

"You flatter me."

"I tell the truth. You are Dora Inch's friend?"

"Not to speak on. We nod sometimes, across the way."

"Yet she told you I was her enemy."

Mrs. Couch waved her pipe. "Sorrow may make a woman confide in anyone. She sorely misses her husband. What dreadful murder!" She shuddered. "I see to my locks now, I assure you."

"Yet you invite in strangers."

"I knew the boy." Ever puffing, watching Mr. Franklin with a fixed little smile, she inquired about his home in America, his family, his business in London. He smiled in turn but gave little reply, only answering with small dismissing waves of the hand and a you-know or a you-see. She was clearly not pleased to get so little from him, yet she kept her smile, and he smiled too, and all was a quiet, barbed battle of politeness. As they thrust and parried I heard women's voices about the house, arguments, sometimes tiny laughs, once a sob. There was the rustle of petticoats too, and three or four times women passed by and peered in. I recognized some of these.

There came a lull in Mrs. Couch's sallies, into which Mr. Franklin deftly stepped. "Did you see or hear anything the morning of Mr. Inch's murder to say who might have done it?" asked he.

"O, I was fast asleep."

"No gentlemen visitors?"

She mimicked dismay. "At such an hour?"

Mr. Franklin gazed about the parlor as if in great admiration. "How long have you resided here?"

But it was Mrs. Couch's turn to parry questions, which she did as well as he, though Mr. Franklin had more skill at seeming not to mind. Another woman arrived, this one older and, though still pretty, much used-looking, like a blown rose, with a great mass of reddish hair hanging undone about her shoulders. Sullen-eyed, she murmured some message to Mrs. Couch, in which I heard the name, Mrs. Mountjoy, which I thought I knew too. Mrs. Couch sent her away and shortly Mr. Franklin rose and said we must be off. He thanked Mrs. Couch for her hospitality. "I wish you and your daughters well," said he as we departed.

In the lane the gentleman shook his head. "Poor young women, to be so used."

I heard a clattering sound and, looking down, saw the girl who had brought Mr. Franklin's sherry. She was emptying a pail of scraps in a dustbin in the areaway. Mr. Franklin saw her too, and, glancing up, she looked terrified to find two pairs of eyes on her.

"If I may help in any way . . ." said the gentleman kindly, leaning over the black iron rail.

She glanced at the area door, as if someone might hear. "No. O, no." Clutching the pail to her breast she shrank back.

"Have you no relations?" persisted he. "How came you here?"

"From M-Mrs. M-Mountjoy," quavered she and fled indoors.

We stepped aside to let a vegetable barrow pass. "It is a cruel world," mused Mr. Franklin, "where people trade in flesh as costers do in marrows."

"Sir," said I, "I have heard Mrs. Mountjoy's name. From Mrs. Inch's lips."

"And what did the woman say of her?"

"I heard only the name. Too, sir, three of the women who glanced into Mrs. Couch's parlor as we spoke—I have seen them at my master's, talking with Mrs. Inch."

"What about?"

"I know not. Mrs. Inch would have flayed me for listening."

He thumped his bamboo on the cobbles. "A pretty pair, Mrs. Inch and Mrs. Couch! Does Mrs. Mountjoy round out the sisterhood?" He polished his glasses vigorously with a cotton cloth. "Though I have been in London but two months I have heard Mrs. Mountjoy's name, with both good and ill spoke of her. Mrs. Couch wished to sound me deeply, did she not? O, she is a sly one! Does she know more about your master's murder than she reveals?" He fit his glasses onto his nose. "Would that I knew her secret thoughts. And now, to the watchman. Mr. Barking's favorite

tavern was the Twelve Bells, was't not? Do you know where it lies?
Nearby? Then lead me there at once."

The Twelve Bells lay in Rooster Alley. It was an old half-
timbered inn which had been proud and prosperous in good
Queen Bess's time. Now, sadly sagging, it was shouldered by taller
houses that looked to bully the breath from it. It had drooping
eaves and a soot-blackened chimney like a crumpled hat; inside,
the floors were sunken, and everywhere the smell of beer. Truly it
saddened me to pass its low, mean portal, for time and again I had
helped Mr. Inch from it when Mrs. Inch cried for him at home.
   This I told to Mr. Franklin.
   "So your master sought refuge here, poor man. Soon, lad, you
must tell me all you know of Inch, Printer."
   We looked about. There was a murmur of talk, and gruff
guffaws. Though a log sputtered in a stone fireplace, the long,
low-ceilinged room was dark as a cave, so it took some seconds to
discover Mr. Barking, at a small round table in a far corner. Two
men sat with him, three watchman's staves, as knobby as their
owners, leaning against the gray, grimy wall as if resting after
much labor.
   We made our way across the room. "Mr. Barking," said Mr.
Franklin softly.
   A skinny neck twisted round, and suspicious eyes glimmered in
the gloom. "Th' man at Inch's, ain't it?" grumbled the watchman.
   "You remember true, sir."
   The crabbed little man shook with silent laughter, as if the
comedy he had witnessed there promised a resumption. "And not
'ere by chance, I'll wager."
   "You win your wager. I sought you out."
   "And why?"
   "May we speak alone?"
   Mr. Barking glanced at his wizened cronies. All three laughed
together. Then the two companions scraped back their stools and
scuttled away grinning as if they never left off jeering at the
world. "O, ye may sit," said Mr. Barking, gesturing. We did so.
The pot-boy arrived, and Mr. Franklin ordered another gin for

Mr. Barking and a sillabub for me, though he took nothing himself.

"Now," said he, leaning forward.

"Aye, now," echoed Mr. Barking, watching with glittering eyes.

Mr. Franklin proceeded to inquire about the watchman's rounds, which ways he took and when and how. In his short hour in the neighborhood Mr. Franklin had got a remarkable picture of its twisting paths, for he spoke of them as if he had lived here for years. Mr. Barking answered readily enough, seeming proud of knowing every alley and mews. At last, after a little pause in which he glanced about as if to assure himself no one might hear, Mr. Franklin said, "And now, sir, you will please to say who you saw return to Fish Lane two mornings ago."

Mr. Barking's brows shot high. "Ye say I lie, sir? No one. I spoke true then, I speak so now."

Mr. Franklin shook his head. "I have already got it from the person, Mr. Barking, and that person is prepared to swear to the magistrate, for this same person feels very bad about withholding facts pertaining to murder. It is a grave matter. Yet I can keep that person from the magistrate, and may keep you from scrutiny too, but only if you confide in me. I assure you, you may lose your place as watchman of Moorfields if you do not speak."

Sparks flew up in the fireplace. Mr. Barking growled warningly, yet his brow creased to a hundred lines. "Damn me, wot's it got t'do with ye?"

"Who did you see that morning, Mr. Barking?"

"But, if she's already spoke to ye . . ."

"She has, but I must know if she lies. Yet if she does, she does so well, and the magistrate may believe her, and then you may spend your nights as well as your days in the Twelve Bells for all the watching you'll be paid to do." Mr. Franklin's voice was soft but adamant: "Tell all, Mr. Barking."

The watchman's yellowish eyes sent a trapped look about the tavern. "Arr!" said he at last, "—the Inch daughter, that's who it were."

"She paid you to say you had not seen her?"

"A shilling, many's the time."

"She was out many times?"

"Six or eight. Sneakin' in when it were still dark. O, that mother o'hers would've spit like a cat t'know it!"

"Where had she been?"

"I dun know."

"And she always returned at the same hour?"

"Aye. Near seven."

"Who else did you see that morning?"

"No un! I swear!"

Mr. Franklin peered close. The watchman fidgeted and rubbed his face hard as if to erase himself from his interlocutor's presence, yet he persisted in saying he had seen no one else. Had I been mistaken that Buck Duffin too had been out?

Mr. Franklin let be. "Now, about the fine coach . . . ?"

"O, ye'll be onto me about that, will ye?"

"Tut, you are too sharp-eyed, sir, to have seen as little of it as you say. Come now, was there more money exchanged hands?"

"Not a groat!"

"But you did see it better than you told Constable Nittle?"

"Wot if I did?"

"Who was in it?"

"I dun know." His eyes grew sly. "But there might o' been a crest on the side that might o' showed the letter B."

"B, is't? And had you seen this B in Moorfields before?"

"Some nights."

"In Fish Lane?"

"Aye."

"Where did this B stop?"

"I nivver looked fer that. It was a some fine lord's, and a lord may do wot he please."

"And is that all?"

"All, divil take ye."

After one last piercing glance Mr. Franklin rose. "Thank you, sir. I trust I shall have no need to trouble you more."

Out in Rooster Alley I gazed up in wonder. "Sir, when did you speak to Tilda Inch?"

"Never," said he with a little smile, "but t'would be a poor angler who fished without bait. My bait was a small lie—and see what we have caught!" His brown eyes danced as he turned on heel. "Let us next cast our line at Inch, Printer, lad."

It had gone two when we came again to Inch, Printer, spreading its shadow across Fish Lane. Mr. Franklin had first spent some time knocking on the doors of those houses whose back windows looked out upon the little yard where Mr. Inch had been struck down, but few souls would speak to him, and those who did said they had seen and heard nothing 'til Dora Inch took up wailing over the body. "Courage, Nick," said the gentleman as we came to her door. "Though Mrs. Inch may protest, yet I believe she is well pleased to have you gone."

The shop was open, and we stepped in, the brass bell tinkling.

At once a storm rose from behind the door, where Mrs. Inch kept her little office, with its shelves and desk with cubbyholes. She loomed up out of it as if she had waited to explode upon us. "You!" cried she, red-faced and trembling, at Mr. Franklin. "And you!" she shot at me, shaking a finger in the old warning way, at which I ducked behind the gentleman.

"Indeed it is we, ma'am," said Mr. Franklin. "We are just come to see if we may offer succor to this house of sorrow. Pray, has Constable Nittle collared the vile robbers who murdered your husband?"

"He has not," said she, "and I want no succor from a stranger. I have thought much on you. Who can vouch for you? I have urged Constable Nittle to inquire into your character. For all I know you may be the very man who brought me to grief by striking down my Eben."

"Grief? You seem not grieving now. As for my character, I should be happy to stand up to any scrutiny. There are many will speak for my good name. May you say the same? Is Mrs. Couch your friend? Will she say you are a fine, upstanding woman?"

Her tiny eyes blinked. "Mrs. Couch?"

"I spoke to her just this morning, in her parlor."

"You snooping man!"

At this moment Buck Duffin stepped in from the printing shop. Wearing his ink-smeared leather apron, he folded his arms and leaned at the door grinning meanly at this show. I felt sorry for the shop, for it must turn out inferior work with Buck at its helm.

It seemed Mr. Franklin would get no chance to speak to Tilda Inch this day, yet he seemed not disappointed but only beamed about as if amongst great friends. All the while since we came in his right hand had lurked in his coat pocket moving about as if he searched for something. Now the hand emerged, and of a sudden he stepped across the shop and heartily wrung Buck's hand. "Pleased to see you again, young sir!" He dropped something small and oyster-colored into his pocket, at once returning to Mrs. Inch. "And you, ma'am, as well!" said he, grasping her hand hard before she could snatch it back with an amazed little shriek. Again I glimpsed a small oyster-colored object drop into his pocket, though I was certain that in their astonishment neither Mrs. Inch nor Buck had glimpsed it. Mr. Franklin tipped his hat. "My regards to your pretty daughter, ma'am."

Out on Fish Lane he gazed across at Mrs. Couch's. "Such a narrow way. It is mere steps between 'em, Nick, is it not?"

"It is very near, sir," said I.

Ten minutes later Peter was trotting our mare back towards Craven Street.

❧ 5 ❧

*IN WHICH I am subject to the scrutiny of a
friend and the threats of an enemy . . .*

MR. Franklin's cold continued to plague him with sniffles
and aches, yet he would not go to bed, though Mrs.
Stevenson pleaded with him mightily. He looked
forward to an evening of pleasant disputation with friends, which
he would not miss for the world.

"I love conversation!" exclaimed he, going upstairs with his
bamboo. "How happy must be the folks in heaven, who have
naught to do but talk with one another, except now and then a
little singing and drinking of *aqua vitae!*"

These friends were, he told me as he merrily readied himself,
Dr. Fothergill, Mr. John Strahan, a printer with whom he had
corresponded for years, and Mr. Peter Collinson, a Quaker mercer
and botanist, who was also a member of the Royal Society.
Though he often hacked and wheezed, Mr. Franklin hummed as
he dressed, even putting on a white-powdered wig. His son
William was also to be a member of the party, and joined his
father at six in fawn-brown velvet with white ruffles. The high tilt
of his chin proclaimed he thought he cut a fine figure, but Polly
Stevenson only laughed.

"The cock flatters himself that such strutting pleases the hens,"
observed she. By the front door she pecked Mr. Franklin on the
cheek and, bundling him up, adjured him to stay out of drafts.
Father and son took coach with Peter.

I was left much to myself. I ate supper with Mrs. Stevenson and Polly and told them of our day, but they knew as little as I what to make of it. Later Polly curled up with Francis Bacon by an oil lamp in the back parlor, though her mother chid her that sewing would serve better than philosophy. I climbed the stairs and peered once more into the room behind Mr. Franklin's, which contained what I supposed to be his scientific apparatus. I hoped he would soon explain all these mysterious gears and wires and bottles. I crept further up too, to the attic, to see where Peter and King slept, and found the space small but cozy, with a little metal stove and the beds with thick coverlets. King sat on a stool by a guttering candle, hands between his knees, looking very dejected. I had heard Mr. Franklin say how unhappy he was, and, gazing on his sad eyes, I wondered how life was for him with his strange black skin alone except for Peter in this city of white faces. This brought to mind how I too had been alone for so long, and my soul cried with gratitude to have been found by Mr. Franklin.

How fortunate that chance had carried him to Fish Lane!

At last I went to the little room which had been set aside for me. Mr. Franklin had but two hours ago presented me with several sheets of foolscap. "This I writ on my voyage from America, in July. Do you know Poor Richard?"

"No, sir."

"Yet you do, for I am he; he is but one of my incarnations." He explained that he often wrote using *noms de plume*. "In jest," said he, "—though sometimes out of prudence, for honestly speaking one's mind may prove some danger. At the age of sixteen I became Mrs. Silence Dogood when my brother would not publish me because he thought me too young. I am Richard Saunders when I compose my *Almanac*. In this preface for 1758, which I call "The Way to Wealth," I am Father Abraham. Will you read it, Nick?"

Lighting my lamp and crawling into bed, I did as he wished. Father Abraham cited many of Poor Richard's sayings, some philosophical, many more practical, and I saw that Mr. Franklin was a man who knew the ways of the world. "Marry your son when you wish, your daughter when you can," Poor Richard advised, and, "The most acceptable service of God is doing good

63

to man." One saying fixed in my mind: "There are three things extremely hard, steel, a diamond, and to know one's self." Lying back, I stared at the night-blackened window. Did I know myself? Could I, if I did not know my mother?

Who had she been?

I held tight to my gold chain and locket as I sank into my third night of sleep at Craven Street.

"Well, Nick, and do you wish to ask me anything?" inquired Mr. Franklin at nine the next morning. "—for there are many questions I mean to ask you."

He sneezed so loud his bedclothes leapt.

The gentleman had not risen but lay propped up with watery eyes and much hoarseness. Grumbling, he drew from his nightshirt sleeve a handkerchief and noisily blew his nose, as he had done many times since I brought him hot cider from Mrs. Stevenson. The good woman was dismayed to find him badly distempered after his willful night out, but she was gratified too, to see her predictions so well fulfilled. "You *will* listen to me in future, sir," said she, touching her mole, but though Mr. Franklin bowed his balding head I saw a skirmish won but not the war.

He winked at me when she was gone.

Now I did not know what to say. The day was gray beyond the bow window. A fire crackled in the hearth. "Come, lad," Mr. Franklin urged. "You have made acquaintance of Poor Richard. What says he of time?"

"That of all things it is most precious."

"Excellent. It follows that the wasting of time is the greatest prodigality. My distemper has taken my legs but not my tongue. Be not shy, but apply to me." He tilted his head. "Or have you all you wish?"

I felt that I should prove myself dull if I asked nothing. Did the gentleman test me again? In truth there was much I wished to know, but though I had often stood up to Mrs. Inch and Buck Duffin, whom I despised, and spoke out even when they beat me, Mr. Franklin abashed me with his kindness. Yet his tone and look said I might make free, and so I said, "I should like very much, sir, to know about America."

"And I should like to tell you." He proceeded to say much of his home, of which I knew little, believing it to be a savage land. Yet there were, he said, great towns—Boston, Philadelphia, New York—and roads and farms.

"And Indians?" said I.

"To be sure," replied he sharply, "but why do you inquire about Indians?"

I felt some awkwardness. "You inquired of them to Mrs. Clay."

He nodded slowly. "So I did."

"Are they strange?"

He was some time answering. "They do not practice English customs," said he at last, "—yet they are human beings, with human hearts and minds. There are many tribes of 'em in America, but there are Indians in London too, did you know, brought to fill the goggling eyes of mobs? Walter Raleigh delivered the first many years ago, to display their savage finery before Queen Bess."

"I see. And what brought you here, sir? What are the Penns?"

"Men, or so they make out to be," said he ruefully. "The first was William Penn, a just man, a Quaker, who had a Royal Charter of land granted to him, which came to be called Pennsylvania. Philadelphia, its chief town, is my home, where my wife and daughter faithfully wait." He explained that, this William Penn being dead, the charter had passed to his sons, Thomas and Richard, arrogant men, called proprietors, and the colony, a proprietary colony. They maintained large estates in Pennsylvania but lived in London and showed a great disdain, refusing to allow their holdings to be taxed. Much vexed, the Pennsylvania Assembly had chosen Mr. Franklin as their agent, to come to England to try the brothers to see what might be wrung from them. But they had treated Mr. Franklin in a high and mighty manner, insisting that of old right their estates were and should remain free of taxes.

At this Mr. Franklin's face flushed scarlet. "And who or what are these Penns? In the province, unsizable subjects and insufficient lords. In London, gentlemen it is true—but gentlemen so very private that in the herd of gentry they are hardly to be found, not in court, not in office, not in Parliament. O, they are low jockeys!"

"Yes, sir," said I at this outburst.

"O. It will be hard to budge 'em, for they are like old trees on a hill, firmly rooted. I must make friends in power, I must discover a fair-minded member of Parliament to present a petition, I must . . ." He railed in this fashion for some moments, thumping the covers and blowing his noise, while I saw with every word how ignorant I was of men such as William Pitt and Lord Bute and even His Majesty, King George II, not to mention the privy council and secretaries of state and commissioners of customs and the board of trade, all which Mr. Franklin must make his way through under suspicious eyes. The wide world was a maze and a mire, it seemed.

"I have gone astray in answering your question, I see," said he at last, reddening.

"Indeed, no, sir. Your answer makes me wish to ask more on it."

"A sound mind is ever questioning. Yet let us leave this subject, for I fear there are weeks, nay months, of it to come. Is there anything else you wish to know?"

"What work was't you wished to have done at Inch, Printer?"

The pink showed brighter in his cheeks. "None, Nick. You have caught me at another lie." He took a sheet of paper from his bedside drawer. "It is time to show you this." Solemnly he passed it to me.

It proved a letter, in Mr. Inch's shaking hand:

Dear Friend,
Though it be many years since we have seen one another, yet I believe you are still generous of heart and would wish to do kindness where'er you may. So, hearing that you are returned to England after so long, I apply to you. There is danger about me, but, though I am a poor, weak man, ruined by drink, I mean to fight the threat, and will, if not for myself then for another. There

is a lad of whom I have grown fond; he is like a son to me, yet he suffers. Will you save him, before things go to ruin? Meet me early Monday morn at my printing shop in Fish Lane, Moorfields.

I count on this. If you do not come the world has changed indeed.

Ebenezer Inch

My eyes blurred with tears as I stared at these words: "fond . . . like a son . . . save him . . ." An aching sorrow rose in my throat, and I began to sob and could not stop. Mr. Franklin held me, and Mrs. Stevenson bustled in exclaiming, "Poor child!" and even Polly was there stroking my hair, all which only made me wail the louder, until at last, after many moments, I was wrung dry and sat sniffing and wiping my eyes.

"Leave us," said Mr. Franklin softly. When the women were gone, he said, "You loved him, did you, Nick? Well, he was a good man in spite of his failings." Sitting me away from him, he peered once more into my face, as if some secret were hid in it. Yet what was there to see?—a plain boy with brown hair. "You know now why I came to Fish Lane that morning. I have fulfilled Eben's wish to save you, yet I owe more—to his sister, to the poor man's memory, perhaps even to you. Did any odd circumstances surround his murder?"

"He was very stealthy the night before," said I, mastering my feeling. "He drew me aside as I headed upstairs, saying I must not be down at five but must wait, for he had someone to meet. You, Mr. Franklin?"

The gentleman pulled at his lip. "Could there have been two of us? Could the first one, man or woman, have killed him?"

"Woman, sir?"

"He was small. And as Fothergill noted, he was first struck on the head from behind. A woman could have done it."

I shivered at this. "O, I am very grateful you took me away!"

"When Eben spoke to you that evening, did anyone overhear?"

"The floorboards creaked—they made Mr. Inch start—but the old house was ever creaking. I do not know if anyone heard."

"Your master's letter spoke of danger. Have you any idea what it might be?"

"None, sir—though in the past weeks Mrs. Inch was harder on him than ever, as if something chased at her heels."

"Chased her?"

"That was how it seemed."

"Had Eben any enemies that you know of?"

"O, no, sir! He was a good-hearted man, well liked." I leaned forward. "But I have meant to tell you this: Mrs. Couch and Mrs. Inch were better friends than either let on, for they spoke often, on the sly. I saw 'em, though Mrs. Inch took great care never to let Tilda see 'em together. 'Mrs. Couch is a wicked woman!' she always said to her daughter."

"Indeed? There were secrets, then, at Inch, Printer? Mrs. Couch—I pity the poor creatures who work for her. The best that may be said is that she saves 'em from thieving and beggary. Yesterday you said you saw some of these young women with Mrs. Inch?"

"Before they went on to Mrs. Couch. They would come to the shop door, shivering and looking miserable. I would fetch Mrs. Inch for 'em, though when she came she chased me away fast enough. Sometimes men came with the young women."

"Men?"

"Sneaking sorts."

"Would you know their faces?"

"They hid behind turned-up collars and hung back and looked away."

"But names, Nick—have you any names?"

"None beginning with B. Yet there is one I recall: Hexham. Mrs. Inch let it slip once. I remember well, because when she saw I may've heard it she struck out at me with her broom."

"Hexham." He sniffed mightily. "Can you describe him?"

"He kept his back to me, but he was a tall man in a black cloak. His voice was gruff, though he spoke like a gentleman. I am sure he was there several times."

"Did he ever speak to Mr. Inch?"

"Only once that I know. There was some dispute."

"What about?"

"I heard only raised voices."

"And how long ago was this?"

"Some weeks."

Mr. Franklin fidgeted with the bedclothes. "It is clear Dora Inch has some part in the traffic with these girls. As go-between? Yet who are the men? And this Hexham . . ." He gazed out at the gray day. At last his eyes came back. "What do you have to say for what Mr. Inch printed, lad?"

It was my turn to flush red. "I am ashamed, sir." In truth I had feared he might ask, ever since he perused the dried pages he stacked in the shop; for though in my early days at Inch, Printer, we had turned out respectable work—pamphlets and small volumes—for several years we had printed bawdy books which made me blush to set in type. I knew they much discouraged Mr. Inch, who was so fine a craftsman and had taught me well. He hated to turn his hand to such licentious stuff, even more hated to see me his accomplice. The books had pictures too, of a sort to make people seem mere rutting animals, and I believe they were why he defied his wife to give me finer things to read, so I might see the world was not so base as the lewd books showed. It was Mrs. Inch brought in the commerce in these things, though she took care never to let her daughter be tainted by them, ordering Tilda to stay away from the printing room under pretext that she might spoil her clothes by the ink. Mr. Inch often protested, but Mrs. Inch would snap at him: "There's money in it, fool!"

All this I told Mr. Franklin. "She kept the purse strings too, and would not hand over tuppence for drink if he balked—yet there seemed more to it, as if she had some hold over him."

"What hold, Nick?"

"Something from his past, yet I know not what."

Mr. Franklin sighed. "The past may be vinegar in milk, to curdle the cream. Mrs. Inch obtained the work? From whom?"

"I never saw. She would be out and about the town, and back with it."

He sighed. "To the morning poor Eben was killed. Tell all you know of it."

I said how I had waked at five, then fallen asleep only to be roused at seven by Buck Duffin's blow. "His bed was empty, and he was dressed as if just come in. As I went down he stood with his back to me, his fingers opening and closing at his sides."

"But no blood on 'em?"

"I did not see. But Mr. Barking spoke true about Tilda, sir. I saw her come in as I hurried down. She threatened me if I said a word about it. Another thing (though it may make no matter), the brass piece that strikes the bell at the shop door was bent so the bell would not ring."

"Oho! Yet it rang when we entered yesterday afternoon."

"I bent it back, when I hurried to send your note to Dr. Fothergill."

"Did someone silence it, to prevent the hearing of anyone creeping in? Remember, the door was unlocked too."

"May Tilda have left it so? Or Buck?"

"Perhaps. Yet I believe Mr. Barking told true when he said he had seen only Tilda. But if Buck was out as you suggest, how did he leave and return unobserved? It may've been Eben himself who unlocked the door, to let in a secret visitor. Mrs. Inch may've done it too. You did not see her that morning 'til she appeared in the kitchen?"

"No—yet her habit was to be down earlier."

Great furrows formed in Mr. Franklin's brow. "It is all a great puzzle. Is there anything more?"

"Again it may make no matter, sir—but I too heard a dog, as I fell back asleep near five."

His eyes narrowed. "Yet why should you recall a dog's bark?"

"It was not usual for Moorfields—that part of Moorfields at any rate, though we sometimes heard 'em. Moreover it was a strange bark, a lamentable yowling that made me pull the covers above my head."

He nodded, as if some notion had been affirmed. "I believe you shall hear more of this dog, Nick—from me. For now, what else do you recall?"

"Why . . . come to think on it, a strange smell. You smelled it too, sir, for you asked if I ate licorice. And I have smelled it in the shop before, though it was faint because of the printer's ink. Yet we smelled it yesterday as well—the anise in Mrs. Couch's pipe."

"Excellent, Nicolas!—Does not inquiring into murder prove very like the scientific investigating of Nature, in which one observes close, questions hard, gathers facts, discovers correlations, condenses them to a truth? We have begun, Nick, we see some facts—yet how may they correlate, what is their truth?" He rubbed his brow. "O, it brings on the headache!"

"But does the presence of the smell mean Mrs. Couch may have struck down Mr. Inch?"

"One of her girls may have done it. One of her 'gentlemen' too, for we ourselves departed her house yesterday with the stink of anise reeking in our clothes. Anyone might have carried it; the knowledge gives us much to ponder—yet there is more to think on. What make you of this? As you know, Dora Inch's office is hid behind the entrance door. Yet I make it my business always to look about where're I go, and I was particularly interested in your little shop of pens and quires, for in Philadelphia I and Mrs. Franklin kept one very like it, to much profit. I glanced into her office when I came in that morning—yet there were no papers flung about, no spilt ink."

"Mrs. Inch herself upset her things?"

"When Constable Nittle was unaware."

"To make it appear robbers had broke in?"

"It would seem so."

"Because she herself—?"

"Struck down her husband? A possible correlation—but does it express truth? Damn me, we must have more facts! The woman told Constable Nittle robbers had broke in once before. What do you know of the event?"

"It was a se'enight ago. Mrs. Inch's office was topsy-turvy, drawers pulled out and flung about, ledgers and letters scattered, the print shop in disarray. When she discovered it she went white as a sheet, even losing her tongue for half an hour."

"An extraordinary event! What was stolen?"

"I do not know. She paid little mind to her money box. It was her record books concerned her. She crawled about, scooping 'em up, muttering as she peered at each one as if none must be lost."

"And what were the daily habits at Inch, Printer, lad?"

For the next quarter of an hour, he probing with questions at every turn, I described how I rose early, and who came down after me and when, and how each hour passed. He asked particularly after Mrs. Inch, and I told of her penny-pinching, her sly ways, her meanness. I described Tilda's spoiled nature and vanity. I told how Buck was Mrs. Inch's favorite, though it was I who had taken over nearly all from Mr. Inch in his drunken despondency.

"What did she have against you, lad?"

"I know not."

"And did the wife never try to stop her husband's slide?"

"She was happy to pay for his drink, if he earned it by doing her will."

"A devilish woman!"

"She was most particular that I should not lurk about the areaway."

He gave a sharp look. "Why?"

"There is a storeroom, under the road."

"There are a thousand such in London. Mrs. Stevenson too has one."

"Mrs. Inch kept the key to this, and went there sometimes with much furtive peering about, as if someone might watch."

"And did you watch, Nick?"

"I dared not."

"O, I should love to see into this hiding place! Mrs. Clay said that Buck Duffin seeks above his station, Mrs. Inch too, wishing to marry her daughter to some fine gentleman. May you confirm this?"

"They are all very proud."

"Yet what to make of it?" The gentleman shook his head. "It is ever thus: answers spawn questions like streams spawn fish. We wade in murky water—I pray it be not quicksand." He sat in silence some moments, wheezing softly and gazing at his own thoughts through his glinting little lenses, while I placed a new log on the fire. Deep and low, King's voice came down the attic stairs in a plaintive song, and a costermonger's cry warbled in Craven Street.

At last Mr. Franklin roused himself. "Enough of poor Eben's murder." His gaze fell on me. "You, Nicholas Handy—how did you come to Inch, Printer?"

I shifted my feet. "I have been there as long as I can remember, sir."

"From a babe?"

"No."

"At what age, then?"

I did not like to be pressed close on this head. "Three or four, I think."

"You do not know?"

"No one has spoke of it for many years. I was four, perhaps."

"But why were you taken in? The Inches are relations of yours?"

"No such. Mrs. Inch was ever at me about how I should be grateful for her sacrifice in placing a roof over my head—I who was a bastard." I stared at my boot toes. "She called me that often. Bastard. To make me see my place."

"Yet you have schooling."

"None. I was always a boy of work."

"But you read and spell. And cipher too?"

These questions seemed to trap me. "A little. Mr. Inch taught me—that is, he gave me books that showed me how, and I worked at them by candle late at night."

"It was he who taught you reading?"

"My mother taught me that," said I through clenched teeth.

I heard him stir and faced him, tucked up to the chin in bedsheets, twin flames reflected in his glasses. "You knew her then?" asked he.

73

I could not answer, but only stared into these twin, licking flames. How could vague memories, a pale, ghostly face, the mere remembrance of kind words and loving hands be knowing? Yet it was all I had, and it was as if, should I speak of this precious store, it would prove mere fancy and crack and blow away.

"Nick, lad . . . ?" Mr. Franklin's voice was urgent, pressing. It seemed to pry where it had no right, to sink a wedge, to break the very heart of me. This—this was what I must pay for his kindness! O, there was ever a price.

"I cannot . . . cannot!" cried I, dashing from his room and from the house.

My headlong rush ended in the midst of Craven Street, in stumbling confusion, my soul writhing in shame. How could I so rudely have run from the only house which had ever shown me kindness? In misery, cursing myself for a fool, I scuffed at dirty cobbles as I wandered towards the Thames. Mr. Franklin was not to blame for wanting to know more of me, and I was a cowardly boy to fear talking of my mother.

A timber yard faced the river; here long planks were unloaded by burly, straining men. At Thames-side, hands glumly pocketed, I watched various craft leave criss-crossing wakes in gray-green swells. An old man cast a line from a small wooden wharf. Two ragged boys played tag nearby, while carts and wagons and an occasional small chaise rattled along Craven Street at my back. East rose a forest of masts, ships from the great world of which I knew so little.

All at once the costermonger's cry sounded near. Then a hand gripped my shoulder. "Apple, young sir?" came a wheedling voice.

I turned. Peering down at me, the coster loomed by his barrow holding out the fruit and nodding, as if he urged me to take it. He was tall but stoop-shouldered, with a large, beaked nose—I recognized him as the man who had watched Mr. Franklin sing his song at the door of Mrs. Stevenson's house. He wore a cap pulled low around a sallow face and had a nest of wrinkles about his eyes. His thin lips smiled to show yellowish teeth, but though the eyes smiled too I shivered at their cold, blue pupils, like little pebbles.

"I have no money, sir," said I stepping back.

"O, a gift," said he.

"But . . . why?"

"You come from Number Seven, dun't ye, lad?"

"I do," said I.

"Where Mr. Franklin resides?"

"Yes."

"Th' same Mr. Franklin was apokin' and apryin' about Fish Lane yestiddy? With a boy? And that boy be ye?"

I took another step back; one more would topple me in the Thames. "I was there with him indeed, but—"

"Pray, take the apple, lad."

"I do not wish to take it." Fearing the man—his wheedling words gave me chill—I made to go, but he snatched my arm and dragged me so close under his great, beaked nose that I could smell his reeking breath. I struggled in a grip like iron. "I expects boys t'do as they're bid," he hissed in a voice that said he would as soon cut my throat as spit, "and I bid ye do this: tell Mr. Franklin he's not wanted about Fish Lane. Yer the boy from Inch Printer, an't ye? Well, yer well rid o' that place—and it o' ye. Thank yer stars, and stay clear. Mr. Franklin likewise."

Thrusting the apple in my pocket, he grinned his awful grin, turned and began keening his high-pitched coster's song— "Apples! Carrots! Potatoes!"—as if nothing had passed between us. Trembling, I stared at his bowed back making its way towards the Strand. There seemed something peculiar about the stringy brown hair that poked out from his cap, and he lurched oddly as he turned into an alley.

Another hand on my shoulder made me jump—but it was only King. "Miz Stevenson says you mus' come in fer tea," said he, wearing his sad, defeated look.

Much shaken, I flung the apple in the Thames before following the servant.

❧ 6 ❧

IN WHICH a young woman floats on air, a dog walks on two legs, and Mr. Franklin accepts an invitation to dine . . .

I longed to beg pardon of Mr. Franklin, but it was not until late in the evening that I was able to see him again, and then in most surprising circumstances. Meanwhile I had tea with Mrs. Stevenson, who told me that the gentleman was sleeping. "Thank the lord he's abed!" proclaimed she. For my part I wished him awake so I might unburden myself of my shame, but this could not be, so I served out my wait performing chores: fetching water from the pump at the top of the road (I kept a wary eye peeled as I went), pulling weeds in the back garden, sweeping the areaway. After supper I ended by polishing a fine copper kettle so bright that Mrs. Stevenson gave me a firm sound hug and sent me off with a smacking kiss on the brow.

I went upstairs.

It was by then very dark, an autumn wind moaning about the eaves, the windows giving back a black sheen. Carrying a small lamp, I climbed to the deserted landing and peered hopefully in Mr. Franklin's room but found the covers thrown free and the bed empty, the fire near dead in the hearth. This somewhat alarmed me, the more because of peculiar sounds issuing from the chamber where he kept his experimental apparatus. This rearward door stood open a crack; a strange light dimly flickered within. Creeping to it, I recognized some sounds: a woman's giggles and the chortling of a man. Other sounds bewildered me: odd, crackling spurts, like the hissing of logs. At each spurt the muffled laughter grew louder.

Knocking, I called, "Sir?" and went in.

A single candle burned on a bench, this quite dim, but my lamp disclosed enough to make my jaw drop and my eyes bulge: Polly Stevenson floating horizontally in air in the middle of the room, Mr. Franklin beside her holding a long metal needle with which he drew spitting sparks of fire from her nose and ears, at which both he and she emitted stifled laughter.

Mr. Franklin raised a brow. "We are discovered, my dear," said he to Polly. He made a dramatic bow. "Enter, young sir, and feast your eyes upon the electrified girl!"

Polly smiled encouragingly. I took three cautious steps nearer and saw that in fact she did not float free but was suspended by silken cords hung from a stout wooden beam. She cradled a large glass tube in her arms.

"Should you like to try, Nick?" asked Mr. Franklin, offering me the needle. This was near twelve inches long and sharply pointed. Placing my lamp on a bench, I took it, though my hand shook.

"How, sir?" said I in a trembling voice, wondering if this was some magic from America.

"Merely hold it near," said he, gesturing.

I approached slowly. When the needle was four inches from Polly's right hand, which she lifted from the glass tube as if to greet me, a blue-white spark leapt from her index finger to the tip of the needle, at which I felt a sudden tingling in my hand and near dropped the instrument. I drew back violently.

"Well? What think you, lad?"

"I know not, sir. It is like . . . like little lightning."

"O, it is lightning indeed—though man-made, and in this form but a parlor trick. Polly rubs the glass tube, which builds up in her an excess of the electrical fluid, which excess I call 'positive.' The silken cords, which are nonconductors, prevent the charge being dissipated. But metal is an excellent conductor; further, pointed objects draw off an electrical charge, hence my needle. You, Nick, as do I, have a neutral charge, while Polly is like an overfull vessel brimming with need to spill its excess back into the general reservoir. When we come near her with the needle, her excess electricity is drawn to us by these sparks, thus demonstrating properties which I have had some small hand in bringing to light."

"You are too modest," said Polly, tapping his arm, which caused her to sway gently in air. "Mr. Franklin is world famous for his electrical writings, Nick. They are translated into many languages, and those who follow his teachings, even as far as Rome, call themselves 'Franklinists.' Indeed, King Louis XV of France once wrote in his own hand to thank him for his proof that lightning and electricity are one."

Mr. Franklin waggled a reproving finger. "Do not urge pride upon me, child. I could tell you of a girl who was observed to grow suddenly proud, yet none could guess the reason 'til it came to be known that she had got on a pair of new silk garters. I fear I have not so much reason to be proud as the girl had, for a feather in the cap is not so useful a thing nor so serviceable to the wearer as a pair of good silk garters."

"O, you wear laurels on your brow!"

"Laurels—or jester's bells?" came a new voice, and William Franklin strode stiffly in, wrinkling his nose. "More tricks? And with this girl? It wants dignity, father."

Polly sniffed in reproof. "Your father has sufficient dignity for *me*. Now, help me, if you please."

William held her hand as she slipped from the cords.

She curtsyed briskly. "Pray save your criticisms for *my* demeanor," said she to him.

William looked pained, which made me wonder if he liked Polly better than he showed. "Pray excuse me," said he. "I have much studying to be done." And he strode out.

"Tut," said Mr. Franklin, "though I love him I fear my son stands far too much upon formalities. Yet he is young, and though age stiffens the joints it relaxes the manner; he will come round. Yet he has a point." He placed a hand solemnly upon my shoulder. "I would not have you misregard the electrical fluid as a harmless toy. It has killed men who attempted to duplicate my experiment with lightning. Indeed I have proposed that it be used for the slaughter of animals, turkeys perhaps. Might your mother, Polly, provide a fine, fat specimen?" He gestured to some large glass vessels, which he called Leyden jars. "A battery of six must be fully charged. Following that, the prime conductor is applied to the head of the bird, killing it instantly." Thoughtfully he tapped his jaw. "Truly I wonder if such a method of execution would not be more humane than our public hangings at Tyburn, which turn justice to a circus. Do you think Parliament would find such an idea whimsical?"

Neither of us had opportunity to answer, for at that moment the gentleman burst into sneezing. "Faugh!" cried he. "I must to bed!"

When we were alone, Mrs. Stevenson having provided Mr. Franklin with one of her soothing toddies, I came forward to beg forgiveness, but he held up a hand to speak first. "I am very sorry, Nick," said he, "to have trespassed upon your privacy. I do not wish to pry."

"Nay, sir, it is I who am sorry!" I assured him my foolish fit had passed and that he might ask anything he wished. "My mother— my memory of her, that is—is all I have had for so long, yet the remembrances are so few and dim that I ran from speaking of them for fear they might prove false. But you are so good, I know I may entrust them to you."

He was silent a moment. "Truly I wish no harm. But it is truth I seek, and truth may sometimes sting. Are you certain, knowing this, that you would wish to talk of your past with me?"

"I am, sir."

"Stout lad."

"But there is something I must tell first." Shuddering, as if the sneaking costermonger's hand still held me hard under his beaked nose, I described my encounter at Thames-side.

Mr. Franklin's countenance grew grim. "A warning, is't? Damned blackguard! You say the dev'lish fellow's hair seemed odd?"

"Yes, sir, as if it was a wig."

"Yet who would wear a dirty brown wig? And he lurched strangely as he turned away into the alley?"

"He seemed to leap."

"Did he perhaps jerk upright, from his bent position?"

"Perhaps so."

"I believe the hair and bent back were a disguise, further attested by the fellow's sallow skin, for true costermen are out-of-doors all days, ruddy-faced. He was no vegetable seller, Nick—yet who may he really be? And you had never seen him before? Mmm. We must treat him as some danger. And yet . . ." Mr. Franklin looked hard at me. "I must confess I am not surprised at this—nor at his choosing you. Certain evidence . . ." But here he sank into his bemused state, trailing a finger back and forth along the edge of the coverlet. At last he looked up. "We must exercise great caution, we must be alert and keep our wits about us. You are not to go out unaccompanied."

"I shan't, sir."

"And now, Nick, may we speak of your mother?"

"If you wish."

"Sit here, on the bed." He folded his hands over his chest. "Tell me about her, lad."

Wind still nipped at the eaves, while blowing leaves ticked at the panes. "Would that my memory was clearer, sir," said I. "I remember a pretty face framed by brown ringlets, and a soft voice that said in many ways that it loved me. I remember sitting with books, and her going over the letters and words and how pleased she was that I was quick to understand and say them."

"Where did you look at these books?"

"In a big house."

"A wealthy house?"

"It seemed so, sir. There were maids and butlers."

"Was your mother mistress of this house?"

"O, no, sir. Yet I know not what she was. There was anger there,

80

and spite. I remember voices shouting at my mother, men's and women's. How I cried and hid!"

"Do you remember any names?"

"Who might have owned the house? No. Nor where it was."

"Faces?"

"It is all such a dream," said I. "Even my mother's face wants clear outlines, I being just four when my life there came to an end."

"And how came that end?"

A lump thickened in my throat. With an effort I stilled my twisting hands. "Someone rudely told me my mother was gone, dead, and I was to be put to work. I understood neither 'dead' nor 'work'—though I came to see what they meant soon enough, for I found myself next at Inch, Printer, never to see my mother again. There I stayed 'til you took me."

"Put to work at four," murmured Mr. Franklin, shaking his head. "And your father, lad—what of him?"

"I know nothing."

"Ah!" in a great wheezing sigh. "But did Mrs. Inch or Mr. Inch never speak of your mother?"

"Mrs. Inch only to abuse me. 'A girl in trouble,' she would say, screwing up her face. 'All the world knows the sense of that: her boy's a bastard!'"

"The heartless woman took pleasure in wounding you, I see."

"And I am not even sure of my name."

"You must be."

"No. 'I named you,' Mrs. Inch told me, 'cause yer handy about the shop, and little enough o' that.'"

He frowned. "Did you believe her?"

"I did not want to." I bent toward him. "O, Mr. Franklin, I want to believe I heard my mother's voice murmur my name to me: Nick Handy. Yet did I? Or is it only a wish, and was my mother a wicked girl who got in trouble by some lord—or perhaps only a coachman—and did not die but just left me?"

The gentleman was silent a long while midst the sighing of the wind. "She may have been," said he at last, his bespectacled eyes projecting a great, sad sympathy that seemed to go past me to the wide world beyond. "The sting of truth, indeed." His head tilted. "And how does it find you, Nick?"

I sat up straight. "I shan't flinch from it."

He smiled. "Bravely spoke. In standing up to it you may make truth lose her venom. But Mr. Inch—did he say nothing of your mother?"

"Little. I do not know if he even knew how Mrs. Inch got me. Yet once he let drop a hint my mother may have lived in America."

"And what hint was that?"

"It was some years ago, but . . ." I struggled to recall. "Boston is a town in America, is it not? Boston, he said, I believe."

"And nothing more?"

"Nothing that I can recall."

"Think on it, Nick. If you come upon more, tell me." He looked away for a moment, pinching his brow, then his bald head swiveled back as if some tip of the scales had been made. "What was your mother's name?"

"Rose."

"Rose," murmured he, seeming to taste the name, as if he bit into some strange fruit. "Should you like to find her, lad?"

"Find her?"

"Alive—or dead?"

"But she *is* dead."

"So you say you were told. Yet you yourself wonder if't be true. I do not say she is alive; she may not be. Yet many lies buzz in the air about Inch, Printer, like flies about carrion. Might her death not also be a lie?"

"But . . . why?"

"We have spoke before on the spawning of questions. This 'why' is yet another. I do not know the answer—yet a man should have his lineage; he should know his place in the world, you as much as any good fellow. I take an interest, Nick. A bastard? May be and may be not; it makes no matter. Bastard is an ugly word—

yet it says nothing of character, only of birth. Neither is it any reflection on the mother, who may have yielded out of love; there is no shame in that. Shall I tell you a fact? My son William is not the son of my wife Deborah, though she raised him as hers. Aye, 'tis true; further, I take pride in him: he is my flesh. Men and women will be begetting, and if they do not take the time to have the act licensed by state or God I see no crime. Do you heed me, Nick? Men will be as they are; to live we must sometimes forgive their errors—and our own."

I said I should take his words to heart.

He patted my hand. "Good fellow. Now." He adjusted himself to a more comfortable position. "I have agreed to help Martha Clay find the murderer of her brother. My business with the Penns creeps like molasses; the circumstance continues to give me leisure. Shall I help you as well? To find your mother—or at least to know more of her?"

"I should be grateful, sir."

He struck the covers. "Settled!" His look gently chided. "Should you not then tell me of the gold about your neck?"

My hand flew to the chain as it had often done at Inch, Printer, where Mrs. Inch and Buck and even Tilda had sometimes threatened to tear the gold from me. "Yes, sir," said I and drew from my shirt the small oval locket which hung from the chain. Unclasping it, I showed him the silhouetted face within.

"Your mother?" inquired he.

"So Mrs. Inch said. It is the one thing which came from childhood with me."

"I am surprised the vile woman let you keep the gold."

"Mr. Inch saw to that. He wavered on many matters, but he was firm on this. 'He has little else,' he told his wife, 'he must have this.'"

Mr. Franklin gazed long at the portrait. "Your mother is pretty, Nicolas," said he at last, relinquishing it. I shut it and slipped it back in my shirt. "Gold chain, gold locket." He wore his deep, speculative look. "There is wealth in this somewhere, lad."

He was silent for some time, while my thoughts turned otherwise. "Sir . . . the dog? I have been thinking. You said I would hear more of it?"

His gaze gleamed. "Things stick in your brain, do they? Excellent. Aye, the dog—or no dog at all, for it walked on two legs, Nicolas Handy, or I'll be hung in my nightshirt." He coughed, but his eyes glittered with a fever that had nothing to do with illness. "You have shown me a secret of yours, I will show one of mine." Reaching in his bedside drawer, he pulled forth the seashells which he had scooped from beside Mr. Inch and held them out in his palm, little flakes of pearl-gray which dully took the lamplight. "They say the sea once covered London. Was't the sea which dropped these by your poor dead master? No. what then—or who? Yet there is more mystery. I have made a study of shells, lad. You will find on my shelves Mr. Reverend Watson's book on them, an admirable work. It confirms my suspicion: these are Atlantic specimens—but from America's shores, not England's. What think you on that?"

"Why, then, sir . . . did an American drop them?"

"An American to be sure. Look." As I bent forward, our heads nearly touching, he pointed to small holes drilled in each shell. "These were strung on a leather thong, likely broke by your master reaching out as he was murdered. The shells were a necklace or belt. 'Wampum' it is called, and it is made by American Indian tribes."

A log collapsed softly on the grate. "An Indian killed Mr. Inch?" said I, staring into Mr. Franklin's brown eyes behind his glasses.

"So it appears. Strange, is't not? I am convinced that the dog's bark that so unnerved you and caused the watchman to take note was the savage's cry as he did it."

I was astounded. "But why would an Indian . . .?"

"Why, indeed? Yet it was not the shells which gave me my first clue but the terrible wound to the back of poor Eben's head. I have seen the like a few times in America. Certain tribes have a practice we call 'scalping' in which they cut the skin from an enemy's head so they may carry about his hair as a trophy.

Fothergill said Eben was killed by a blow to the head. Why then the bloody sawing at his skull? To take his scalp, Nick, I know the marks."

I did not know what to say. An American Indian killing harmless Mr. Inch? At last I found voice. "Why did not the Indian complete this . . . this scalping?"

"He may have feared discovery. Perhaps someone surprised him at the bloody task."

"No one at Inch, Printer spoke of such a thing."

"That is true."

"And the Indian cried out."

"An incautious act if his aim was to remain undiscovered. The answer then may be—" But, shutting his lids, Mr. Franklin did not complete this thought, though I glimpsed an idea writ furtively in his eyes before he hid it, deliberately it seemed, and for the first time I wondered if his knowledge of the matter went further than I supposed. Yet if he kept things to himself it must be for good reason, must it not?

Shortly he urged me to bed. In my little room I pulled the covers over my head, for I had strong food for nightmares that windy night: savage Indians and threatening costers.

Yet hope banished fear: might I truly find my mother?

"Now, lad," said Mr. Franklin next morning, "I have thought how you might earn your keep, if't be agreeable to you."

"I am eager to begin, sir," said I.

"I knew you would be game." Yet Mr. Franklin looked not game but much worse than last night, with running nose and swollen eyes and a hoarseness to every word. He lay in bed. Pointing to his desk, he asked me to show some of my handwriting.

This I did gladly, copying out some lines of Mr. Addison's. Mr. Franklin pronounced the result very decent. "And now, young sir, I shall show you another writing, of my invention." I conveyed to him the small bed-table which Mrs. Stevenson had supplied, and with much sniffling he made several rows of odd, curling little marks, some of which reminded me of letters and

85

words, though I could make head nor tail of any. "I have writ the same as you," said he when done, "but, look you, in one-fourth the time and space." Pointing with his quill, he showed how each brisk little mark of his was equivalent to one of my words, and sometimes to two or three. "I call it 'short-hand.' O, other men have made some such thing, but I have much improved it, I believe. Do you think you might master it, Nick?"

"I believe so," said I. In truth I was taken with how one might write so quickly.

"Excellent! I shall give you lessons this very morn, so you may begin your apprenticeship at once. Indeed I have long wanted for help in setting down thoughts which I wish to preserve. Too, you may be of use in these new investigations, in which an exact record of our interviews may prove vital."

I practiced some few strokes. "This suits me very well, Mr. Franklin. Yet it seems so little to repay you."

"I have other thoughts. Did you note the print shop next door?"

"Yes."

"Its proximity is one reason I chose Number Seven, to be near printing. I love the smell of ink! You may do a little smouting there, when I do not need you. Indeed I have already spoke to Mr. Tisdale, who says he can sometimes use an extra hand, especially one so expert. When I described your talents he was all for setting you up as apprentice. You would find him a fine, fair master, Nick." At once he grew flustered and red. "But yet . . . forgive me . . . how foolish to have been so forward in claiming you first. O, I o'erstep myself. Naturally you must choose. You need not work for me if you would prefer a printing apprenticeship." He peered above the tops of his glasses. "Should you prefer Mr. Tisdale, Nick?"

"Why . . . I do not know him."

"He is very fair and upstanding, an excellent fellow."

"You . . . you wish me to go?"

"Certainly not . . . yet what is best . . . and naturally if you desire . . ."

This greatly distressed me. "But, sir, I am happy here!"

86

There came a great relieved smile, which touched me. "As I hoped! And I am happy to have you." A fit of coughing overtook him, followed by curses and an angry blowing of his nose. "Damned distemper!" Wheezing, he fell back upon the pillow. "I must sleep, Nick, or Mrs. Stevenson will lock me in for a fortnight, which must not be, for I must make myself well for tomorrow eve. Look you, lad." He plucked a folded rectangle of fine rag paper from the bedside table. "An invitation to dine with Lord Bottom." He winked. "Bottom with a B, does that not strike a note? It came early this morning by a liveried man, with request for quick answer. Naturally I said yes, and I mean to be there if I must go wrapped in bedsheets! Lord Bottom, whom I know no better than His Majesty, says he longs to meet the famous natural philosopher from America. Is milord's interest truly in science? We shall see. Yet there is more. His friend, Mr. Hexham, longs to meet me too, he says—Hexham, the name you said you heard from Mrs. Inch's lips." In spite of their rheum Mr. Franklin's eyes had the eager gleam of a fox's on a hen. "Hexham and Lord B— who are those fellows? We seek truth—yet truth seems to seek us too. Shall we be sharp enough to spy it? I shall keep my eyes open tomorrow night, young Nick, and when I return you may practice your short-hand on my discoveries, for I shall surely reveal every bit of 'em."

❦ 7 ❦

IN WHICH Mr. Franklin relates an adventure mingling pleasure and dismay . . .

"SHALL you hear all and write all, Nick?" asked Mr. Franklin at ten o'clock Sunday morning, churchbells ringing in crisp, clear air.

"I am ready, sir," said I, poising a newly-shaved pencil.

We sat in his room, I at the desk, he in his armchair by the fire with his legs wrapped in woolen blankets. I had spent Friday and Saturday practicing his short-hand and though far from proficient believed I had it well enough to set down his words. For his part, amidst much sneezing Mr. Franklin had yesterday been bled and cupped by Dr. Fothergill. "What is to prevent draining the healthful humors along with the distemper?" he had protested, his foot over the bowl.

Yet the doctor was adamant: "You shall be bled!"

"I shall get well in spite of purging," wheezed Mr. Franklin when Fothergill was gone, and indeed with much rest he had recovered sufficiently to make his way, bundled like a bear, to Lord Bottom's last night.

This, from my short-hand, is what he told of that adventure:

. . . . Milord's house is in George Street, Nick, near Hanover Square. O, it is a fine brick pile and blazed with lights when Peter drove me to its door, a white-wigged footman bowing me up the

88

marble steps. Inside was everything that could be expected, with much gilt plaster and fine carpets and paintings and spacious rooms with fires all lit. Yet it was not the house but the master whom I wished to see.

My interest was soon gratified, for I was at once shown up some grand stairs into a large parlor or greeting-room, where I discovered I was the last to arrive and a sort of guest of honor. This much discomfited me (I am better at ease with two or three close friends over some pints of beer), yet here half a dozen of strangers swept upon me in a pack, Lord Bottom first among 'em.

And what shall I tell of him? That he is a villain? Yet he seemed a kind, gracious gentleman, of middle years, slender yet vigorous in a fine gray wig. He has a lean, lined face, very intelligent, with inquiring brown eyes which are capped with spiky brows that stand up like little porcupines. Showing no lordly affectations, he wrung my hand. "I too am an investigator of natural phenomena," proclaimed he, "though only an amateur. I take it an honor to have the famous Benjamin Franklin under my roof."

I waved this aside. "My discoveries belong to Nature, milord. I am merely the humble gardener with a spade, who chanced to dig 'em up."

He laughed merrily. "Too modest by half." I looked about. The windows were covered in deep crimson damask, the walls hung with paintings of English country scenes. A servant delivered sherry. "I long to talk of the electrical fluid," said my host, taking my elbow, "but for now you must be met."

He proceeded to introduce me round, first to his daughter, a young woman of eighteen, all in blue, the sweetest girl one might meet, with milky skin and soft brown eyes and auburn hair worn in a simple style that showed off her fresh beauty. "A pleasure, Mr. Franklin," said she, curtsying. Some women know not how they take a man; such was Miss Bottom. O, to be twenty! She spoke with shy modesty and moved without flirtatiousness, yet she bloomed with charm. Anne is her name, the apple of her father's eye—he beamed upon her like the sun upon the earth.

"And, your wife?" inquired I.

"Dead these several years," said he, looking sad.

There remained four guests, two men and two women, the Hexham family. I shall save the father for last. Sweeping upon me, the daughter, Lydia, proved a handsome, dark-eyed beauty who offered her hand to be kissed as if she were a princess, all the while fluttering her lashes like fans to keep off flies. She used as much art in her appearance and manner as Miss Bottom used none, having thoroughly powdered and painted. She wore not one but three patches and a high white wig full of ringlets, and her hard little laugh leaped forth whenever she bid it as if it were trained. (Indeed I imagined her trying poses daily in front of a looking glass.) O, she has natural beauty, but her brows were ever arching in ironical little salutes. Her long dress fairly crackled when she moved.

Next, the son, Bertram, or Bertie as he is called, as handsome as his sister—and as artificial. He is perhaps thirty-two and tall and slender with a determined, square face and tiny eyes. He clicked his heels at me. He has a waxed military moustache and a soldierly walk, with which he spent much time striding about to be looked at in his fine velvet suit. He often entrapped poor Anne in some corner, though she tried her best to elude him.

As for the wife—a mystery, a pinched, squinting little woman, a prune in green satin. What signify those darting eyes? Yet there is something of flint about her—backed into a corner, she would fight like a ferret.

And Jared Hexham? I should give much to know his business with your dead master's wife! He proved a tall, burly, swarthy man with black hair and black eyes—and, I assure you, black ways. He alone hung back when the rest came forward, though his burning gaze stayed fixed on me; but at last, bullying forth, he squeezed my hand as if he would crush it. "Well," said he, going up and down on his heels, "so you are Benjamin Franklin."

"I confess it."

"Confess? Is't then some crime?"

I could not at once answer this rudeness, for, peering into that

90

jowly face, I discovered news which took my breath away: I knew Jared Hexham! Did he recognize me? I believe so, though he gave no clue. It was a trial to compose my features, yet I mustered some small assenting gesture. "I begin to think it may be a crime, sir, so ill treated am I by the Pennsylvania proprietors."

"Aye, I have heard of your business. Useless, I tell you; the proprietors have their rights."

"You know much of American affairs?"

"I am a merchant from America."

"From Boston?"

He peered close. "You know of me?"

"O, no," said I hastily. "Many prosperous merchants live in Boston."

He rocked smugly on his heels. "I live in London."

"You have settled here?"

"A dozen years now, and no regrets. I am much pleased to've left the damned colonies behind. Here a man may truly make something of himself."

"And one may not in America? I have always held that a man rose in the world by natural talents. Why 'damned' colonies, pray?"

"They are low and inferior."

"Tut, I cannot agree. No doubt they are not so settled, nor have they so long a history as the mother country, yet I have always been of opinion that the foundations of the future grandeur of the British Empire lie in America; and though like other foundations they are low and little seen they are nevertheless broad and strong enough to support the grandest political structure human wisdom ever yet erected."

Hexham's eyes flashed. "Broad and strong? Grand structure? Bah, I say! They are savage and turn out a very inferior sort of man."

"Did not they turn out you?"

"Ha, I have you there, for I was born in England. And I am heartily pleased to be back in her bosom!"

I merely nodded. "Then I pray that she will nourish you. And what do you intend to make of yourself here that you could not in America?"

"Why . . . a lord, like our good host!" He slapped Lord Bottom resoundingly upon the back.

The others had stepped aside, Lydia Hexham and her mother peering at a painting of Salisbury Plain, Bertie Hexham pursuing Anne, much distressed, to the fireside. Sipping sherry, I took the opportunity to examine the two fathers. A greater contrast could hardly be imagined: the slim, well-bred Lord Bottom with a face like the bust of Tacitus, against the hulking Hexham, whose dark visage would more suit the point of a pike on London Bridge. At the slap on the back his lordship near lost his gracious smile. Could he truly be Hexham's friend? A momentary faltering look suggested he even feared the merchant.

"But one must be born a lord," said I.

"Ah, there you err once more," sneered Hexham. "One may marry a title. One may also buy one. Have you not heard that a man may buy a title?"

"I have heard that nowadays money buys anything, if't be piled high enough and placed where the greedy may find it."

He drew himself up. "I intend to have my title."

At this I could but nod while Martha Clay's words ran through my mind: "There is ambition at Inch, Printer." Clearly it was to be found in the Hexham household as well.

A liveried servant announced, "Dinner is served."

The lovely Anne flew to my side like a hare seeking succor from hounds. "Please, Mr. Franklin, do me the honor to take me in?"

"My honor, ma'am," said I, patting her hand while Bertie Hexham glared for being thwarted, as if I were his greatest enemy.

Dinner was a fine affair—or would have been were it not for Jared Hexham, who had a way of taking conversation by the throat and shaking it like a dog shakes a rat, ever disputing, as if no one could have opinion save he. His wife's few words he quickly squashed, his daughter contributed little but her hard, practiced laugh. Only to his son did Hexham sometimes defer, though this young fop expressed the most vaporous of ideas that one might blow away with a breath. But the father beamed upon him. Clearly it is the son he favors—and why not? Only a son may carry on the family name.

Then I glimpsed something which alarmed me more than Jared Hexham, for across the long dining room, past the white damask cloth and fine porcelain china and flickering tapers in polished silver candlestands, was a servant in black dress and white apron hovering in shadow by the sideboard, a heavy, sullen-looking woman with knotted hands and downcast eyes. Her task was to bring in dishes and then stand by them while two liveried men served us. This she did with slow, defeated movements—and she was an Indian.

Truly, Nick, there was no mistaking the high cheekbones and dark hue of the skin. Lord Bottom sat at the head of the long table, I to his right, his daughter opposite me. Taking care to make it appear a mere trifling question of the moment, I asked milord about his servant.

"Indeed she is an Indian, Mr. Franklin. A . . . an . . . what is it, Jared?" he called to Hexham at the other end of the table.

"Algonquian," said Hexham. "They reside about New York and other parts of New England."

"I know they do," said I. "How came she here?"

"Jared did some traffic in Indians," said Lord Bottom, "as servants."

Or slaves? thought I. "And is she a good servant?"

Lord Bottom seemed not quite able to meet my gaze. "As to that . . . she . . . she does her work well enough . . . yet she is unhappy."

"I too might be unhappy far from home," said I.

Bertie Hexham sat at his father's left. "You *are* far from home," put in he in a high-pitched voice, spitefully, as if he heartily wished me back in Philadelphia. "Very far from home." And he gave a yawping laugh.

To this I but smiled. "On the contrary, sir, I am home here. I am an Englishman, which far too many on this happy isle wish to forget. That Indian woman's nation, however, lies miles across the sea."

Jared Hexham sawed ruthlessly at his beef. "No matter."

"O, no matter to you. But to her . . ."

"She is a savage."

I saw by a flickering of the Indian woman's eyes that she listened. "If savagery be judged by deeds rather than lofty words spoke in parliaments," said I softly, "then many so-called civilized nations are savage indeed. The Indians generously helped many early colonists to survive hard winters. Further, they—"

Hexham's knife clattered to the table. "She is a savage, I tell you, they all are, with little feeling and no sense. Do you say they are civilized? They do not wish to own land but believe all is every man's. Is that civilized? They will work no more than to feed themselves. Civilized? Further, they steal horses and keep many wives. Can you call that civilized?"

"Stealing horses but not land? Openly keeping wives rather than secretly keeping mistresses? Savage indeed!"

His black brows bristled. "Do you mock me?"

"I should not presume. I wonder you do not cite scalping as more evidence of their savagery."

"Aye, scalping," said he, thumping the table, while I peered to see if my words wrung anything from the Indian, but she appeared unmoved.

"Yet poachers in England still receive such punishment," said I.

I believe that if his shriveled little wife had not sat between us Hexham might have grasped my collar. "Are you or are you not an Englishman?" growled he.

"Proud to be one—and proud too that two Englishmen may politely disagree. I say only that that poor woman, torn from her native land, may suffer, just as an Englishman in Barbados might—more, for she has little hope of returning home."

"Pah, you waste your pity, sir!"

"I never think pity a waste."

94

"I would not waste this fine burgundy," put in Lord Bottom hastily, ordering the bottle poured round. Lydia Hexham laughed her brittle laugh. Bertie Hexham fixed a fierce moon-struck look upon Anne. Mrs. Hexham seemed to shrink into her green dress like a snail in its shell, while her husband hacked hard at his beef. At all this Lord Hexham's porcupine brows signaled distress. As for me, many vexing speculations ran through my brain. A large tear trickled from the Indian woman's eye to drip down her cheek, with only me to notice it. The Algonquian are proud; such open show of feeling speaks of much quiet suffering.

After dinner the women left us, and leaning back with crossed legs we gentlemen smoked pipes and drank port. Lord Bottom remained well-bred—my estimation of him only grew—yet I saw that there was some agitation about him, as if a subject might burst forth which he would rather stayed hid, and his fine brown eyes were ever traveling between Jared Hexham and me. I learned that Hexham had sailed for America in 1726. There over the course of a dozen years he had risen to wealth and position in Boston 'til he had three ships and a counting house of his own on the wharf. "What did you trade in?" asked I, but he seemed not to care to give answer, though he let out that his dealings with the Indians had begun in furs, which he conceded they were tolerably skilled at trapping. My opinion of his son changed little. Bertie Hexham is a spoiled, vapid young man, mean-spirited; I would not care to cross him. Indeed the whole family seems dangerous. Lydia Hexham would break a heart as soon as swat a fly, and her mother might flog a servant for spilling tea.

Lord Bottom talked eagerly of scientific matters, and I found his mind quick, his knowledge first-rate. (Hexham drummed fingers as we spoke; his son yawned rudely.) Milord invited me to see his library, which I was delighted to do. This proved to be at the far end of the house, down a long corridor—but when we got there a servant called his master to some business belowstairs, and I was left alone. This suited me. The room was circular, a wheel of wooden shelves stacked with all manner of volumes, handsomely bound, which I wandered among as a favored angel in heaven, free to sample what I might. There was Dr. Johnson's *Dictionary* and Mr. Nicolas Rowe's Shakespeare, as well as many works of philosophy and nature study, even my own slim book on electricity, keeping its modest sphere in the orbit of Newton's great *Principia*.

Yet I was puzzled. The room displayed a handsome symmetry —save at one spot, to the right of the door. One might expect from the design of the room to find bookshelves here, echoing those on the left, yet there was but wood, fine and polished. Why? Ever curious about anomalies in art as well as nature, I felt along this wood—to be amazed when my fingers chanced upon some secret catch. At this the wood flew open, to reveal, behind, several score of volumes. The reason for their hiding was plain: Lord Bottom possessed an extensive collection of erotica, from the Orient and ancient Rome and modern Paris, as well as from London, including books from Inch, Printer. I looked with great interest at those your master had done, Nick, some dozen or so. In spite of their subject they were finely crafted; Eben Inch turned out excellent work. Did you have a hand in some, lad? You may be proud of your skill. One thing I noted: each title page was numbered by hand, as one of a printing. This is not unusual, yet each of the books from Inch, Printer, bore the same number, as if Lord Bottom subscribed to the books, a certain volume of each printing being reserved for him. Was this the meaning of the numbers?

Yet I had no time to speculate, for at that moment Jared Hexham strode into the room.

The lamp in its sconce cast his shadow long and black, and I was not pleased to find myself alone with him. I did not like his threatening air nor those sly, dark eyes. Coming close, he breathed hot breath upon me as he leered at the book in my hand as if we shared some wicked secret. "Aha, you have a taste for it, I see."

"No more than any man," said I.

He nudged me. "Come, Franklin, confess. A library full of books, and you choose this?"

"I chose other books before this. Yet I confess this one catches my eye. 'Diary of a Country Girl, set by Ebenezer Inch, Printer, of Fish Lane, Moorfields.'" I pointed to the title page. "The man does excellent work."

"Tush, in such stuff 'tis the matter not the art."

"Yet I know good printing, for I was a printer many years." Replacing the book and shutting the secret door, I peered hard into his face. "Do you know anything of the printer's craft, Mr. Hexham?"

His quick, angry stare confirmed my earlier suspicions, which you shall soon hear, Nick. "I know nothing of printing," growled he.

"But do you too collect erotica?"

For answer he poked my shoulder, hard. "I do not care for books, I say. But as to other subjects . . ." He glanced about, as if someone might listen. "I tell you, Franklin, your business in London is useless. Be advised by me: leave it."

This took me aback. It was not easy to remain composed gazing up into his twitching nostrils, yet I paid him sense for nonsense. "My business with the proprietors? If by 'useless' you mean difficult of achievement, I find every day that you are correct. Yet a challenge stirs my blood; it is like bracing morning air. Further, I am charged by the people of my colony; they put their trust in me; I cannot leave off their wishes. Even more, right is on our side; the proprietors must be taxed. Nay, I shall never leave it off."

"Then you are a damned stubborn man!"

"Proud to be so, when justice fills my sails. Yet my course may be altered by reason."

"The devil take reason. Fear steers many a man who claims to reason."

"Fear steers a coward, sir, and you shall not find me that." Hexham's fists knotted at this, but I faced his impudence, though he might strike me. "Come, why should you so fervently wish me to leave off?"

"I wish you back in America."

"Why?"

"Because it is where you belong!" He drew himself up. "Here's reason for you." He shook so in anger that I fully expected him to strike me—yet instead he snatched a gold sovereign from his vest pocket and thrust it under my nose, turning it this way and that. "Pretty, eh? A very paragon of reason. I won't concede fear can't buy you, but I'll give you a chance to be paid by kinder metal. Come, take it. There's a hundred to follow—and your passage back to boot." He laughed. "The Pennsylvania Assembly? Merely tell 'em the proprietors won't be budged."

I stared at the coin, not with any intent to take it but in a sort of fascination at the gall of the man. My voice felt sullied by having to pronounce words to him. "Are you in the pay of the proprietors, sir?" But there came no answer, for just then Lord Bottom stepped in, with that same shamed, wary glancing from Hexham to me, as if he had known some low business was afoot, and I could not help wondering if his being called off had been part of a plan.

"Talking of books?" said he with a strained smile.

"Aye, books," snapped Hexham, thrusting coin in pocket and stomping to the door, "—though for my taste your Mr. Franklin takes too great an interest in books." He blustered out.

There followed a small silence. With some sheepishness Lord Bottom gestured towards the door. As we returned to the front of the house, I took opportunity to ask how he and Hexham chanced to be friends.

At the word "friends" the man blanched. "The world is changing, Mr. Franklin," said he stiffly. "Wealthy merchants and titled lords may find some common ground."

"Shrewd men of business are the new aristocracy, you mean?"

"Many long to be."

We paused at the entrance to the great hall. "Mr. Hexham wished to meet me, your invitation said; yet—forgive me—I find myself bewildered by his intents."

"O, Jared has whims, hard whims, which are difficult to deny. He is rough-hewn. I am sorry he has been so disputatious."

"I revel in dispute."

"Surely not his kind. I should have invited you and you alone. Your work on electricity—wonderful! We must converse sometime, if you would be so kind. As for Jared Hexham, you will not meet him here again."

I went ahead of Lord Bottom to join the ladies and gentlemen. Candles blazed in the salon, and Lydia Hexham and Anne strolled arm-in-arm, though I thought Anne showed ill ease. All the while Hexham's black eyes fixed me with such malice that I knew he longed to fit me for a shroud. Did he somehow fear me? As for Lord Bottom, in spite of his graciousness, did he too wish me back in America? There is more to milord than appears. Many gentlemen collect erotica, yet he seemed not the sort.

The time for parting approached. Near it Lord Bottom had words with his daughter. She is his pride, yet the subject was heated, she refusing some request with a desperate toss of curls. I longed to know the matter, but the father had drawn his daughter into a far corner, and not a word of their quiet dispute reached me for the silly, braying lecture on painting with which Bertie Hexham regaled us: "These dabblers merely color our walls!" asserted he.

"As Nature merely colors the earth?" offered I, at which he turned scarlet. I cared not. My heart went out to Anne, who looked near tears. For his part Lord Bottom was agitated and when he rejoined us shot such a look at Jared Hexham as might strike a horse dead.

At the very end the wizened Mrs. Hexham drew me aside. Prudence is her name. Her face, turned up to mine, was like a dried crabapple, and her thin, pinched smile was like vinegar.

"I too am from America, Mr. Franklin," says she.

"O?" says I.

"Yes. But I am not so grand or reknowned as you. I come of a poor family, tillers of the soil. No great estate, but a little plot of rocky land."

"Tut, I am not grand, ma'am. My father was but a candlemaker. The man you see before you is self-made and humble.

"O, humble! Yet I too am self-made, after a fashion. I did it by helping my husband rise in the world. When he was poor and just come to America Mr. Hexham saw something in me, and I have struggled to live up to it always."

What he had seen, I began to believe, was a shrewd, unscrupulous woman. "Admirable," said I.

Her smile fled. "You must not provoke him, Mr. Franklin," said she. "Much depends upon it. Heed me, sir, do not provoke my husband." And, rapping my arm with her fan, she walked off, leaving me to make what I might of her sharp adjuration.

The Hexhams' coach departed first—driven by an Indian. Yes, Nick, a second of the breed, a lean, hawk-nosed young brave in scarlet livery, with a purple scar upon his cheek and a fierce look that showed he had spirit. Yet there were signs of dissipation too, a blearing of the eyes, a weakness of mouth. Did Hexham hold his man in check with drink?

The brave's whip cracked: Lydia Hexham's laugh twittered in George Street; then they were gone.

I turned to my host, a splendid figure, full of breeding. Yet he is strained to breaking by some torment. "Your daughter—charming!" said I on the front step. "Your only child?"

"My only child, and my happiness."

"Forgive me, milord, but . . . is your estate entailed?"

He gave a weary smile. "No. There is no near male relative; everything, title and lands, will fall to Anne."

"Let us hope it falls to no one else," said I, wishing him well. I took coach midst much sneezing. It is the last I may report of my evening . . .

Putting down my pencil, I turned to Mr. Franklin where he sat with a brooding look, pulling at his lower lip, by the fire. A wintry light suffused the room. Downstairs Mrs. Stevenson's grandfather clock struck eleven of the morning. "Two Indians, sir?" said I.

"Two." Fitfully he adjusted the blanket about his legs. "Did one of 'em strike down Ebenezer Inch?"

"Were the carving knives at Lord Bottom's table like the one used on my master?"

"They had ebon handles—as do knives in many a fine house."

"But, what could an Indian have against Mr. Inch?"

"Damn me, Nick, did your master know something which wanted silencing?" A deep look suffused his face. "And yet I have other thoughts about his murder which, though they unfold new mysteries, may tell why he died." His soft brown eyes seemed to pierce me. "You, Nick—is't *you* who are the answer?"

Ice congealed about my heart. "I, sir?"

He rubbed his balding brow. "I do not know, I do not know. Family, Nick—or famiies; there is some answer there: Jared Hexham and his prunish wife and haughty brood; Lord Bottom and his dead wife and their Anne, in line for estate and title; the Inches at Fish Lane, the father murdered but the wife smoldering with ambition for her Tilda; even Mrs. Couch and her so-called 'daughters'; and last—yet perhaps most significant of all—you, Nick, and your unknown mother."

"And my father, sir?"

"Aye, lad, he too."

"But I am no one, sir, a boy of work."

"No one to murder for, you mean? No, I do not say you were the cause of Eben Inch's death. But yet you are in't somewhere. I feel that you are. Does it come to this: to help Martha Clay we must pursue your birth?"

I shivered at this. "I do not know."

He smiled of a sudden, with round, red cheeks. "Never fear, Nick. Whate're may come, you have a home in Craven Street. Now . . . as to my shock at meeting Jared Hexham, this is its source: I knew the man for a blackguard. He had grown a full thick beard, and time has marked its changes, so he must pray I do not recognize him, but there is no mistake. Eben Inch knew him too." He rubbed his hands. "O, the threads are weaving together, forming a fabric. It was on my first journey to England more than thirty years ago, when I was but eighteen and run away from home. Shall I tell you of it? Truly I shall—but first . . ." He appeared to listen, then said in a lower voice: "Hark you, lad, fetch Peter to bring a carriage—but take care Mrs. Stevenson does not hear. She is a dear soul, but I have no wish to be chided." Throwing off the blankets, he went to his wardrobe. "Hurry, Nick. We go to Watts' Printing House." He winked. "On our way I shall tell you of Jared Hexham and Eben Inch and Benjamin Franklin when they were young."

❦ 8 ❦

*IN WHICH Mr. Franklin travels
thirty years into his past—and is followed
there . . .*

WE headed north from the Thames, Peter in yellow
livery perched on the box of our small open chaise,
which proved all that could be hired on a bustling
Sunday noon in London, churches great and small letting out
their flocks. I did not know what it was to go to church, Mrs. Inch
ever leaving me to drudge about Inch, Printer, while she and Tilda
in their finery (Mr. Inch was most often left abed) trotted off like
great ruffled hens to services.

Six days, near a week, since Monday last, when I had
discovered my old master dead in his yard. What a change had
come to Nicolas Handy!

It was gray and chill. I wore a woolen scarf about my neck. Mr.
Franklin, nose sniffling, eyes watering, sat likewise bundled
against the cold, with a round beaver hat upon his head. Our
breaths were frosty plumes.

"My father made and sold candles at the sign of the Blue Ball in
Milk Street, Boston," the gentlemen told me as we jounced along.
"There were books about, thank God; my maternal grandfather
had taught the Indians to read. One of my brothers, James, kept a
printing shop, and when I was twelve he took me on as

apprentice. A fancy to write for his newspaper, the *New England Courant*, grew upon me, but he thought me too young and inexperienced, so at sixteen out of slyness I invented that good dame, Silence Dogood, to see myself in print. This earned me some grudging respect, yet still I was not satisfied and some time thereafter determined to run away. I ended in Philadelphia, where I improved my printing skills and made some small name for myself, enough to garner a promised letter of credit from the Governor of Pennsylvania to buy printing equipment in London. It was only when I was arrived at the great city on Christmas eve, 1724, that I learned the Governor's promises were the whims of a well-meaning dreamer. He had not writ the letter. I was all on my own.

"But, O, to be in London then, the city of Walpole and Lord Chesterfield, of Newton, Hogarth, and Pope! Even Voltaire resided here, escaped from France, which would not have him except in two pieces, head severed from body. It was a printer's city, I a skilled journeyman, and I soon found work at Palmer's in Bartholmew Close, where I stayed near a year before moving to a yet larger printing house, Watts', near Lincoln's Inn Fields, where I worked six months before sailing back to America."

Mr. Franklin glanced behind us as we turned into the Strand. "It was at Watts' that I met Ebenezer Inch and Jared Hexham, Nick— or the man who calls himself Hexham, for that was not his name then. Eben's sister, Mrs. Clay, spoke of a time her brother had known me; his pleading letter told of it too. Well, 1726 was that time, and Hexham was known as Gerrold Bixer. Watts' employed near fifty fellows, and Bixer, Eben Inch, and I were three such together, young journeymen, all eighteen or twenty. I may tell you that Eben was even then the paragon of his craft. Alas, he had also fallen prey to that fondness for beer which plunged him in mischief. Do you think we are followed, Nick?"

I felt a shock. "Followed?"

"Glance over your shoulder. Discreetly, lad! That's the way. See you? A black, closed carriage, rather shabby? It has been with us since Craven Street."

Indeed I saw it, driven by a coachman muffled to the eyes so his face could not be seen. My heart thudded, for I could think only that we were pursued by the coster who had threatened me.

"Do not be alarmed. It may be coincidence." Mr. Franklin leaned forward. "A little faster, if you please, Peter." We moved on at a spritely trot, while the gentleman proceeded as if there had been no interruption. "Bixer was as bullying a fellow then as I found him at Lord Bottom's, yet he is crafty too; he could not have risen in trade if he were not. He is not one to underestimate, Nick. Ah, what turns a man? Bixer would have gone far on the straight path, yet he was ever seeking the crooked way, as if he took pleasure in tightening the screws on men and watching them squirm. He lured his fellow printers into gaming and dice, at which he always won. He had acquaintance among low women and, I heard, among knaves who passed on stolen goods. O, I stayed clear of the vile fellow—but poor Eben, gullible and weak, proved a victim made for his cajolery. Bixer plied him with drink, and Eben fell deep in debt. What a misery he became! The long and short of it is: I determined to save him, for he had a good heart and talents which I hated to see wasted; besides, I despised Gerrold Bixer and longed to see him thwarted.

"One night, at a game of cards which Bixer had urged among some five or six of players, I joined in. Eben was there as always, feigning good cheer, which the beer helped him to do, hoping to win back what he had lost but with a great, sad air of hopelessness in his eyes. I knew Bixer cheated; further, I knew how, for, merely for the pleasure of the thing, to see its secrets, I had one time studied the tricks of cards. Further I had made myself adept at these tricks, much better than Bixer, who was clumsy at 'em, knowing just enough never to be caught out by the simple souls he inveigled into gaming. And what was the end of this evening? To his joy Eben discovered he had won back all he owed, with some two or three guineas to boot. What pleasure I took in Bixer's gnashing looks, never mind my knowing he suspected me of guiding Eben's luck.

"Next day Eben was not to be seen in London, for I had found him the printing job in the Midlands to which Martha Clay alluded. It was but three weeks after this that I sailed for Philadelphia, and I have not been back these thirty years."

"Did Bixer never try to get at you for what you did?"

"Perhaps he tries to get me now."

This caused me to glance round. "The black carriage still follows, sir," said I.

"Does it?" Mr. Franklin poked my ribs. "And yet you took the wind from Buck Duffin's sails. You shall protect the both of us in case of danger." He winked broadly.

Shortly we turned into Wild's Court. "Hurrah, we are arrived!"

Peter pulled up under a hanging wooden sign, JAMES WATTS, PRINTER, and we got down. Wheezing, Mr. Franklin beamed at a long, two-story half-timbered building. "My old home!" I could not feel so at ease. We were in a sort of mews, very narrow, with sloping eaves looming above our heads. I looked behind us. The black carriage was not to be seen—might it lurk just round the corner, unknown eyes peering out?

"Why have we come here, sir?" asked I.

Mr. Franklin tapped his fur hat. "To jiggle my memory. Thirty years, and there are things I am not remembering . . ." He spread his arms. "Ah, it does my heart good to revisit the scene of such useful labor!" The place was shut up, but he strode to the door and banged hard, calling out, "James Watts! Dear God, thirty years, I hope the fellow is not dead." He pounded twice more with no result, and we were about to climb back in our chaise when a shutter banged open, and a grizzled, scowling face popped out.

"It be Sunday! No printin' o' Sunday!" The shutter slammed— yet it opened again slowly, and this same grizzled face, with an expression first of suspicion, then of wonder, looked Mr. Franklin up and down. "Ben Franklin?" quavered the man. "B'God, if't be not Ben Franklin!"

Grinning broadly Mr. Franklin waggled his head. "Have I changed so little, Francis Crook?"

106

A warm chuckle. "Aye, time's wrought upon ye, as it has on me—yet I knew ye still. How many years has it been?"

"Thirty."

"Thirty? But yestiddy, I say! Come in, come in!" And a moment later the barred oak banged open, and we were heartily ushered into the smell of printer's ink. Francis Crook and Mr. Franklin warmly shook hands and clapped backs. For my part I gazed in wonder through a second door into a sprawling room containing half a dozen fine big presses and many trays of type, with what seemed hundreds of sheets hanging to dry, and a large, handsome bindery as well. Inch, Printer, was shamed by this plenty.

With much chuckling and shaking of his head Mr. Crook urged us upstairs to two jumbled rooms, a bedroom and sitting room, which he called home. Smears of ink covered everything from waterpitcher to coverlet. A round little table sat by a window overlooking the mews. Here we took chairs while Mr. Crook poured beer.

"Success to printing!" cried Mr. Franklin, raising his flagon.

Even on Sunday Mr. Crook wore his leather printer's apron, and his nails were so blackened his hands looked as if they had been steeped in ink when he was born. "Ye remember the old toast, Ben?"

"Have I not every reason, Francis? For I was a printer many years in America." Briefly Mr. Franklin told his history.

"And ye're now the Pennsylvaney agent, here to treat with good King George? Aye, ye were ever a coming lad!" He raised his glass. "Then I call for success to printing—and to Benjamin Franklin too!" We all drank. Mr. Franklin introduced me, though he said nothing of where I came from. He asked after the printing house, and Mr. Crook informed him that James Watts was dead eight years, the business passing to his son. "But I am master, young Watts having more interest in the money of the shop than in presswork. It suits me to the ground, for I am given these rooms and may live among ink and types, as I like." The two men fell to reminiscing about old times, while ever and again I glanced out the window.

"Bless me if those were not good years," said Mr. Franklin after some twenty minutes. "And do you recall Ebenezer Inch?"

Mr. Crook thumped the table. "And how could I forget, him bein' the best hand ever was for settin' type—after you, o' course, Ben? But you ask after him at a sad hour, for he died but days ago, murdered by some thieves."

"How did you hear of his death?"

"Him and me stayed friends. He looked me up when he come back to London some dozen year ago. We'd meet sometime at the Twelve Bells, in Rooster Alley, though I didn't see much of him of late, for that wife o' his kept more and more a sharp eye on him." Mr. Crook rubbed his jaw. "Too, somethin' was much on his mind, some worry. And then a lad come five days ago to say he was passed on."

"A stocky, dark-haired lad?"

Mr. Crook's grizzled brows rose. "Aye. Ye know him?"

"I have been to Eben's print shop since I came to London."

"Have you, now? Poor Eben. Of good heart, he was, though ever one for the beer. O, it is the curse o' many a pressman!" Mr. Crook nudged Mr. Franklin's arm. "I remember Gerrold Bixer too."

"What prompts you to think of Bixer?"

"Why . . . you know." The old fellow winked. "Because they was two together, him and Eben. Not the same sly sort, mind you. No, as different as night and day—Bixer bein' the night. But there was somethin' betwixt 'em, was there not? Bixer had poor, good Eben in his clutches; he squeezed him hard. Aye, 'twere a sorrow to watch! Come to think on't, you helped him get free, didn't you, Ben?"

"I did."

Mr. Crook gave his gravelly chuckle. "I thought as much, though I never knew for sure."

"Whatever happened to Bixer?"

"Did you not know?" Sailed to America, same as you, and not long after, neither."

"Why did he go?"

"Said he was fed up with London. Said there was grand

108

prospects just awaitin' a bright young fellow across the seas. High and mighty he was about it—but what I think is, he ran afoul o' the law and had to fly. Truth of it is, Eben was the one made me b'lieve so. Him and me were in Baggot's Alehouse just before Eben left Watts'. It was Eben's lowest time—Bixer was asqueezin' the last juices from him. 'Thinks he's got me where he wants me,' Eben said, bleary-eyed, '—but I've got something on him, and if he tries to make me do it, I'll . . .' Well, he never said do what or what he had on Bixer, and I never knew, though as if t'was gold he waved a sheet of good tenpenny linen paper with some writin' on't under my nose."

"A paper, you say? What writing?"

"Couldn't say."

Mr. Franklin merely nodded. "A mystery, is't not? So long ago! Have you seen Gerrold Bixer since he sailed to America?"

"And how could I, if he stayed there? Did you ever run across him?"

Instead of replying, Mr. Franklin gestured towards the window. "This lad you said came from Eben's print shop to say his master was dead—is that he?" This startled me, for I had not glanced out for some moments. We all gazed down—and indeed there was Buck Duffin half-hid in the shadow of a thatched eave not twenty paces from our chaise, pumping his big booted feet up and down and staring with his stubborn black look at the door of Watts' Printing.

"Why . . . that's him all right," proclaimed Mr. Crook, rising. "Why's he here?"

"The question," said Mr. Franklin, "is why he came here in the first place. You say it was to tell you Eben was dead? He must then have been sent by Mrs. Inch. How kind, how thoughtful! And did you ever receive such courtesy from the woman before?"

Mr. Crook dropped back in his chair. "You may count upon it, I did not! Suspicious of ev'ry friend of her husband's, she was, and heaped curses on any of 'em! But that sneaking lad . . . come you mention it, that was not all he were after. He kept askin' if there was other friends of poor Eben who might like to know he'd died. Had any been to see me lately? You, Ben, is that who he meant?"

"May be."

"Mrs. Inch is akeepin' a eye on ye?"

"I do not know. The truth is, Francis, Eben may not have been murdered by thieves. I mean to discover who his true murderer is."

Francis Crook's eyes rounded. "Yer a wonder!" exclaimed he.

Buck shortly vanished from under the eaves, and when we left Watts' near three he was nowhere to be seen. "Was it he in that black coach, sir?" asked I as we climbed in behind Peter and set out.

"Would Dora Inch hire a coach for such a spy? More likely Buck footed it. Did he follow us—or is he keeping an eye on Watts' Printing?"

London smoke was thickening, forming a stinking fog. As we turned out of the mews I saw to my relief that no black coach lurked. "But why should Mrs. Inch want watch kept on your old print shop?" asked I. "And, if not Buck, who followed us?"

But Mr. Franklin's mind was elsewhere. He pulled hard at his lower lip. "I pray," murmured he, looking very grave, "that there is no chance of another murder."

By the time we were returned to Craven Street it had turned an even grayer day, with no wind to carry off the smoke of a thousand chimneypots. Our coach pulled up to Number 7 in a brown murk. I expected Mrs. Stevenson to fuss at Mr. Franklin, for he had snuck past her in leaving, but she was civil.

The reason sat within earshot in the front parlor: Mrs. Clay, come to see how her agent fared.

Mr. Franklin spent some half an hour with the lady, giving many assurances that he was on the scent yet saying nothing particular of the odd turns in the matter. "At your first visit you hinted you had reason to hate Dora Inch, other than her treatment of your brother," said he. "You would not speak of it

110

then. Have you perchance reconsidered? Do you not think it wise to tell me all?"

The thin red-haired woman's hands twisted in her lap. "It is something a respectable lady hates to speak of," said she, her jaw stiffening. "And yet—" Eyes downcast, near tears, she explained that in those long-ago, desperate days, when she had sent pleading letters to her brother which he had not answered, one reply had come from Mrs. Inch, showing that indeed she intercepted the letters. "In it she haughtily asserted that beggars could not be choosers and suggested I turn whore. Further, she assured me she had means in London to find me a house in which to do it."

"An outrage to such a lady as you."

"I suffered much from it."

"Did she ever broach the subject again?"

"Thank God, no."

A moment later Mrs. Clay rose to go, as she did so reaching out and touching my hair with a great, stricken look. "You are truly fortunate in Mr. Franklin, child!"

Mr. Franklin kept the woman but a moment more. "Did your brother ever say anything of the circumstances of Nick's coming to Inch, Printer?" asked he at the door.

"No. I assumed him to be an orphan." Mrs. Martha Clay departed into the smudged, gray day.

"Tut, Nicolas, a bedeviling business!" Mr. Franklin led me quickly upstairs.

"Now, Nick—" said he in his room, the door firmly shut. He drew a plain leather-bound volume from his shelves, "I have had several of these made up by Mr. Tisdale next door, blank pages for convenient carrying and jotting. Certain ladies use such books to embellish the boredom of their lives. For myself, I have made scientific observations in some; in others I write of human nature. This is yours, Nicolas. I wish you to set down what passed today, what we did and saw and heard. Write with truth as your aim.

111

Practice style. Mr. Addison may serve you a good model. Will you do this?"

"Gladly, sir."

He looked pleased. "Thus your education may be made by observing life."

It is from this journal—and many like it—that I tell this story.

I spent the remainder of the afternoon setting down our journey to Wild's Court. Mr. Franklin rested but was up in an hour, scribbling letters to influential men about London, striving to find sympathetic ears for Pennsylvania's cause, even, he told me, to Lord Granville himself, President of the Privy Counsel. "My lord Granville and I have met once, poorly I may say, I arguing right and he law. I ask you, should not law follow right, rather than being led by the nose by custom?" Near four o'clock a sharp-tongued man named Robert Charles called. "My fellow agent here," sniffed Mr. Franklin when the man was gone, "a vexatious fool who has done little to further sympathy. There is much I must overcome!" Dusk settled about the house. Polly hummed gaily belowstairs. William Franklin popped in and popped out for one of his nights on the town. Dr. Fothergill arrived near eight, accompanied by two men whose names I knew from Mr. Franklin's mentioning: Mr. William Strahan, a stout, jolly Scot whom Mr. Franklin affectionately called "Straney," and Peter Collinson, the Quaker textile merchant with whom he had corresponded for years. Mr. Collinson practiced botany. Mr. Strahan printed many newspapers and journals. I was given the honor of being introduced and the privilege of sitting with the gentlemen in the parlor whilst they talked of politics and science. Enthralled by their wit and sense, I longed to be as splendidly versed in the world as they.

At one point Mr. Franklin left the room.

"His health, Fothergill?" inquired Mr. Strahan softly, in a thick Scots burr.

"He cannot be made to rest. It is the success of his venture that I doubt. What will this continual failure do to him?"

"Indeed," put in Mr. Collinson, shaking his head, "he is looked upon with suspicion in near every political circle."

Mrs. Stevenson had set out some pippins in a pewter bowl. "Handsome apples!" said Mr. Franklin to her when the gentlemen were gone. "Pray, is there some new coster plying his trade in Craven Street, a hunched-over fellow with a beaked nose?"

"No such. Only Mr. Digges."

"You have not seen such a fellow? I am mistaken then." Mr. Franklin tossed an apple from hand to hand as he mounted the stairs.

In his room, where a fire was laid and crackling, he settled heavily in his chair and blew his nose. "Now, Nick, we must make a summation."

"A summation, sir?"

The flames flickered in his eyeglasses. Looking away, he leaned back and tapped his nose while a wind blew up about the eaves. "Imagine a picture, sketched in for painting. There is yet no color—but one may see outlines. Thirty years ago Jared Hexham (for so I shall call him) inveigled Ebenezer Inch into debt. By this he meant to coerce Eben into abetting him in some enterprise—a nefarious one we may be sure. Eben struggled against it and at last got his hands on some evidence against Hexham, something writ on a piece of good linen paper. I effected Eben's escape; the result: he had no use for the paper. In fact, in saving Eben I may have spared Hexham too, for the paper was never used against him. Nonetheless I incurred his enmity by the act; yet, no matter, one would suppose, for mere weeks later I was gone to America, and though Hexham took ship shortly thereafter it was surely not to pursue me for revenge. Likely Francis Crook was right: the blackguard was only fleeing the hot pursuit of the law. Did he flee the same matter that was writ on that paper? What happened to the paper?

"Leave that. Dora Pulley, who became Dora Inch, is in the picture too. Did she meet Eben merely by accident? She must have come north from London, for Mrs. Clay tells us she knew at least one bawdy house here. Was she then a young whore of Jared Hexham's acquaintance? Did he send her to seek out Ebenezer, to discover if he truly posed some danger? Yet Hexham was forced to fly, leaving Dora Pulley free to do what she might. Finding in her hands a young, skilled printer, of good heart but little guile, she tricked him into marriage, then bent him to her ways. O, I have no doubt his prospering may be laid to her shrewd managing; she knows money and business as he did not (though she knows morals as much as a cat). Clearly she and Hexham still have some association. Why does he visit her?"

Mr. Franklin was silent some time while the coals hissed softly on the hearth and shutters rattled in a rising wind. For my part I wondered if there was something he left out. He had known Jared Hexham and my old master. He and Jared Hexham had been thirty years in America. I hardly dared think it: did Mr. Franklin have some part in this all?

The gentleman looked up after a time. "Damn me, Nick our picture is too much a sketch—the coster . . . those Indians—we must fill it in! Tomorrow I revisit the good Lord Bottom, and you shall go with me."

❧ 9 ❧

IN WHICH I meet two Indians and learn a new use for wax . . .

"HANDY . . ." mused Mr. Franklin as we set out the next afternoon at two, "not a common name—yet not uncommon either. There may be hundreds in England."

I turned to him in his beaver hat and heavy brown greatcoat. We had this day a closed coach. It had rained night and morning, and our wheels made a squelching sound in the muddy streets. "And in America, sir?"

"Fewer." He pulled the traveling rug tighter about his knees. "Yet I have bethought me, I myself knew one such family, numerous and widespread, a sort of clan. Puritans, they were. The Reverend Josiah Handy shepherded a flock near Philadelphia, I believe, but most of 'em resided in Boston. I knew a Handy there."

"Boston is the town Jared Hexham settled in, is't not? Were you there often, sir?"

"I was born in Boston; I had relations there. But I spoke of one of the Handy clan. Arthur was this fellow's name, a printer; that is how I knew him. Many's the time I sat at his table in Boston, amongst his numerous brood and ate his good wife's suppers. Would that the seas did not separate us; I should like to quiz him, for I confess the name Jared Hexham struck a note even when I first heard it from Lord Bottom, and I now think Arthur may have

115

spoke it to me, though I do not recall just why. Well, the best I may do is write to him, though it will take months for answer. Still, if he may tell us anything of Jared Hexham we must have it, though I fear it may arrive long after it be useful. Does anyone follow today, Nicolas?"

I leant out the window. "Not that I see, sir."

"America," Mr. Franklin murmured, blowing a plume of frosty breath, "how does it attach to this affair?"

Ten minutes later we arrived in George Street, before a handsome brick town house with marble steps and a fanlight door and gleaming brass knocker, which Mr. Franklin vigorously thumped.

A periwigged servant showed us in. The house was grand, but I hardly saw the splendid rooms past which we were led for thinking of the Indian woman Mr. Franklin had seen. Might she appear?

Lord Bottom met us in his study, surrounded by books. He was as Mr. Franklin had said, with a lean, fine-featured face as noble as a Roman's. He wore no wig, but just his thinning salt-and-pepper hair. His brows were truly as spiky and upstanding as porcupine quills and gave his gaze a lively cast. He greeted Mr. Franklin very deferentially before turning on me a pleasant, inquiring smile.

"My young friend, Nicolas Handy," said Mr. Franklin, watching milord closely as he said my name.

For my part I could discern no alteration in Lord Bottom's kindly look. "A friend to Mr. Benjamin Franklin must be a friend to me," said he, giving me his hand. He turned to Mr. Franklin. "How good of you to answer my offer of hospitality. I did not look for you so soon but am the more pleased by the surprise." He rubbed his hands. "Scientific conversation, eh? I have a small laboratory in which I have duplicated some of your experiments. May I show it you? I should be happy for your advice—or perhaps for some new direction of inquiry . . .?"

"I should be pleased to see it," said Mr. Franklin, "but first—may I ask a question?"

"Anything."

"Is Jared Hexham truly your friend?"

A change suffused Lord Bottom—an instant pallor and a pinched look about the eyes and mouth. "A blunt question," said he.

"Honest and direct," replied Mr. Franklin. "Should you prefer otherwise?"

"No. The world shows little enough honesty, I have no wish to turn it from my door. Yet—" He glanced at me.

"O, you may speak in front of Nicolas," assured Mr. Franklin.

Lord Bottom lost none of his dignity, yet there followed a moment of grave indecision. At last he yielded: "I have known Hexham some years, but, no, I cannot call him friend."

"Enemy, then?"

"He is my torment!" burst out Lord Bottom, shuddering. He sank into his chair. "Dear God, I do not know why I tell you what I would tell no other man."

"You may trust me."

Lord Bottom's brown eyes lifted. "Indeed, I believe I may." A pained smile played about his lips. "Do you know, it much relieves me at last to say how I truly feel about the man?"

Mr. Franklin lowered himself into a scrolled chair beside Lord Bottom's writing table. "Why do you hate him?"

"Ah!" Milord gestured out the window. "There is my reason." We all turned to look, into a small garden of yews and myrtles with little flowered borders, in it: a pretty young woman, who must be his daughter. She strolled under the gray sky in small circles, aimlessly, with an unhappy look upon her face, and my heart was moved by her prettiness and her sadness. "My Anne," said Lord Bottom feelingly, "whom I would harm for nothing in the world. And Jared Hexham dares to wish to marry her to his booby of a son!"

"You need only say no."

"Would it were so simple, but if I deny him . . ."

"Jared Hexham has some hold on you?"

Lord Bottom's grim silence served for answer.

"And this knowledge would also harm your daughter?" pressed Mr. Franklin, sighing. "Scylla and Charybdis." He bent earnestly

117

toward his host. "Sir, I have reason to suspect Hexham of nefarious dealings. The bringing to light of these should considerably diminish the man—might even lift your burden. Will you tell me all you know of him?"

Milord glanced toward the door, as if there might be spies in his own house. Lifting a silver letter opener, he let it fall dully. "I know only the general outline of his career in America, though as you shall see it is sufficient to damn his character. He began by exporting indentured women from England, ostensibly as servants, but when they got to Boston they were turned to service in houses of call. All defenseless, they were sorely abused. He traded in slaves too, and cheated the Indians of their furs. He cheated white men too, if he could, so I have heard. Over the years he amassed money. His reputation in Boston was none of the best, though gold may gild any man, and there are fools enough willing to wink at the perfidies of a wealthy, glittering knave. So it was with Jared Hexham. And when he had greased sufficient palms with his tainted gold in the New World and made himself large in its society, he set his sights on London and came with his ships and set up along the Thames. A dozen years he's been here, prying into men's lives, ferreting his way up. He looks to buy a knighthood; further, he looks to set up his damnable son in my house and fortune."

"How long have you known him?"

"Too long if t'were a minute, but 'tis three years since he thrust himself upon me and six months since I saw his black design. He is a ferreting devil!"

"And blameful for it," said Mr. Franklin. "Honest ambition is a virtue, but sneaking ambition is a pox. I too should like to prevent the man. By and by, your library—young Nick is a lover of books; may he peruse yours?"

Lord Bottom blinked. "Why . . . I should be happy."

"No, do not trouble yourself. I shall point the way." Leading me into the corridor, Mr. Franklin bent close. "Is this the house, Nick?" whispered he. "Is this the grand house which you recall?" and gesturing me to be off he returned to Lord Bottom.

At this I was taken aback. Why should Mr. Franklin suspect

118

Lord Bottom's grand house might be that in which my mother had raised me? Yet I would do as he bid. Feeling dwarfed by the vast rooms, I went in the direction he had shown, my plain buckled shoes echoing on fine marble amid tall columns and gilt plaster and grand paintings decorating the ceilings. Was it here where my mother's hand had stroked my brow and soothed my fears and run along the words of books to show me how to read? I listened for sounds from the past. Her voice? The harsh voices which had scolded her? I could not imagine hateful words here, yet that niche by a window in the spacious sitting room—was it there I had curled beside her while she read to me of princes and fairies? And those grand stairs sweeping up—did they lead to our little rooms, which we made a sanctuary by our love? And the tall fireplace in the drawing room—had I once warmed myself there? Though I found the library, I felt lost. What was true, what was true?

Bewildered and shaken, I spent some moments among the books in the wood-paneled room, noting the hidden door which Mr. Franklin had described. I had just drawn out a volume of Plutarch's *Lives*, when a voice startled me with its "Hello."

I turned to find Lord Bottom's daughter gazing inquiringly from the door.

"H-hello, ma'am," said I, thrusting the book I had taken back in its place and bobbing my head in an awkward little bow.

She was small and slender in a pale green dress, and her auburn hair hung to her shoulders. Her dress rustled as she came forward. "Pray, who are you?" asked she in a musical voice.

"I came with Mr. Franklin. He sent me to look at the library. I am a lover of books."

She smiled. "So is my father. All kinds of books. Mr. Franklin is here? And what do you have to do with Mr. Franklin?"

"I write things out for him."

"What sort of things?"

"A record of his days. His thoughts."

"You are fortunate. Father says he has wonderful thoughts." She spoke to me but a moment more before leaving to pay her respects to their guest, but it was long enough for me to see that

119

though she was composed and smiling on the surface there was a sadness beneath, as there was beneath her father's dignity. She was winning—eighteen years old, Mr. Franklin had said. I felt deep sympathy. What had been my mother's age when I was born? Had she too suffered under terrible sadness?

I returned to Lord Bottom's study twenty minutes later with no sure answer whether or no I had lived in his house, but the study proved deserted. The gentlemen must have repaired to the laboratory—yet where might that be? Waiting some moments to no effect, I determined that Mr. Franklin must wish me to seek them out. "His lordship's experimenting room lies below," informed the periwigged servant, directing me to some narrow stairs. These I descended but found myself in a dim-lit corridor unsure which way to turn. I tried left, yet this led only to the kitchen, a great room filled with the rich smell of simmering stew and the clang of copper pots, a white-capped cook laboring with sweating face at a huge brick stove.

There was a second person present.

I found myself face to face with an Indian.

Though I had never before seen an American Indian, I was at once certain from his burnt-looking skin and high, strong cheeks and strange, deep-set eyes that this was one, though he was dressed as an English manservant. He gaped, as startled to discover me, it seemed, as I to chance upon him. Yet it appeared worse for him, for his fierce eyes squinted, then widened; his mouth fell open, and he held his hand in front of him, palm out, as if casting a spell upon me to make me vanish from the spot. He was young, not over twenty, and tall and lean and light-footed as he stepped back. Too, there was the smell of liquor about him, a vague blearing in his eyes. I recoiled from him as he from me, our gazes momentarily locked, and my heart pounded at the unsettling mixture of emotions twisting his features: vexation, anger, fear.

I was terrified. Turning, I dashed back down the corridor—only to run into a woman as I rounded a corner.

I stared up into the face of another Indian.

She was shorter than the first and heavier and older, with streaks of white in her black hair, surely the woman Mr. Franklin had seen at dinner. O, the sadness in this house!—it was on her face too, etched in leathery lines. Smelling mustily of herbs, she caught me in strong hands and held me away, hardly looking at me but setting me aside as if I were made of straw and striding away from whence I had come, and I was amazed at the effortless stealthy silence of her movement, as if she might creep anywhere and not be heard.

At this I was breathless, hardly aware for some seconds that Lord Bottom's and Mr. Franklin's voices came from the room outside which she had been standing. Listening?

All this I told to Mr. Franklin as our coach rattled away from George Street some quarter of an hour later. "The Indian man stared at me as if he saw a ghost," said I.

"A ghost, you say?" Mr. Franklin pulled at his lip. "And he had a purple scar upon his cheek? Then he was the same brave I saw driving Hexham's coach Saturday night. What's his relation to the Indian woman?" He peered at me. "And Lord Bottom's house, Nicolas—was it there you and your mother once lived?"

"I do not know, sir. May be, may be not. I recognized nothing for certain, though I prayed to have found the place."

He sighed. "We shall continue to search. The black coach is with us once more, have you seen?" I started, but he squeezed my hand. "Do not be alarmed. Our pursuers, whoe'er they be, tell us we are on the right road." Chuckling, he thumped the box with his bamboo. "Drive faster, Peter! Give 'em a merry chase!"

Rain lashed Craven Street upon our return. At the end of the road the Thames churned muddily. Splashing through puddles, we ducked under streaming eaves.

"Lord 'a mercy!" exclaimed Mrs. Stevenson, greeting us dripping in the entranceway. "To go abroad in such weather!"

"Dear Mrs. Stevenson," replied Mr. Franklin as he shrugged his greatcoat into the gloomy King's waiting hands, "it was not raining when we departed." He sneezed loudly, thrice.

121

The good woman firmly touched her mole. "I warned you of this. O, when will you be guided by wiser minds?"

Mr. Franklin bowed his head, "Guide me now, dear lady," and suffered himself to be prodded upstairs like a sheep driven to fold. "I am in your hands." In his room wrapped up next the fire he sipped one of his landlady's warm medicinal libations—but the moment she was gone he threw off his blanket.

"She has walked down, Nicolas. Hurry, into my laboratory!"

He led the way, I feeling very foolish creeping to escape Mrs. Stevenson. When we were in the laboratory he closed and locked the door. Rain beat at the small glass panes; the light was dim. Firing two lamps, he hung them high, then turned to me and reached auspiciously into his waistcoat pocket, from which he drew out a chased brass snuff box. "Come close," said he, setting the box on a rough wooden table much stained with acid. From the box he carefully removed three small oyster-colored flakes. "Wax, Nicolas," pronounced he, and I saw they were the same as the oyster-colored bits he had seemed to take from Buck's and Mrs. Inch's hands when we visited Fish Lane. "Observe." Nearby was a miniature ink brayer. Delicately he flattened the little curves of wax and with equal care inked each small disk. Drawing forth a sheet of paper, he pressed the first onto the paper, revealing a pattern of curving lines. "Lord Bottom" he penned beneath this. Under the second, which also revealed a curving pattern, he printed "Anne," and under the third he printed "Indian woman." He beamed proudly. "Fingerprints!" said he.

"Fingerprints, sir?" said I.

He nodded. "From early days when I worked for my brother in Boston I noted these prints everywhere, for the men's hands were always covered in ink. Further, as I was even then of an observing nature, I soon saw that each finger of each hand made a different print, and that no two hands or prints were ever alike. Is't not wondrous, Nick, that as a man's face is his own, unique to him, so are the tiniest lines of his fingertips? I became used to playing a game with the workmen, which much perplexed them but to which they never discovered the secret. Indeed I have kept it to myself until this moment. I would set out three plain pewter cups, which I had taken pains to polish. I would then fill them with beer and leave the room, having first invited the workmen to choose three among them to sample my beer. Upon my return I pointed out the three workmen and the exact cup from which they had drunk. How? I had memorized the characteristics of each man's prints—O, it is an easy task—and as their hands always had some quantity of ink they always left prints. Thus it was the mere matter of glancing at the cups to say who had drunk from each."

I had to laugh at this story, yet I did not see its point. "But . . . what is the consequence of your game in this case, sir?"

"I shall show you." He drew forth a paper from a metal box. "Here I have collected some of Buck Duffin's and Mrs. Inch's prints by the method you have just seen: I soften wax by my hand in my pocket, then press a small ball of it against the thumb or finger of a person before quickly slipping it into my snuff box so it may not lose its impression." From the same large metal box he removed the ebony-handled carving knife which he had taken from under Mr. Inch's body. "Look closely at this." He pointed to some white powder dusting the smooth ebony handle. "The powder is snuff; it brings to light the hidden history of who has held this knife." I peered close. Visible in this fine dusting were some three or four of what he called fingerprints. "Now, who made these prints?" asked he.

"Why . . . the person who killed my master."

"And—?"

I saw at last. "And if you may discover the person whose prints match these," said I eagerly, "you have discovered his murderer!"

"Capital, Nick! I hope it may be so simple." He adjusted his glasses. "Nature thus provides a method to bring miscreants to justice. Is not her study rewarding? I may write of this some day. Do you think it would prove useful, or should I be deemed a madman? Leave that. Compare Buck's and Mrs. Inch's prints to the prints on the knife."

I did so. They did not match. I looked up at Mr. Franklin. "Neither of them killed him, then?"

"Neither held the knife. We must remember, however, that he was first struck on the head from behind. And now let us compare our three new samples, though I expect nothing from Lord Bottom's or his daughter's." Indeed they were like none of the prints on the knife handle, nor were the Indian woman's.

"How did you obtain her prints?" asked I.

"I glimpsed her in shadows as Lord Bottom and I descended to his experimenting room and drew her out and squeezed her hand. O, I took milord aback by doing it." He laughed. "Indeed I am certain he begins to think me eccentric." He gazed out the rain-swept window. "Would that I had the prints of the Indian you saw in the kitchen. What was his business belowstairs at Bottom's? Visiting? I inquired about Hexham's bringing Indians to England, and his lordship said the rogue imported whole families of 'em. Could the woman be the mother of that brave? We have spoke of families before, young Nick. Is there yet another which we may sketch into our unfinished picture?"

A strong wind set up a creaking about Number 7. "Sir," said I, "did you sweep pieces of Mr. Inch's type into your hat to get fingerprints from them too?"

"You saw me at it, did you? Then you are as sharp-eyed as I at your age. Truly I looked for fingerprints, for even then I did not trust Constable Nittle to see further than his nose." From the same box he drew forth a leather pouch and spilled the metal letters on the table. "Buck's prints are here, and what I take to be Eben's. And yours? Shall we try you, Nick?" He dabbed some ink on the thumb and fingers of both my hands and pressed ten prints onto a new sheet of paper, which he labeled "Nicolas Handy." Examining the types, we found my marks at many places on 'em. Mr. Franklin moved the knife to the paper, carefully so as not to disturb the dusting of snuff. "See?" He peered at me above the tops of his glasses. "Proof that you did not wield the instrument. Shall we examine my prints also? In fairness we must." He inked his own fingers, all ten, and pressed them onto yet another sheet of paper and compared them to the knife. "Neither of us attempted to steal your master's scalp, it seems."

124

"His scalp . . ." echoed I. All at once the rain at the windows made me feel I was drowning. The knife-point yet had blood on it, brownish smears, and, staring at it and knowing that the white-dusted prints on its wicked black handle were those of the murderer of poor Mr. Inch, I blanched, and trembled.

Mr. Franklin wiped his hand clean on a cloth. "Aye, it is a terrible business, Nick. Murder and who knows what may be?"

"I . . . I am sorry to be so affected, sir."

"Do not apologize. You, a child . . ." His ordinarily composed features shook with fury. "Damn them for what they did to you!"

"And the button which you took from Mr. Inch's hand?"

That too was in the metal box. He removed it. "See, stamped with a pinnace on the sea. From some suit of livery? Made specially? I have sent King round to several metalsmiths to inquire, but none that we have found cast the button."

"Might it have been made in America?"

He cocked a brow. "Quite right, lad, indeed it may." Replacing everything in the metal box, he locked it and put it into a drawer. Supper was served him on a tray in bed, as Mrs. Stevenson insisted, to which he acceded as if she were Juno to his Jove. Polly looked in, and later Mr. William Franklin. The son spoke much of the adamancy of the Penns, showing himself very knowledgeable in his father's suit. I sat all the while by Mr. Franklin's fire, practicing his short-hand. Everything was cozy, the logs crackling, the storm held at bay, and it was hard to believe that threatening costers or Indians or mysterious pursuers in black coaches might lurk outside.

In bed, warm under my comforter, my thoughts ran on about the mystery we followed, which was a road with many turnings. America was mixed up in it, surely; the Indians—if nothing else—said so. Recalling the dog's yowl, which had proved to be not a dog's but a savage's murderous cry, I pulled the comforter over my head.

What more might prove false to its seeming?

☙ 10 ☙

IN WHICH Mr. Franklin causes much stir at Inch, Printer, and we visit a floating house of pleasure . . .

"DAMN me, Nick!" said Mr. Franklin next morning, gazing out his window at a blustery day, "it is more than a week since your master was struck down, and we are far from knowing who did it or why, with the trail growing cold so that even a keen-scented hound might lose it! Yet, here comes King." Having spied his servant in the street, the gentleman seemed in some agitation, pacing and blowing his nose waiting for him to come up.

"Out?" asked he sharply when the melancholy black man appeared hat in hand at his door.

"Out, sir," delivered King in his low, defeated voice.

Snatching his fur hat and bamboo Mr. Franklin turned to me. "Your coat and cap, Nicolas, quickly! We must be off!"

In very short time we were in a hackney coach rattling east along the Strand, past St. Clement Danes. "Out, sir?" asked I.

He gave a low chuckle. "Someone watches us—may we not watch in turn? Thus I set King these past few days in Fish Lane, to see Dora Inch's comings and goings. She has just left Inch, Printer, with the appearance of staying away some time. Now is our chance to look about the place."

In a quarter of an hour we were at the leaning, half-timbered house in its crooked lane, and once again I found myself in the little stationery shop, with its pen nibs and quires of paper and pounce boxes set out on high wooden shelves. It filled me with unease to be there, as if I might be reclaimed by the place, snatched up and eaten whole, swallowed and digested and never again seen in the world of kindness and light, and I stuck close to Mr. Franklin's side.

Tilda kept watch over the trade in her mother's absence, behind a little counter. Plump and coarse, tiny eyes squinting, she had on a blue ruffled dress finer than any shopgirl's, which she wore with airs, like a grand lady, fluttering her fat arms so that its pink lace ribbons flew about. "You *dreadful* boy!" squealed she at the sight of me, poking out her fat little chin. "I hoped *never* to set eyes on you again."

"How delightful to meet you once more," said Mr. Franklin.

"O!" Coyly she blinked. "You are the gentleman here the morning my poor papa was found."

"Indeed I was present on that sad occasion. I am Mr. Franklin." Grasping her hand, he kissed it, and I saw a little lump of oyster-colored wax drop deftly from his fingers into safekeeping in his waistcoat. "Is your mother at home?" asked he.

Tilda patted her straw-colored ringlets. "She would not wish to see *you*."

"Pray, why not?"

"I do not know, but she rails against you. You had best leave before she returns."

"Yet I have business here."

"Printing business?"

"Business with you, for one," said he. "You were out the morning your father was murdered. Where had you been?"

Her pinched gaze flew accusingly to me. "O, you . . . you boy! You weren't to tell, you weren't!" And she stamped her foot.

"Do not blame Nicolas," said Mr. Franklin. "Mr. Barking, the watchman, saw you many mornings." His voice pressed her. "I repeat, where were you, Miss Inch?"

127

A wordless squealing set up in her throat, and her ruffles and laces flew about as if in a gale. "I *shan't* tell, I *shan't*!" puffed she, her plump cheeks purpling as if her face might burst.

"Why, then I must put the question to your mother," said Mr. Franklin.

She gaped. "Not Mama! No!" And she moaned so mightily, swaying back and forth and flinging her arms about, that though she had ever snubbed and abused me I pitied her.

At this moment Buck Duffin stomped in from the printing room wiping his inky hands on his apron. "'Ere now, wot's this? You!" barked he at sight of me, bunching his fists. "And you?" said he more doubtfully at sight of Mr. Franklin. He turned his scowling face to Tilda. "Wot've they bin askin'?"

"They want to know . . . they want to know—"

"Never mind. You git upstairs. I'll talk to 'em."

Tilda planted her hands on her ample hips. "You'll not tell me what to do, Buck Duffin!"

He thrust his face in hers. "I'm master 'ere, when your mama's away, and she's away now, and you'll do wot I say. Now, either git upstairs, my girl, or," he hooked a thumb at us, "tell 'em all they want t' know and be damned."

Tilda stared, sputtered, choked. Wailing, she flew into the printing room and up the stairs.

"Now, sir," demanded Buck of Mr. Franklin, leaning hard on the counter, "wot's yer business?"

"Questions, young sir. You were out the morning your master was murdered. Where?"

"Me? Out? Never. I wuz abed."

"You were out."

"I wuz in bed, I say!"

"You returned at seven in the morning. You struck this boy from his sleep."

Buck glowered at me, and I could see his mind working behind his sharp black eyes. He drew himself up. "So wot if it be? What matter?"

"Great matter if you were in your master's yard, waiting. Were you? Did you strike down Eben Inch?"

Buck's mouth fell open. "'Ere now!"

"Did you?"

"I never . . . !"

"Can you prove it?"

"I'm a innocent man! I've no need t'—"

"Why were you lurking about Watts' Printing on Sunday?"

"Lurking? Why . . . why—'cause Mrs. Inch told me to, that's why. There's no law 'gainst bein' in a place."

"Being there to do harm?"

"I mean no harm."

"Yet you are a sneaking bully of a lad, my eyes and ears give proof of that, and I should be happy to deliver it to any magistrate in London. Why did Mrs. Inch set you after us?"

"How should I now? I does wot she sez. She thinks you murdered her 'usband fer all I knows. Just you watch out—it may not be only you speakin' out b'fore th' magistrate."

"Did you ride to Wild's Court in a black coach?"

He laughed. "Black or brown, t'isn't likely I'd ride in a coach. I footed it. I'm quick on my feet, I am, and no horse goes so fast in these city streets but what I can't catch 'im."

"The night your master was murdered—were you out with Tilda?"

"Tilda?"

"She returned near dawn, as did you."

At this Buck began to sputter. "She? Out? Why . . . why . . . how dare she?"

"You did not know that she was out?"

"How should I? But I know now, and I'll . . . O, damn Bertie Hexham!"

"Bertie Hexham?"

But Buck looked sly once more. "Never you mind. You're not wanted 'ere, and you can leave or I'll 'ave the constable throw you out."

"Then call Costable Nittle at once. I should be happy to hear his news of your master's murder. What has Bertie Hexham to do with Tilda Inch—or should I apply to the father for news of the son?"

"Do as you like. Mr. Hexham'll toss you in the street, he will."

"You know Jared Hexham?"

Buck's chest swelled. "I do. He's a gen'leman. He brings this shop custom, and when I'm master 'ere I'll be as proud to know 'im then as I am now."

"Master here? How will you become that? By marrying Tilda? So Jared Hexham and Mrs. Inch do business? And do they do it with Mrs. Couch? And with Mrs. Mountjoy too?"

Buck sneered. "Mrs. Mountjoy? Aye, Mrs. Mountjoy. Go ask yer questions of 'er. You'll get somethin', you may count on it— though it will not be wot you expect."

All at once a familiar rude commotion sounded at my back, quick steps and puffing breath, and I flinched. Mr. Franklin and I turned as one, and indeed there came Mrs. Inch in a large, flapping bonnet, bearing down upon us like a coach upon its post, carrying an enormous wooden-handled embroidered bag which she swung in great arcs as if she would smash the room and its contents, ink pots, pens, persons alike. Even Buck ducked his head.

She halted, snorting like a bull. "I do not wish to see you here, sir!" she bellowed in Mr. Franklin's face. "I do not wish to see you ever again, did I make that clear upon your last setting foot in my shop?"

"Why then did you send your apprentice to keep watch on us, ma'am?"

"What?" Her angry look fell upon Buck. "You! Back to work!" Buck darted from the room.

She whirled again upon Mr. Franklin. "As for my apprentice, I do with him what I wish!" Yet a great alteration overcame her. Her tiny eyes lowered. "O, sir, begging your pardon for such a show," she murmured. "It is just that . . . that the death of my poor Eben has turned his poor widow topsy-turvy." She wobbled and leaned upon the counter and held her head as if she would faint, yet I saw her peer slyly at Mr. Franklin to see how he took this.

"Pitiable woman," murmured he. "You have my sympathy. Eben was my friend, did you know that?"

There was a small stiffening, but she only replied in the same lost whimper, "No."

"He never told you I saved him once, from the clutches of a man named Bixer?"

"Never."

"No doubt the circumstances were too painful for him." He peered close at her. "You are certain you know no Bixer?"

"I have said so, have I not?"

"Indeed you have. Mmm . . . I wonder whatever became of the rogue, there are things I should like to tell the law about him. But I came not to burden a poor widow with the past—except in one regard. This boy here, who has caused you so much grief." He placed a hand firmly upon my shoulder. "Who was his mother?"

Her little eyes shot up. Was there a flash of fear? "Why . . . who does the boy claim his mother may be?"

Mr. Franklin only gazed pleasantly, as if he had asked the way to Westminster with eternity to wait for answer.

"As to that," said Mrs. Inch at last, "I never knew his mother. I got him from the foundling home, has he not told you so?"

"You named him, then?"

"I did."

"Handy?"

"I thought he might be handy. He turned out sneaking and lazy."

I longed to protest but held my tongue.

"Yet you told him his mother's name was Rose Handy," pursued Mr. Franklin, "and that he was a bastard."

Her gaze flicked to me, and I was very glad to have Mr. Franklin's protecting hand pressing my shoulder. "He told you that? Perhaps then I did—but I only made it up, meaning no harm."

"Made it up? Why?"

"To shut him up from asking. To keep him in his place."

"I see. And which foundling home, may I ask?"

"Surely I cannot be expected to remember—it has been so many years."

131

Mr. Franklin nodded. "Memory oft fails me too." His gaze hardened. "Yet soon or late I recall what I wish."

"Why do you take such interest in this boy?"

"I mean to discover the truth of his parentage." He cocked his head. "Naturally, not knowing the mother you would not know the father?"

"Naturally," said she.

"Do you do business with Jared Hexham?" asked he.

"Jared Hexham?"

"I met him the other evening. A splendid fellow! His son looks to marry Lord Bottom's daughter. You have a daughter, have you not? We spoke to her just now, a sturdy girl."

But Mrs. Inch seemed to have heard but one thing. "Bertie Hexham looks to marry Lord Bottom's daughter?"

Mr. Franklin nodded blithely. "I believe the father approves his son's choice. Truly the lady Anne is lovely. So you do know Hexham? Your apprentice said as much. What business does he with you? Printing? What printing might a merchant require?"

Mrs. Inch gripped the counter hard. "I am feeling dropsical," moaned she. "I must be up to bed."

"Poor woman! May we assist you?"

"Buck will assist me." She snarled his name, at which he darted back. She leaned heavily on him as he steered her into the printing room, though who led whom was in question, for she gouged a hand into his back and cursed under her breath, and I was very happy to know that it was he who must face her wrath when we were gone.

Out in Fish Lane the rain had started again, a dreary pelting. Rivulets of muddy water slithered at our feet. Mr. Franklin frowned into the areaway of Inch, Printer, its bolted storage door just visible under the stairs. "Dora Inch is secretive about what she hides there, is she?" he mused. "I should like to know why."

Just then I glanced at Mrs. Couch's windows across the way. A lace curtain suddenly fell as if someone had kept watch. "Sir," said I, tugging his sleeve, but Mr. Franklin must have seen it too, for he made a motion that I should show no notice.

"We visit Mrs. Mountjoy next," said he clambering into the coach and rubbing his hands and smiling as he settled back. "The world is full of fools who think themselves clever! To the *Folly*, Peter."

We went west against the rain, past Lincoln's Inn Fields and Drury Lane and Covent Garden, Mr. Franklin taking pleasure in pointing out landmarks. I saw that in his short time in London he had got to know the city well, and I began to fancy that I, a child of Moorfields, knew her too, stretched out along the Thames in a crowded, smoky, roiling jumble of poverty and wealth and surging life.

"And what is the *Folly*, sir?" asked I as we passed St. Martin's Lane.

"An establishment like Mrs. Couch's, though grander, where a man may satisfy his desires."

This establishment proved to be a fine, large barge moored in view of Charing Cross, amongst a churning of smaller craft. It had two stories, with a pavilion at the front, under which I was surprised to see in spite of the rain a band of six or eight musicians playing light airs which floated over the choppy waters. Peter halted on the embankment and clutching our hats we scurried down a gangplank to the shelter of the pavilion. Above us gay little flags of red and green bravely fought the sodden breeze. Ahead lay a wide door with FOLLY painted in bright curling letters above it. This we entered to discover all pipesmoke and clinking glasses and jollity within, with more music being played and pretty girls in low-cut dresses strolling about a broad, comfortably furnished room or sitting on gentlemen's laps, very coy and seductive. These gentlemen sprawled at ease, unbuttoned, and I knew enough to see how it was with Mrs. Mountjoy's and to guess what went on in the rooms upstairs.

I glimpsed a dark-skinned girl nearby. Her eyes flashed at sight of us. "Mr. Franklin," said I urgently, but a small gesture said that I should say no more. Tapping his bamboo, he looked about with a ready smile as if he were here for naught but pleasure.

133

At this point a plump bustling woman appeared through a far door and began to sail about the room, greeting its patrons by name or title: "Good day, Caleb Greene," "How well you look, Sir Bond," "O, milord, we are so honored!" with pleasant laughter. She had a warm, humorous voice, loud and cracked. She was much watched, many men smiling her way and greeting her. Her skirts floated so huge about her that she seemed to glide on 'em. Above the waist was scarlet velvet trimmed in white ruffles, then a powdered bosom and a powdered face, with red-painted lips and a beauty spot on the chin, last a high white wig stuck with pearls. She had a small pointed nose.

This woman came near us. "Good day, sir," said she to Mr. Franklin, thrusting this sharp little nose good-humoredly into his face. She reeked of perfume.

He made a little bow. "Good day, ma'am."

Her powder had made her seem younger, but now I saw she must be fifty. "I am Mrs. Mountjoy," announced she in her cracked voice, looking him frankly up and down. "You are welcome, sir, yet I do not know you. What is your name?"

"Why . . . Silas. Silas Dogood."

She gave a hearty laugh. "Dogood, a name to conjure with!" Winking, she tapped his arm. "Well, sir, you may not do good here—but you will surely do well. And the boy? You have brought him to introduce him to pleasure? No better place, I say, though we are not used to 'em so young. Yet we shall give him all he hopes for, he shall be satisfied. Pray, how do you know of the *Folly?*"

"O, from Mrs. Couch." He cocked his head. "Or perhaps from Mrs. Inch?"

I knew he watched her close though he made no sign. I watched too. One of her black-painted brows rose a quarter inch. Her smile stayed fixed upon her face, yet suspicion stirred in her deep brown eyes.

"They are ladies of my profession?" asked she cautiously.

"Very like it, I believe."

"Yet they recommend me? How strange."

134

"There are stranger things in this world. You do not know these ladies?"

"I begin to think I do not know you."

"I am a man."

"Prove it, sir, by taking one of my girls."

"I should prefer their mistress."

"Oho! yet their mistress is not to be had."

"I wish her only to ask questions of her."

"You insult me, sir!"

"No insult intended, ma'am. You are handsome." Gallantly he kissed her hand. "Indeed your ripeness shames the callow, unformed beauty of your girls. Any man must be grateful for a moment of your favors."

Mrs. Mountjoy's false black lashes trembled while two spots of pink glowed through her powder. "Why, sir—you make me think I spoke wrong when I protested I was not to be had. Your words move my heart."

He spoke in lower tones. "I wish they might stir your tongue, for there are things I must know."

She stroked his arm. "Might these things be preludes to acts where words do not suffice?"

Mr. Franklin discreetly gestured toward a gentleman near a window. "That fellow . . . Bertram Hexham, is he not?"

Mrs. Mountjoy's gaze turned towards a slim young man in night-blue jacket and breeches. He wore shiny boots and lolled in a broad red-leather chair a dozen paces away. His wig was askew, and his face was wrapped in a vacuous stare, yet he had a mean, petulant air. He held on his lap the dark-skinned girl who had stared at us as we came in, grasping her about the waist. I thought she did not like him, though she kept a smile on her dusky face and let his hands wander where they would, from waist to bosom.

"Yes, that is Bertie Hexham," said Mrs. Mountjoy softly.

"Does he visit here often?"

"He is a frequent guest."

"And the girl—she is an American Indian, is she not?"

"She is. The *Folly* caters to many tastes. We have women from

Africa and China, even a girl who speaks the tongue of Araby—though her voice is not the best of her charms."

"The Indian girl's name?"

"I cannot pronounce it. She tells us it means cornflower, and that is what we call her."

"Cornflower," mused Mr. Franklin. "Do you do business with Bertie Hexham's father?"

Mrs. Mountjoy placed her hands on her hips. "I see your compliments were meant only to flatter, to wheedle answers of me."

Mr. Franklin shook his head. "No flattery. I spoke true. Am I not of an age to savor mature charms? These girls are green apples, with no pleasure in the picking, while you are ripe. I repeat, do you do business with Jared Hexham?"

She stroked his arm once more. "I do not know why I do not have my man toss you in the Thames, indeed I do not! Yes, I do business with Hexham. It is he supplied the Indian girl, besides several others in my employ. I pay well for 'em, to boot. He knows it; it is his chief trade."

"His chief trade?"

"O, he wears airs of fine respectability, and it is true he exports some trifling British goods to the colonies. Yet his money comes from smuggling off the Irish coast and the trade in slaves and women. There is rumor he wishes to turn it to a knighthood, perhaps even higher title."

"And are there no other rumors?"

"As to that," coyly she wrapped his arm in hers, "—let us talk of it in my chambers. The boy may choose a girl, if he please."

"Keep watch, Nick," said Mr. Franklin before acceding to Mrs. Mountjoy's tugs, and shortly the far door closed upon one of her throaty laughs.

I felt much at a loss. Choose a girl? Many of the women were pretty, but I flushed at their smiles and took a place for a time in a corner hoping no one would notice me and fidgeted with my hat uncertain what I should do. My gaze was drawn to the Indian girl. She had long, blue-black hair and a strong-boned face and wore no powder but displayed her savage origins proudly, though she was forced to submit to Bertie Hexham. Had she some connection to the Indian woman at Lord Bottom's or to the Indian man who drove Jared Hexham's rig? Indeed she resembled that young brave. I found I pitied her. Bertie Hexham grew more intimate, yet she resisted him, at which his voice grew loud, slurred with drink: "Come, you wench, I *shall* have you!"

And then she struck him—not slapped as an English girl might have done, but struck him on the side of the neck with such sharp vigor that he gasped and fell to the floor, where he crawled about choking and coughing as if he would expire. "Doxy!" sputtered he again and again, falling back against a table, legs askew, but she had fled through the outer door.

His bleared eyes fell on me. "You! What do you stare at?" Pulling himself up, he cursed his way out amidst uproarious laughter, the patrons appearing to take this as part of the revelry while the music lost not one measure.

For my part, I was wracked by sad thoughts—had my mother been reduced to such as this, called upon to deliver herself to any man with a sovereign in his pocket?—and I dashed out into the wind of the day, driving before it a slanting rain that hissed on the stone embankment and pelted the gray-brown Thames, causing me to turn up my collar, pull my hat low and bury my hands in my pockets. A narrow walkway encircled the barge. Hunch-shouldered, lashed by the storm, I made my way along it feeling very down. Find my mother? How could that be? And if it meant finding her, even her history, in such a place as this, I thought I could not bear it.

And then strong hands grasped my shoulders and spun me about. It was the Indian girl, soaked to the skin, her straight black hair streaming in the rain. She held me hard, peering into my face; and, recalling with what ease she had felled Bertie Hexham, I made no resistance but stared with bewilderment into eyes that seemed to pierce my soul. These eyes searched me while her lips formed incomprehensible words, her Indian tongue I guessed. She seemed to ask a question, urgently shaking my shoulders, but

I knew not what and could only plead helplessly, "Please, ma'am . . . please—"

At last she delivered haltingly, "Boy . . . Inch?"

I nodded my head, and she gave a great cry not unlike the terrible cry I had heard the morning my master was murdered, which made my blood run cold. Lifting her hands she flung her head high so her streaming hair flew up like wings. Her strong, dark face writhed with despair, and she staggered back, turned and fled round the corner of the barge.

"Damn me, boy! You again?" came another voice, and I was roughly jostled by Bertie Hexham, lurching along the walkway, his sullen face twisted in fury. "Was that the Indian wench? I shall teach her a lesson!" Pushing past, he near toppled me into the Thames.

Shivering with more than the cold, I hurried to find Mr. Franklin, discovering him under the pavilion peering about anxiously under his beaver hat.

"Nicolas," said he. "I feared for you."

Breathlessly I said why I had gone outside and what had passed. He sent one of his deep looks out over London. "Worse and worse." His gaze returned. "You must take special care, Nick."

"I, sir?" Then I recalled something. "The Indian girl—she wore a chain of shells like those you found near my master's body!"

He pulled at his lip. "Could *she* have struck down Eben Inch?"

We returned to Peter, who had drawn our conveyance under the eaves of a wharfside shed. Mr. Franklin climbed into the coach. As I made to do so I sent one last glance back at the *Folly*, long and low in the churning waters. The embankment chanced to be deserted just then, save for the figure of a tall man in a long black coat and a wide-brimmed black hat. He stood far away, at the very edge of the Thames, yet before he ducked his head to hide his face I knew him: the beak-nosed coster who had threatened me.

"Mr. Franklin! The coster!" cried I, pointing, and was astonished to discover the gentleman out of the coach in an instant and dashing toward the man in black.

I was more astonished to see this man leap into the Thames.

I hurried after Mr. Franklin, reaching him at riverside in time to see that it was not the river but a small boat into which the man had leapt. Rowed by two men, this swift craft quickly disappeared round the corner of the *Folly.*

Mr. Franklin struck the embankment with his bamboo. "Damn me, who is he?" He gave a great sneeze. "A warm fire and one of Mrs. Stevenson's potions for me!" When we were in the coach, rattling toward Craven Street, he said darkly, "Things grow to a pretty pass. We must take strong measures. Housebreaking, Nick—would you think ill of me for proposing it? Yet it must be—and tonight." He laughed wryly. "O, the irony if bumbling Constable Nittle should catch us at it!"

✖ 11 ✖

*IN WHICH I turn housebreaker and
face up to a magistrate . . .*

I T did not seem criminal but only what must be done for truth
as we crept along a winding way in Moorfields that very same
night. It was near two A.M. and dankly cold amongst the deep
shadows, with only the ceasing of rain and a bright moon to be
thankful for.

Abruptly Mr. Franklin drew me into a doorway. Lamplight
wavered ahead, and shortly wiry old Mr. Barking came peering
along the puddled lane, though he did not see us. "Thank heaven
he is not so sharp-eyed as he claims," breathed Mr. Franklin as he
led on, I keeping close at his side. I was again amazed, for after
but three visits to these precincts he knew their ways as well as I.

I kept my misgivings to myself. What if Mr. Barking should spy
us? What if he sounded the hue and cry?

At last we came to Inch, Printer, its shabby sign creaking in a
sharp breeze. "The areaway, Nick," whispered Mr. Franklin. With
but a single glance round he stepped over the iron rail, grasped
two spikes firmly and with a soft grunt lowered himself onto a
barrel, from which he dropped to the ground below. I too peered
about. Mrs. Couch's house had never felt so full of eyes, though I
saw no light; indeed it and Inch, Printer, seemed to bend heads
together over Fish Lane like two watchful gossips, ready to cry
out. Quickly I joined Mr. Franklin below.

140

The long rectangle of the areaway was dank-smelling and at first seemed black as ink, though a dim ray of moonlight soon let me see. Mr. Franklin was at the storage door that led under the road. "Locked and bolted," murmured he at its formidable iron bar and chain, "yet we may find a way." At this he removed a large ring of keys from his greatcoat pocket. "Jemmies," said he, "—at least that is what I am told the lockpickers call 'em. Peter found 'em for me; I did not inquire how. Let us hope they do what they ought." Quickly he drew forth a small metal cylinder with a wick. "An improvisation for this occasion, a tiny lamp," said he, striking flint. "Hold the light, Nick, while I work."

This I did to the soft clink of keys, he trying one after another, prying and twisting, while I thought of what the day had revealed. After her first fury Mrs. Inch had appeared afraid of Mr. Franklin. Why? Yet for all his questions we still had not discovered the secret of Tilda's and Buck's nocturnal forays. As for our time at Mrs. Mountjoy's, that lady had had little to add to what she told us about Jared Hexham, so Mr. Franklin had informed me on our way back to Craven Street. "Yet she confirms he is ambitious," said he. "And she confesses she knows Mrs. Couch and Mrs. Inch. The picture grows clearer. They are go-betweens for Hexham. They receive the girls and pass 'em on to him—some of 'em at any rate—and he distributes the chattel to bawdy houses in London and about, or sends 'em to the New World to suffer what fates they may."

"How did you persuade Mrs. Mountjoy to speak of it?" asked I.

"O . . . e'en at fifty I have a way with the ladies. I find I like the woman. Hers is no ordinary bawdy house. . She is good-hearted and watches out for her charges, and I fancy when she hears of Bertie Hexham's behavior she will take the Indian girl's part. Ah, if only we knew the truth of that sad creature!"

My ruminations were stopped by a soft cry of satisfaction. "Done!" said Mr. Franklin, sliding a huge lock from its chain. "Now . . . what has Dora Inch hid within?" Amidst the gloom he pulled back the heavy, creaking oak, and, I holding the lamp high, we stepped into the storage room.

The space was small, perhaps six by ten feet, its walls lined with wooden shelves. My flickering light revealed nothing extraordinary: books and ledgers, stone jars of preserved food-stuffs, old implements—a broken broom, a rusted garden rake. There was a dusty smell—yet something more.

"Anise!" said Mr. Franklin as I too recognized it.

"But why should the smell of Mrs. Couch's pipe be here?" whispered I.

"That is what we must find out." Rapidly he moved to the shelves, I following with the lamp. First he examined the books, hundreds, packed close and taking up much of the space, which proved to be copies of volumes we had printed: *A Maid's Diary*, *The Life of a Rake*, *Scenes from Old Rome*, and the like, stored here against future sales, I supposed. He peered close at several title pages, but none had hand-lettered numbers as had been in Lord Bottom's books. Next he turned to the ledgers. Some were records of shop goods—pens, ink, paper—and some of printing supplies. Others showed what books had sold. And one, finer-bound than the rest in sturdy red vellum, had names such as Lord Bottom's and other gentry, with numbers by the names. "Mrs. Inch kept careful record of what fine folk subscribed to your master's special printings. See?—the number by Lord Bottom's name is the same as that printed in his books. Might it prove an embarrassment to some of these gentlemen to have this known?" Carefully returning this volume to its place, he picked up the one remaining, a shabby thing, its binding chewed by rats. In it were dates beginning a dozen years ago, monies listed by each, the words, "Received from America," written by each sum in quarter-yearly installments from 1745 to the present.

When I glanced up from the yellowed pages Mr. Franklin's face was hid by a hand rubbing his brow. "Money from America—what does it mean, sir?" asked I.

The hand briefly trembled. "It means that though the picture grows clearer its colors prove dark." He pushed his glasses hard against his nose. "O, there is danger, Nick!" He stiffened. "But what is this?" Some old cloaks were hung on the wall by the

142

broken broom. My gaze flew there to discover these moving in ghostly fashion, trembling, as if they had living souls within.

My blood near froze in my veins, but Mr. Franklin was not daunted. Striding to 'em, he pushed 'em aside, revealing a narrow passageway where a small breeze blew. "The answer to more than one question, Nicolas. Follow me." With no more ado he bent and fitted himself into this hole.

Swallowing hard, I scurried after. Seconds later we reached another door, not nearly so well-bolted as Mrs. Inch's, which Mr. Franklin's jemmies handily opened. We emerged in Mrs. Couch's areaway ten feet across the lane. "So," said he, glancing back, "a tunnel between the two houses. It is my guess that Buck Duffin came and went this way; that is why Mr. Barking never spied him. Dallying with one of Mrs. Couch's girls? Did your master's murderer use this route also, coming direct from her house with the smell of anise on his clothes? Well, Mrs. Inch can no longer deny she is friends with her neighbor. Mmm, Fish Lane is so narrow that the digging of the passage must have been pretty easy labor and well worth it. No doubt it eased the dealings in girls, too, it might serve as a hiding place or escapeway should officialdom decide to raid Mrs. Couch's. Is there any more to discover?" But Mrs. Couch's storage room contained little save warped wooden shelves, and we were soon back across the way and clambering onto the barrel to Fish Lane, the doors carefully locked behind us.

The sign INCH, PRINTER still creaked in the wind. A reeking fog began to curl from the cobbles. "Sir!" cried I. A human form had seemed to lurk where the lane twisted into black shadow—yet the instant I spoke it vanished like smoke. "I thought I saw—"

"Aye, Nick," murmured Mr. Franklin, grasping my arm, "it is time to be home in bed."

We scuttled like cutpurses along the twisting alleys to where Peter waited with our coach beneath the scudding moon.

Next morning at Craven Street Mrs. Stevenson tut-tutted at Mr. Franklin, propped up in bed. "Did I not hear the front door open and close very early this morning, sir? And did I not hear coach wheels twice at my stoop?"

Mr. Franklin peered innocently over the tops of his spectacles. "O, I cannot say what you heard, kind lady, but I heard the very same—or dreamed I did—and wondered who might try the folly of such early hours."

He sneezed mightily. Clucking her tongue, Mrs. Stevenson placed the tray of porridge and bread and fresh boiled egg on his lap before departing with a tragic air, head high, as if the world were lost if it escaped the hands of housewives.

"To my view, Nick," said Mr. Franklin when she was gone and the door closed, "Jared Hexham and Dora Inch are two of a kind, villains yoked in some way we cannot yet see clearly. We know they trade in those poor girls."

"Sir . . . might my mother have been one of 'em?"

"I pray not, lad. Yet she may prove to be. If so—"

"I am determined to face the truth."

"I hope to uncover it for you—and for myself." Tucking a white cloth at his throat, he cracked his egg. "But there is more than the girls," said he, scooping the white with his spoon. "The numbered list we discovered last night tells so. It is my guess that Hexham catalogues the sins of influential men who might aid him in his rise. Ambition, Nick; it drives him and Mrs. Inch to wicked measures! Hexham has ferreted out something to blacken Lord Bottom's character, which he means to use to advance his son, no matter that milord's daughter loathes the very sight of Bertie. Yet what can poor Anne do, caught in such meshes? Ah, women are ever victims! Clearly it is extortion which is Jared Hexham's means—yet is't murder too? But if it is . . ." Here he gazed in his distracted way, spoon halfway to his lips, while I shifted on the stool at his desk where I had gone to write out our nocturnal venture.

At last Mr. Franklin swallowed his egg. "Our abiding mystery, set by Martha Clay, is to discover who murdered her brother. Finding motive for the deed may yield the answer. Surely good-hearted Eben did not connive with his wife—yet did he know something that threatened some ambitious plan? I cannot but wonder: might we seek motive for the wrong murder?"

"What do you mean, sir?" asked I.

He looked suddenly furtive, as if he had not meant to say so much. Harumphing, he adjusted his glasses. "One thing I mean is that I fear more murder. Hexham and Dora Inch pull the same cart, yet the yoke begins to chafe. Affairs between 'em may have run as smooth as cream 'til now, but their aims do not mix; Mrs. Inch's apoplexy upon hearing that Bertie Hexham is intended for the lady Anne tells so. The cream curdles. A falling out among thieves may have fearful consequences. One murder has occurred. May there not be more?"

"Whose, sir?"

"We must see it is not ours."

Our hours ticked away indoors that day, the ninth since I came to Craven Street. Outside it was gray and bitter-cold October, indoors cozy, with a parlor fire and bedroom fire springing merrily. Wheezing and coughing, Mr. Franklin had been set back by our creeping amongst dank, narrow ways and stayed abed complaining of wasted time, though he used it well, scribbling long letters to his wife and daughter in Philadelphia, letters too to members of Parliament whom he hoped might aid him in his cause. His handsome son joined him some while to speak of the obstinacy of the Penns. Again William showed himself knowledgeable, though he was more inclined than his father to see the Penns' side, which caused some friction. I noted how the son paid little mind to me, though I sat not six feet from his back fashioning imitations of Mr. Addison's style; more, I noted how the father himself spoke of me as little as possible to his son, and I had the sense that William was unaware of the truth about Fish Lane—my long years of captivity and my master's brutal murder. I was certain he was not told of our search, and I wondered why— he being confidante to his father in all else—this should be kept secret.

Twice I peered out the window upon hearing a coster's jaunty song, but both instances proved only Mr. Digges, Mrs. Stevenson's customary purveyor, though I was more uneasy than relieved when no sight of a beak-nosed man in black or a shabby black coach met my eyes.

That evening Mr. Franklin roused himself and once more beckoned me into his laboratory. There in soft-spoke confidence by the rough, acid-stained bench he showed me that Mrs. Mountjoy's fingerprints did not match those on the ebony knife handle. Nor did Tilda Inch's. "Would that I had got the Indian girl's," he muttered. "Bertie Hexham's too."

"But, sir, have we not determined that it was an Indian did the murder?"

"We take the cry you heard to be an Indian's, and the dreadful hacking at the root of Eben's hair seems the prelude to a scalping—yet I draw no sure conclusion. Scalping is neither a custom nor a privilege confined to the red man. It is known in England, too, certain Christian souls who have spent some years in America are known to have learnt it and practiced it, calling upon God as their witness and justification. One cannot name the Indian hypocrite, Nick, and there is a good deal of deviousness in this, O, I do not wonder that the red man sometimes seeks the white man's scalp."

At this he moved to new subjects, for I could not but gaze with keen interest about the room, nor could he restrain himself from displaying its contents. This he did as if he were a child eagerly showing toys. In one corner stood an elegant mahogany box on legs, containing rows of glass hemispheres which he set in simultaneous rotation by a treadle. This he called his Armonica, a musical instrument of his invention which produced bright singing tones when the spinning disks were touched with wetted fingers. He played a few bars by Handel. Elsewhere a giant bone rested on a shelf. "A fossil of the mammoth," pronounced he, "which leads me to speculate that the climate of our world has changed vastly, a theory I may sometime write on." Demonstrating the electrical spark once more, he pulled speculatively at his lip. "I wonder . . . were a man to harness this might it be used to light a small space of room, perhaps enough to read by at night?"

This led him to show me his electrical battery, as he called it. This sat on a table, several panes of sash glass armed with thin leaden plates pasted on each side, placed vertically and supported at two inches distance on silk cords. "The whole may be charged together, with the same labor as one single pane. Do not touch that wire, Nick! Much of the electrical fire is presently stored here, to the peril of the unwary. Indeed I have done demonstrations in which I felled six men with much less than is kept here. On the occasion of one such demonstration I placed myself inadvertently under an iron hook which hung from the ceiling down to within two inches of my head and communicated by wire with my battery. Moving to discharge it, I did so—but perceived none of it, for the charge went through me. I neither saw the flash nor heard the report nor felt the stroke but came to my senses on the floor, my company much agitated and assuring me there had been a sound like the crack of a pistol. Truth to tell, a man might die so, though it would prove the easiest of all deaths."

That night I dreamt of sparks flashing all about me. These gathered in a shadowy void to form the sweet shape of my mother, ghostlike, crying out for me—but my mother had the face of the Indian woman, then the Indian girl, then Lord Bottom's daughter, then Mrs. Couch and Mrs. Mountjoy and Martha Clay, last, most horribly of all, Mrs. Inch, who called me bastard and struck me with her broom, and I shot upright in a sweat, trembling and whimpering, groping in the darkness.

At that Poor Richard tapped me on the shoulder. "Three may keep a secret if two of 'em are dead," murmured he in that black night.

The next day, a Thursday, which dawned with the sun struggling its way through London's smoky brown haze, Mr. Franklin breakfasted with us at the round table belowstairs. Indeed he appeared the heartier for his hours abed, with even his gout, he assured us, much improved, so that he capered a little and pinched Mrs. Stevenson's cheeks, making her round face glow as red as a forge.

"A letter for you, Mr. Franklin," said Polly, passing across the tablecloth a small white envelope, "—perhaps a love note from some smitten dame?"

Mr. Franklin smiled at this jibe. Unfolding the letter, he read, and read again, his manner changing but little, there being still a smile, yet he asked, "Pray, how did this arrive?"

"O, a boy delivered it," replied Mrs. Stevenson, passing round hot muffins under a checked cloth.

"What boy?"

"A boy."

"In livery?"

"No indeed."

"How dressed then?"

"In boy's clothes. As a boy. Neither rich nor poor, but a boy."

"His face?"

"A boy's face. Not so handsome as our Nick, but much of Nick's age, if perhaps older—or younger. His face a bit dirty, I think, though all boys' faces gather dirt."

"You did not know him?"

"I do not believe so, though I take little note of boys."

Mr. Franklin laughed. "I'll swear before the magistrate that you do not!"

"Why do you inquire, sir?" asked Polly peering close at him.

He tucked the paper quickly into his waistcoat. "It is a dunning note from a tailor—yet damned if I owe the fellow. He does not even name his shop."

But, "It is no note from a tailor," pronounced Mr. Franklin gravely when we were once more rattling our way along London's streets, Peter in the box. "Read it," said he, passing me the paper.

I opened it. On ordinary foolscap was writ in a workmanlike hand: *You are observed, Mr. Benjamin Franklin. Mind your business or suffer.* There was no signature.

Mr. Franklin's deep brown eyes were fixed on me. "What do you make of it, lad?"

"It frightens me, sir. I do not wish you to suffer on my account. Nor on Mrs. Clay's. My master is dead. Nothing will bring him back, and—"

He placed a hand on my sleeve. "Allow me to fear for myself. Truly I am more angered by this than affrighted." He crumpled the paper before thrusting it in his waistcoat. "I hate these low threats! O, an honorable enemy shows his face!"

I acquiesced uneasily. Along the Strand a surging midmorning throng jostled our carriage to a snail's pace, and I could not help thinking of the coster's warning, his evil, beak-nosed face thrust into mine. Strangers, some beggars, some gentlefolk, pressed against the sides of our conveyance. Eyes occasionally peered in, speculatively it seemed, as if measuring us, and I sat nearer Mr. Franklin, seeing with what ease our progress could be told, and with what quickness a blade or pistol might be thrust through a window or strong arms reach in. "Where do we go, sir?" asked I.

"To Bow Street. You have read *Tom Jones*. I have long wished to make acquaintance of its author's remarkable brother."

Bow Street proved a cobbled lane of large dwellings much out of the way of traffic. "It is not so fashionable as when Wycherley, Gibbons, and Kneller lived here, so I am told," Mr. Franklin informed as we surveyed the row of two-story brick and slate, "but Number Four lends it a distinction which may someday surpass theirs." Peter drew us up before a green-shuttered house, on the west side of the street, and we got down to be met inside by a wizened peering fellow who seemed with his bulging, watchful eyes to be sizing us for very tight-fitting suits of clothes.

"Brogden. Joshua Brogden, sir," said he briskly, giving Mr. Franklin's hand a rapid squeeze. "Mr. John Fielding's clerk. A remarkable man, Mr. Fielding! So too was his late brother, Henry, God rest his soul, whom I also had privilege of serving. Now what may I do for you?" He rubbed his hands eagerly. "A robbery, is it?"

"More like murder," said Mr. Franklin.

"Oho! This way." He led us with a gleeful, hopping walk into a room containing a large desk, behind which a portrait of King George glared down with a fearsome froglike look. "Our Justice Room," pronounced Mr. Brogden proudly though there seemed little enough to justify his pride. Some ten or a dozen plain wood chairs sat facing the desk. A smaller desk and high clerk's stool stood in an inconspicuous corner by a narrow window. Repairing here, Mr. Brogden bustled among some papers, drew forth a pen, brightly bulged his eyes. "The details, sir, if you please."

"Begging your pardon, it would more please me to present them to Mr. John Fielding himself."

"But it is customary—"

Mr. Franklin raised a hand. "O, I am a great respecter of custom, where custom may serve," said he with firm politeness. "Yet in the case of this murder it will not. I must speak direct to Mr. Fielding."

Mr. Brogden blinked. There followed some stammering cavil, but Mr. Franklin held his ground, and at last the clerk yielded: "Very well, with no promises I shall apply to Mr. Fielding," and shaking his head he hopped through a far door.

Mr. Franklin strode impatiently about the room. "The dangerous state of London's streets is a disgrace. Cutpurses and bludgeoners everywhere! Yet we keep no militia to maintain order as they do on the Continent. Our mistrust of standing armies, we say. Well, there is justification in that—yet some remedy must be found or it may soon prove unsafe to step from one's door, and riot will rule. The answer lies here, in Bow Street, I have heard. This," he gestured round, "has become the central criminal-fighting office in London. It is less than ten years since Henry Fielding took the oaths as Justice of the Peace for Westminster. He was already sick and had but a short reign, yet he accomplished much. Crime and misery appalled him; thus he brought all his intelligence and organizing powers to bear on fighting it, ending by forming a permanent force of public-spirited constables. These men are still called 'Mr. Fielding's People,' and anyone who seeks true justice applies to them. Henry's half-brother John has succeeded him as Principal Metropolitan Justice. He too possesses energy and dedication, I hear, even going so far as to seek care for young prostitutes and homes for orphans." Mr. Franklin tapped the ridge of his brow. "Let him prove equal to his reputation, Nick."

At this point Mr. Brogden returned, and we were shown into a small, plain office with one large window admitting fitful sunlight. Mr. Franklin was bid to sit before a modest desk. I stood at his side.

Seated before us was a great, doughy man, with a pale face, fleshy cheeks, pendulous lips. Three chins rested upon a black cravat. This imposing gentleman wore his worsted coat open, with fat hands folded across a large belly. His slow breathing seemed to fill the room.

Joshua Brogden withdrew, and I became aware of the ticking of a clock. More silence ensued, which Mr. Franklin seemed content to endure, with two hands crossed over the top of his bamboo. At first I thought Mr. Principal Justice Fielding examined us, but his eyes were strangely downcast, yet he exuded a sense of sharp awareness, as if his great seashell ears, showing under his white wig, heard all the way to Wapping Dock.

And then he raised his eyes, and I saw with a shock, from their unfocused blankness, that he was blind.

"Aye, stone blind," rumbled he curtly, as if he read my mind. "From age eighteen. O, it is a trial, yet I make do, I make do. You, sir, are Mr. Benjamin Franklin, from America?"

"I am."

"So my clerk tells me. Yet there is someone with you. I hear him. A small person, from his step as he came in. He stands by you, does he not? On your right-hand side. A boy. Ten or twelve, is he? My clerk has told me none of this. Speak to me boy."

"W-what shall I say, sir?"

"What should a boy say?—that he respects his elders."

"I respect my elders, sir."

"And the law."

"And the law, sir."

"I shall never forget your voice, boy. Twenty years from now I shall recognize it, for it is in my mind as firm as your face should be if I could see that. And your way of moving, the very sound of you. Ha, people say I am not fit, but I fool 'em. Do not you try to fool me, boy, for you cannot do it. You are a good boy, I can tell that too. Do not fall afoul the law, for I shall remember you, and your name, which is—?"

"Nicolas Handy, sir—at least that is what I am told."

His black brows lifted. "What? A boy not sure of his own name? How can this be?"

For the next half hour, the clock still ticking loudly, Mr. Franklin retold all that had occurred since that morning ten days ago when he first came to Inch, Printer. Through it all Mr. Fielding sat unmoving as stone yet sharply alert, sometimes interjecting questions.

At the end he harumphed. "Indeed, a boy should know his parents—though in these wicked days even those who find two names plainly writ in the church register may be none too certain, eh, Mr. Franklin?" He chortled a laugh. "As for my helping you, my constables are hard-pressed just now. Ah, if only parliament could be persuaded to vote us more men! Yet you seem to do well, without aid, I doubt one of my trained fellows could have discovered so much."

"Tut, you flatter me. Yet I came not to ask for men but to meet John Fielding, of growing reputation. We are alike investigators, you of the world of crime, I of Nature's laws; alike too, we seek practical ends: to bring truth to light for the betterment of mankind."

"You put a fine face on my work. Would you speak in Parliament for me?"

"Begging your pardon, but I find I am not allowed to speak in Parliament for myself. Yet you may help me by saying if you know anything of Mrs. Inch and Mrs. Couch and Mrs. Mountjoy and their dealings with Jared Hexham."

"As to that, we try, sir, to know of bawdy houses, from which riotous behavior may ensue, and to keep the license of liquor from 'em. Yet they multiply like fleas upon a dog. No, I know naught of

152

Mrs. Inch nor Mrs. Couch, little fish. Mrs. Mountjoy now——every man knows of her; she is a woman of fame indeed. Yet would that all such were like her, for she holds her guests in bounds, and they must behave or be tossed in the Thames; many a lord's house is not kept so orderly as hers, and I might be proud to sup at her table. Jared Hexham? Quite another matter. Do you know, sir, it is the petty thief that is ensnared by Mr. Fielding's People, but the knave that makes thievery profitable is rarely known? I mean the go-between, the receiver of goods. True, some inconsequential fellows are found out, men who pass on trifles. But the big fish . . . mmm, I have become aware over the years of a criminal organization in London which casts its net over robbery, bawdry, even murder. Further, I know enough of Hexham to suspect he may be part of it, though I have no proof."

"But if a man might deliver such proof?"

"Why, then, I would nab this Hexham by the collar! But there is Quimp, sir . . ."

"Quimp?"

"Aye, Quimp." A shadow fell across the huge man's features, and for the first time his fingers stirred, fitfully, on his belly. "'Tis but a man's name—yet it is the name of him who heads the criminal organization I spoke of. I do not know his face, though it is not blindness keeps it from me but the damned villain's guile, for few men know it."

I stirred at Mr. Franklin's side.

"What is it, Nicolas?" asked he.

With a lump in my throat I addressed Mr. Fielding. "Sir, does . . . does this Mr. Quimp have a great beaked nose?"

"He may, though it is hard to name the blackguard's true countenance, for he is reputed to be a master of disguise. Think you he was the hunchbacked coster who warned you? If so, you are among the few who have heard his warnings and lived. I am one such, for he threatened me too, when first I took this office and came near to spoiling one of his plans. O, I shall not forget that sly wheedling voice! Yet he has never laid hand on me—nor sent one of his minions to harm me either. I believe he admires an able enemy and is loath to dispatch a man with whom he may thrust and parry. You, Mr. Franklin, may be one such, yet I advise you, watch your step lest Quimp tip you to the devil, for he is as deadly as the adder for those who come too close to him."

"Quimp," pronounced Mr. Franklin darkly as we headed away from Bow Street. "He may explain much, Nicolas. Dora Inch's plans for her daughter were near fruition, so were those of Jared Hexham, both for himself and his son, to rise to a title. Imagine what these two desperately unscrupulous people might be led to in order to assure that their aims were not thwarted. But imagine how much worse if they took foolish chances that might threaten Quimp's black enterprises—what means might he seek to protect himself?"

"We come near to some truth which threatens all of 'em?"

"We do, Nicolas—and that truth threatens us."

I shivered at this. It was then just noon. Dark clouds had wrestled with the sun and won; the city was shrouded in a choking, gray pall, and I longed for the warmth and safety of Craven Street. Peter drove east along High Holborn, then turned into Dorrit Street aiming for the Strand. This way showed little traffic.

Suddenly I heard Peter's cry, heard the loud, quick rattle of other carriage wheels, and felt a jolt which flung both Mr. Franklin and me about, sending his beaver hat flying. Ours was a small rig. Glancing out the window, I discovered the shabby black coach which had pursued us roaring fast at our side, its heavily muffled driver brandishing his whip. With a cry, he drove it amongst his dappled pair, simultaneously jerking his reins, which sent his larger vehicle once more against us. I was this time thrown topsy-turvy. There came the sharp crack of a snapped wheel, a sickening yaw—and we were full tipped over into a tangle of horse, driver, and carriage crashing into an ironmonger's.

❧ 12 ❧

IN WHICH I find a house I know well, we pick two more locks—and there comes another cry of death . . .

"AND, Peter, have you paid the ironmonger for his damaged building, as I instructed?" asked Mr. Franklin.

"Yes, sir," said Peter at Mr. Franklin's closed bedroom door.

"Excellent. I would not wish him to suffer on our account—nor on that of the blackguard who tipped over our carriage. The man from whom we hired the conveyance shall be paid also, but that must wait. What say you, John, am I fit or must I be put to pasture?"

Mr. Franklin sat in his fireside chair. Dr. Fothergill rose from fixing a plaster to a cut which the gentleman had suffered above his left eye. "You are fit," pronounced he sternly, "no bones broke. And both your servant and this lad are unscathed save for some small bruises—a miracle, my friend. But what are you about that someone wishes you such harm?"

Mr. Franklin made an airy gesture. "O, you know how I am reviled for what I attempt in behalf of Pennsylvania. I am called the 'Judas of Craven Street,' have you heard? Ha, we are likely attacked by the zeal of some patriot, who mistakes an act of war for justice!"

155

Fothergill shook his white-wigged head. "I do not like to think an Englishman would engage in such an act."

"Of war?" Mr. Franklin pulled himself to his feet. "Much may come to war."

"Indeed it is a kind of war," spoke Mr. Franklin ringingly when we were not half an hour later in a newly hired coach, driving east along the Strand under threatening clouds. The gentleman looked none the worse for his cut and bruises but sat with a fierce air, almost of triumph. He thumped his bamboo on the coach floor. "Yet we shall not stand still to be laid siege to, Nick! We shall attack!"

He had given an address and Jared Hexham's name to Peter, and I felt a chill to think that I would shortly meet this unscrupulous and dangerous man, whom Mr. Franklin had thwarted thirty years ago and whom he dared to challenge again. Was it Jared Hexham who had murdered my master, pursued us, sent the threat note, ordered our carriage dashed to ruins? Fortunately Mrs. Stevenson had been out when we returned, limping, to Craven Street, or we would presently be prisoners to the good landlady's ministrations, with broths and poultices as warders. Polly too had been gone, but William Franklin was there—yet Mr. Franklin took pains to be unseen by his son until he had on his beaver hat, which covered his bandage; and to young Mr. Franklin, who accosted us as we left, he was scrupulous to say nothing of our near disastrous adventure. Why so circumspect with his son? That remained a mystery.

In twenty minutes we were at Jared Hexham's house, near Berkeley Square. I was surprised to find it even larger than Lord Bottom's, a dozen mullioned windows in span and three stories high, with a curved drive and a square, white-columned portico under which a carriage might go, and a manservant stiff as a rod by the door.

"A fine façade, to be built upon black deeds," murmured Mr. Franklin as we rattled near.

Peter drove under the portico just as large wet drops began to spatter the drive. I felt a strange tingling as we stepped down, an unsettling mixture of fear and longing, as if the looming house brought us nearer truth than I cared to go.

The manservant held our coach door. He was thin and tall. My eyes stood level with his gold-embroidered waistcoat, at which I stared, for a secret was revealed by it. Yet I had no chance to whisper it to Mr. Franklin, for we were already shown up three wide steps to a broad door beyond which lay a large, paneled entrance hall. Mr. Franklin placed his card on a silver salver that was whisked away by yet another liveried man who bore on his waistcoat the same news as the first.

I was about to tell this discovery to Mr. Franklin when Miss Lydia Hexham swept into the hall.

She was as Mr. Franklin had described her, sulkily beautiful, with dark eyes and a slim, elegant figure. Coming to a sudden stop before us in a whirl of rustling silks, she showed off this figure in a practiced way, swaying and gesturing her white arms. "Why . . . Mr. Franklin, is't not? Has your card been sent up to father? He is sure to be delighted by this visit." Her painted brows drew together petulantly. "This weather is very vexing!—I hoped to amuse myself at Vauxhall Gardens but now must stay indoors. What shall divert me here? Not my foolish brother. Pray, who is this handsome boy?"

"Nicolas Handy, ma'am," said Mr. Franklin.

Staring into my face, she touched my cheek with long, painted nails, though she frowned faintly, abstractedly as she did so, as if my name or appearance gave her pause. Yet her piqued look might well have been caused by the rain. "Perhaps I shall go out nonetheless," said she abruptly. "I believe I shall. Fie to this weather! Pray, excuse me, gentlemen." And with a curtsy she turned and swept back out the door through which she had come.

Again I made to draw Mr. Franklin's attention to what I had seen, but my mouth was stopped a third time, by a woman's voice which I knew too well: Mrs. Inch's, shouting and protesting. Her raucous cries grew near. Abruptly she burst through a far door, a large manservant gripping one of her arms, forcing her towards the entrance. This poor fellow had a battle of it, for Mrs. Inch was strong and resisted with kicks at his shins and a windmilling of her heavy arms. Blood oozed from claw marks upon his cheek, but his face stayed grim with purpose.

A burly, black-browed man appeared behind these two, keeping well back from the struggle. He was dressed in a handsome, gold-embroidered, burgundy-red coat, though the fine cut of the cloth seemed not to suit his stocky shape, which looked more fitted to coarser stuff. His dark eyes projected thunder.

Jared Hexham, thought I.

Mr. Franklin and I stood by a carved, mirrored hallpiece. None of the trio noted us, so occupied were they. "You *shan't* put me out!" cried Mrs. Inch over her shoulder.

"O, but I shall," shot back Hexham.

"Your Bertie is promised to Tilda!"

"You are mistaken, ma'am."

"He is, and you know why! And if you dare to go back on your word I shall see you sink like a stone in the Thames and leave not a ripple, and where will be your fine airs and your plans then, eh?"

Hexham paled at this. "Be reasonable, ma'am. You must see that—" Here his eyes lit on us. "What . . . ?"

Mr. Franklin made a small nod of the head, while I drew close to his side.

Mrs. Inch saw us too, and ceased her struggle. "You? Here?" sputtered she to Mr. Franklin. "And . . . *you?*" said she to me, her eyes bulging. Beginning to wail, the color draining from her fat, shaking cheeks, she slumped against the servant, who grunted at the sudden weight. With much stumbling he maneuvered the moaning woman to the door. "After what has passed between us, Jared," cried she plaintively to Hexham before the servant struggled her bulk from view. As the oak closed on dashing rain, I peered up at Mr. Franklin. Was it he who had caused Dora Inch near to faint?

He directed a cool, inquiring look upon Jared Hexham.

"Do you not have a card, sir?" demanded this man with beetling vexation, opening and closing his hands at his sides.

"I do."

"And do you not send it before you?"

"Always."

"I did not receive it."

Mr. Franklin only tilted his head gently once more. "I placed it on your man's tray. Perhaps Mrs. Inch distracted you—or perhaps she frightened your man." He gave a small smile. "To be sure, she is formidable; one would not care to cross her. Do you fear her, Mr. Hexham?"

Hexham drew back his shoulders. "I do not wish to talk of Dora Inch. What is your business?"

"Questions. For you."

"And if I choose not to answer them?"

" 'If'? Tut, sir, we are not children; let us have nothing to do with 'if.' Pray, hear me like a man."

At this Hexham stared. His expression turned yet blacker, and he glowered and fumed. But at last he said curtly, "Very well, come with me," and led us with heavy steps up some curving, red-carpeted stairs. As we went, I felt a strange oppression, as if the house whispered evil in my ear and these stairs led to doom. With every tread my breathing came harder, and there was a pressure about my temples, a sort of swooning dizziness, yet I made myself climb on, panting, my heart thumping in my breast.

We went some way along a second-story corridor, where Mr. Hexham gestured us into a small matter-of-fact study, with a square, plain desk and some ledgers on a shelf and hunting scenes on biscuit-brown walls. It looked the room of a man who had little to do with nonsense. A window gave onto the back of the house. Below in the rain lay a garden and coach house. With a catch of breath I saw in this garden the Indian brave whom I had encountered in Lord Bottom's kitchen, making an oddly weaving path beneath some dripping yews.

Mr. Franklin faced Jared Hexham, who stood with his glowering, suspicious look behind the desk.

"I see you have not taken my advice. You remain in England," growled the merchant.

"Was it only advice? You seemed to wish to bribe me. Why, sir? That question still vexes me."

159

Hexham merely folded his arms. "Bribe? Nonsense! Yet I would be happy to have you gone from England."

"Again, why?"

"Because you are a snooping man."

"I confess I look into many matters. Yet a man who would call it snooping may be a man with something to hide. Are you such a man, Jared Hexham?"

"Damn you, Franklin, I have nothing to hide!"

"Is that honest . . . Gerrold Bixer?"

Hexham paled.

"Come, you know me, do you not?" insisted Mr. Franklin.

"Know . . . you?" Hexham appeared robbed of words. Sitting heavily in his chair, he pulled out a white cloth and wiped at his broad, cruel mouth.

"Watts' Printing," pronounced Mr. Franklin, pressing his fingers upon the desk and leaning over the merchant. "Thirty years ago Gerrold Bixer and Benjamin Franklin were journeymen there. I am that same Benjamin Franklin, and you are Gerrold Bixer, though you call yourself Hexham. That is why you wish me back in America, is't not? Because I know your true name and know too that you fled England to escape prosecution by the law?"

Hexham gripped the arms of his chair. "You know no such. You cannot prove—"

Mr. Franklin straightened. "I can prove nothing—at present. Yet you fear that I may find means to do so, do you not? That is why you wished to bribe me to betray the people of Pennsylvania, whose honest trust placed me on these shores."

Hexham's eyes glittered. "I admit nothing," said he.

"Not even that Dora Inch wishes to marry her daughter to your son?"

"O, you must ask *her* about that."

"I have no need. I heard what passed between you just now. Yet you fear her, I see that too. Because she holds the proof which I lack?"

Hexham rose. "Damn you again, Franklin."

"Proof which you might murder to regain?"

"What!" The burly man's eyes flashed. "I have murdered no one."

"You plan to wed your son to Lord Bottom's daughter, do you not?"

"That is none of your business."

"I make it my business. His lovely daughter loathes your foppish son, with good reason; I shall not let you take advantage of a young woman again."

"Again?"

Mr. Franklin glanced at me. His round cheeks glowed red, and he turned and paced to the door and back before facing Hexham once more. "I cannot respect you, sir. Long ago you took advantage of Ebenezer Inch; I have not forgot that, and I have reason to believe you began squeezing the poor man sorely again, when he returned to London, lured by Dora Inch, who was once Dora Pulley, the woman you sent to inveigle him before you buried your true name in America. Was she your doxy once, sir? Too, your traffic in helpless young women is vile, and your extortion of Lord Bottom is not to be stood. I shall prevent it, sir, I warn you, unless you desist." He drew a hand over his brow. "The Algonquian woman who serves Lord Bottom, and the young Indian woman at Mrs. Mountjoy's, and the brave who drives your coach—they are related, are they not, mother and children?"

"So what if they be?"

"It is proof that you are a destroyer of families."

Hexham laughed. "No magistrate will sentence me for that."

"Likely not . . . yet—" Mr. Franklin peered hard through his glasses, "—do you know a man named Quimp?"

At this Hexham blanched. His teeth ground, his jowls shook, and from the fury that contorted his face I believed him indeed capable of murder. But he only made fists and glared.

"I see you do," said Mr. Franklin coolly.

"And do *you* know him?" rejoined Hexham. "I see a wound upon your brow. Take care the next be not fatal."

"And you," said Mr. Franklin, "—are you in no danger? This boy, who stands beside me. You have said nothing of him."

161

Hexham gave me a contemptuous glance. "Why should I?"

"You might wonder why he accompanies me."

"I care naught for your serving boys."

"No? I shall give you another name. Arthur Handy. Did you know Arthur Handy in Boston, sir?"

"I knew many men in America. I knew no 'Handy.'" But I thought Hexham swallowed hard before he spoke.

Mr. Franklin gazed at him searchingly. He sighed. "I did not expect you to admit to anything, though the manner of your denials reveals much. Come, Nick." He went heavily to the door. "I shall take no more of your time, sir. But be warned," he thrust out his bamboo, "you have much on your conscience. Only if you are truly innocent of murder may you 'scape punishment." His voice softened, almost pityingly: "You too have a family. Think of them, I beg you. Ambition may not serve their best interests—or yours. Good day, sir. You need not show us out."

Hexham did not move. The door closed upon his stolid, brooding figure, and we went down, Mr. Franklin very grim and shaking his head. As we descended the curving stairs past huge staring portraits I felt yet another wind of ill ease, as if at any moment some ghost might blow up in my face. The air of the house felt stifling, my nape hair stood on end.

At the foot of the stairs a woman's voice accosted us: "Mr. Franklin!" It was dry and reproachful.

We turned. In a doorway stood a small, pinched woman in a green watered-silk dress, with a great clutch of pearls at her throat. Her eyes in nests of wrinkles were as tiny as currants, yet their venomous depths leaked poison.

"Mrs. Hexham," said Mr. Franklin with a small bow.

Without a word the tiny woman turned and stepped into the room beyond, we following into a large conservatory with a spinet piano and brass harp and handsome rose-upholstered furniture placed about. Tall windows looked onto the rainy back garden, but the Indian was no longer in sight.

Mrs. Hexham tapped her foot. Her hair was built up very high, making her appear precariously balanced, as if her head might at the wrong twist of her neck snap off like a weed-top. She was formidable nonetheless, with a sour, disapproving scowl on her jutting face.

Her voice was high-pitched: "You provoke him, sir. I adjured you not to provoke him, yet you do't."

"Who, pray, ma'am?"

"Mr. Hexham, sir, as you very well know." She shook a finger. "At Lord Bottom's I most distinctly told you that much depended on your giving Mr. Hexham his head, yet you persist."

"Much?"

"Much."

"But, what may that 'much' be?"

"Happiness, sir, what else? My family's." Her eyes took me in. "Perhaps your happiness too."

"Perhaps, ma'am, I am the one provoked," offered Mr. Franklin.

She stamped a foot. "Mr. Hexham is not a provoking man!"

"Mr. Jared Hexham, ma'am?"

"Mr. Jared Hexham indeed, whose wife I am, and a dutiful wife, who has ever striven to rise to his expectations. I am proud to say I have done so, and I tell you, sir, that he is not a provoking man. *You* are provoking, sir. You set foot in our house. You bring that . . . that boy."

"The boy is provoking?"

Here she sputtered, her head wobbling dangerously. "He provokes *me*, sir, and I say: take the boy out, and yourself, and never show either of your faces at our door again!"

Mrs. Prudence Hexham strode from the room in a rustle of indignation.

"Well, Nick . . ." said Mr. Franklin, peering bemusedly over the tops of his glasses, but I hardly heard him. A door led off the conservatory. It drew me, and I turned and passed through as if drawn by an irresistible call—as indeed I was, for the call was my mother's. Here was a small library, with books to the ceiling and a cozy windowseat backed by dripping windowpanes. Well I knew the wallpaper of tiny yellow poppies, foxed by time. I saw my mother there on the seat cushions reading to me, and I saw myself

163

curled at her side, three years old and following the words which her slim, pale finger gently traced for me as she spoke 'em in loving tones.

"So. This is the house," said Mr. Franklin softly at my side.

"Yes, sir," said I, understanding at last why I had felt so strangely moved ever since we came here.

"And there your mother sat and read to you?"

"Th-there," said I, hardly able to speak the word.

Mr. Franklin turned me by the shoulders and gazed down at me. "You are certain, Nick?"

"My heart tells me so," said I.

"We must trust your heart. Yet I guessed this was the house. Indeed, I have suspected so for some time, would that it were not." He shook with such fury that his fringe of longish brown hair trembled. "O, Jared Hexham and Dora Inch have much to answer for!"

At this came a crashing musical chord from the conservatory. Mr. Franklin and I returned to this room just as the Indian brave staggered a second time into the spinet, which emitted a protesting dissonance. He was dressed in livery like the other servants, yet he looked incongruous in it, seeming to diminish these clothes, as if they were a civilized folly, and he should be more magnificent, better dressed, in natural savage nakedness. He was clearly drunk, and pitiful for it. Yet as his bleared eyes rose in his dusky, lost face, struggling to focus upon us, I could picture him moving with stealthy freedom through some green New World forest, and I felt heartsick to see him brought low by his captivity.

He saw us. Mobile lips drew back from white teeth. Slitted nostrils flared, and a terrible howl escaped him. Of fury? Fear?

"Here, sir," said Mr. Franklin, gripping the tall fellow's arm to steady him. Bending near, he spoke words which I did not understand but to which the brave listened with a white-eyed stare. He seemed to come to himself, yet he still looked lost and miserable. He made some guttural sounds. These Mr. Franklin responded to in the strange, clicking tongue, pointing once at me, at which the Indian quavered.

164

A stomping came from the door by the stairs. "What's this?" cried Bertie Hexham, striding into the room in gleaming black boots. Mr. Franklin and the Indian drew apart, and young Hexham glared at the Indian. "You, fellow, drunk again? You have no business here. Leave at once!"

The brave retorted in the Indian tongue.

"Speak the King's English, damn you! You know it well enough. Get to the coach house and see to the horses. Miss Lydia wishes to go out."

The Indian shot such a look as would have made me quake, but Bertie Hexham seemed too foolish to be fearful. With a last hooded glance at Mr. Franklin the Indian crept out, with the same amazing softness of step, though he was drunk, as that with which the Indian woman at Lord Bottom's had moved. I stood nearest the door. As the savage slid past me, almost with loathing, as if I were a thing unclean to him, I glanced at his dark brown waistcoat. It had the same large brass buttons as the other servants', showing a pinnace upon the sea, exactly like the button which Mr. Franklin had taken from my master's dead hand. That was the secret I had wished to say to him. Yet there was more: one of the Indian's buttons was missing, the third down, with only a bit of thread to mark its spot, and I was struck cold to think that the murderer of Ebenezer Inch passed not three feet from me as he went out the door.

"Hexham knew you, Nick, make no mistake," said Mr. Franklin as Peter took us east against a driving rain, our wheels sending up gouts of muddy water. "He pretended to pay you no notice, yet I saw the fellow go pale when he first got sight of you. He is not subtle—I wonder as I did thirty years ago how he gulls people, yet some men are blind to the worst; their innocence is the path upon which evil speeds its mischief."

"Thirty years ago, sir," said I, "—did Hexham do something not only to Mr. Inch but to you, which caused you to be his enemy?"

Mr. Franklin peered at me. "Did he?" Yet he gave no clear answer but mused with his faraway look, drumming his fingers: "The felon's willingness to twist other people to his ends, no matter the harm it caused, was what first turned me against him. It is that which makes me oppose him now—though I do not hold grudges and should let him be if he should repent and desist."

We jounced on, the wind and rain whipping the leather coachtop as Lincoln's Inn's Fields slid by wetly on our right. I examined Mr. Franklin's round, pale face by the gray afternoon light. Peering into some unknown in those gloomy coach shadows, he seemed momentarily a stranger, and I shivered. Did he have secret reason to hold a grudge? In any case I did not believe Jared Hexham would leave off his wicked ways. Should I myself hate the merchant? Had he mistreated my mother in that grand house? Had he given me to Mrs. Inch?

I wanted to cry out. What had happened to my mother?

Mr. Franklin patted my hand. "So that indeed was once your home. Yet the family denies you. Damn me, how then shall we find your mother, for it is clear they wish to hide the truth of her?"

"You believe I may be related to the Handys of Boston?" asked I.

"They share your name, and Hexham resided in Boston. Surely he lied when he said he knew of no Handy there. He must at least have heard of the family. Family, Nick—we return to it once more. Would that we could put 'em all—fathers, mothers, and childen—into a sum and add and subtract to see all resolved, yet such simple ease is rare in human affairs. Mrs. Hexham knew you, did you see it? Lydia Hexham may have, also."

"And the Indian?"

"He quailed at sight of you. I tried to wring the why of it from him, though without success. I learned the Algonquian tongue in some negotiations with the Indians in western Pennsylvania, but I am not adept at it. I spoke the language to him in hopes it might make him trust me better. One thing I discovered: it was indeed his mother and sister whom we saw at Lord Bottom's and Mrs. Mountjoy's, but I was unable to wring more from him because of Bertie's Hexham's interruption."

He had, however, got wax impressions of the fingerprints of each person we had met. I had observed his sprightly trick of

166

hand, these clues now resided snugly in the little pewter snuff box in his waistcoat, waiting to be compared to the ebony knife handle.

"Sir, the servants' buttons," exclaimed I, suddenly recalling, "—they have the same design as the one you took from my master's hand, a ship upon the sea!"

"So I saw. I have seen none like 'em elsewhere. Hexham must have had 'em specially made. Yet, the Indian's waistcoat—did you note that too?"

"With its missing third button?"

He nodded. "Thus we may have found our murderer—but not the why of the deed. O, I suspect . . ." But he did not complete this thought. He blew his nose vigorously. "I fear more murder, Nick. The answer lies, I believe, with Dora Inch; the woman may be in danger. The break-in a week before your master was killed was a search for her secret, but she is too shrewd to hide it where simple robbery might unearth it. Nor did we discover it in her storeroom—though we did find a list of great men and a ledger recording payments from America."

"Was my master murdered in order to get Mrs. Inch's secret?"

Peter had been instructed to keep a close lookout for looming black coaches. None apparently had been sent to pursue us, for he proceeded without incident into Craven Street as Mr. Franklin's gaze narrowed gravely. "He was murdered, Nicolas, because of that dusty, rat-chewed ledger of payments. I am coming upon the truth, lad, but I may not speak of it yet, for reasons I hope you will know some day."

This took me aback, but I said sincerely, "I trust you, sir."

Mr. Franklin blew his nose once more. "I pray I may trust myself," said he.

That evening at eight Mr. Franklin and I were once more creeping along a London byway in deep shadow, this time east along the Thames, at St. Saviour's Dock, where Jared Hexham kept his counting house and ships. The rain had turned to fine, frigid needles; fog rolled up from the lapping Thames. Cobbles glistened at our feet in the wreathed light from dim-lit lamps which barely fought the shrouded dark. The Thames stank here, of pitch and offal. To my right, above black, sloping rooftops, I could just make out a forest of masts bobbing like warning fingers against the cloud-wracked sky. The creak of wood on wood and the occasional mournful clank of a buoy rose to us. My heart thumped in my chest, but Mr. Franklin seemed unaffected by our dire surroundings, moving purposefully past a tavern that burst with light and drunken song, then on into inky, silent lanes.

At last we came in sight of Hexham's counting house, by Thames-side.

It was a plain, single-story wood building with none of the ostentation of the house near Berkeley Square. "One would take little note of it, eh, lad?" whispered Mr. Franklin. "No doubt as Jared Hexham wishes it." Dim lamplight revealed a small plaque with the single word HEXHAM affixed above the door, which faced the river.

We took a post at the dark corner of a leaning old shanty, I shivering at the trickles of rain that ran down my collar. To prevent being followed from Craven Street we had crept out through Mrs. Stevenson's back garden, slipping up a narrow, little-used lane to the Strand, where Peter waited to drive us across London Bridge. To prevent any alarm which coach wheels might render we had been set down some distance away. Now Mr. Franklin glanced about. No one appeared in sight, only the looming hulls of ships amidst the sodden gloom.

We scurried to the counting-house door. In less than a minute Mr. Franklin's jemmies admitted us to its precincts.

I felt all the strangeness of our previous break-in, a crawling fear about my shoulders—puzzlement too. Mr. Franklin broke the law by these acts. Mere pickpockets sometimes had their fingers cut off. What drove the gentleman to take such risk for me and Martha Clay?

There was no time to ponder this, for he began at once to look about, with the aid of a small bull's-eye lantern. There were two rooms, a clerk's room in front, with two high desks piled with foolscap, and an office behind, where ledgers sat on shelves behind a broad oak desk. The clerk's room offered nothing; we went at once to the office, where Mr. Franklin began to pore over the ledgers. "If I may find proof against Hexham I may save Lord Bottom's daughter," muttered he as he turned pages.

Holding the lamp, watching his fingers move, his eyes dart down the entries, I wondered if my mother had once found herself in the selfsame position as Anne, forced to marry a man she despised. What man? Was it the preventing of a new wrong of this same unjust sort which so sparked Mr. Franklin's zeal?

"Pah!" exclaimed he after some twenty minutes, thrusting the last ledger back in its place. "All appears respectable, with mere linen stuffs and sugar and the like recorded here. No slaves, no human cargo, no stolen goods. Hexham shows well, does he not? O, he is clever in his rascality!" He glowered at a squat iron safe that sat beside the desk. "Would that that would yield to us." But after some moments of kneeling with the jemmies he stood with a groan. "These keys will not work those wards. The attempt but inflames my gout. Come, Nick, his warehouse—it is our final hope."

We slipped from the counting house back into the drizzling dark, Mr. Franklin carefully locking the door. Peering about, he led me into yet blacker shadow, to a long, looming wood building that abutted the lapping water. Its great iron lock fought his key but at last gave in, and with an eerie creak of the great door we stepped inside.

A rat scurried away, squealing, in the beam of our lamp. The interior smelled of spices and coffee and chocolate—yet it proved near empty, with but a few bolts of cloth on shelves and a mere half-dozen bags of salt and two boxes of China tea in a far corner. "Hardly prosperous," murmured Mr. Franklin. "Are we defeated, Nick? And yet—" His bulls-eye lamp found a steep ladder to our left, half-way across the long room. We went to it, and he began at once to climb, wheezing mightily.

I followed.

We were truly defeated at the top, it seemed, for this was but another storage room, chill and musty, under the sloping roof, where Mr. Franklin could barely stand without scraping his beaver-hatted head. It was thoroughly empty, our light showing nothing in any corner save dust. I felt disappointment—but relief too; fear of being caught grew upon me, and I longed for the safety of Craven Street.

Mr. Franklin sharply cocked his head. "What . . . ?" exclaimed he softly, and I saw that he frowned first at one end of the room, then the other. "See you, Nick," he pointed, "the ladder rises from the center of the room below, yet it does not emerge in the center here." I observed that this was true. Passing me the lamp, he went to the nearer wall, at the short end of the room, and tapped it and ran his fingers along it. Abruptly he began to butt his shoulder against it—with the startling result that after three such blows a rectangular piece of the wall, just under the roof beam, suddenly gave way into darkness.

"A door," breathed I.

"Aye," said Mr. Franklin drawing me through it. "Shine your light."

This I did and was near blinded by a glittering brightness. Jewelry set with diamonds and sapphires and emeralds, and finely wrought silver—cups and bowls and handsome plate—sat on shelves, close-packed, in this small, cramped room. I gasped to see it. Truly a warehouse full of teas and spices could not have matched the wealth that shone before us. There were, too, cunning clocks and fine silk purses and gold chains and rings and buckles and brooches, all excellently wrought. And mirrors and watches and inlaid boxes. And pearls and pendants and tortoiseshell combs. So engorged was this tiny closet, so crammed to tiptop, that Mr. Franklin and I bumped against one another to keep from sweeping the wealth to the floor.

Mr. Franklin chuckled warmly. "So, stolen goods, all, or I am not Benjamim Franklin of Philadelphia!" He did a sprightly jig, which flung a silver teapot to the floor. "O, Jared Hexham shall not marry his son to Lord Bottom's daughter after all, if we may but speed Mr. Fielding's men here before the merchant passes on these goods!"

"Yet, I behink me, Nick," mused Mr. Franklin when we were once more in our coach, Peter speeding us back over the black, surging Thames, "that there may be no great hurry, for Hexham does not know we know his secret." The gentleman had carefully replaced the teapot and shut up the secret door as it had been and locked the warehouse tight. "No doubt the goods come and go in his hidden room. Tomorrow a diamond necklace may find a new throat to grace, while a jeweled fan, snatched from its rightful owner, will take its place amidst the hoard. Hexham's secret is our secret, and safely may be so for a time, until we know all." He thumped the top of the coach. "Fish Lane, Peter!" His face, turned to me in the encompassing night, was a mere dark smudge in the shadows. "There are a few more knots to untie, Nick. Mrs. Couch must supply some untwisting, or we shall urge Mr. Fielding to harry her like a hound does a fox."

It was near ten when we drew up before Mrs. Couch's tall house, opposite Inch, Printer. As ever the scene of my captivity brought a sour taste to my mouth—yet as we stepped down in the narrow lane I felt less fear than before. Mr. Franklin's guardianship heartened me. Nonetheless I had disturbing knowledge to ponder. At Craven Street this afternoon the Hexham family's fingerprints had joined Mr. Franklin's collection, along with the Indian's—and indeed it had proved to be the brave's prints which matched those on the ebony knife handle. This made me unaccountably sad. Surely my poor murdered master had been innocent. Was innocence then no protection in this world?

The rain still fell steadily, splashing from eaves, gushing from lead pipes. Save Mrs. Couch's, all the houses in Fish Lane showed little or no light, while her two street windows glowed behind pulled curtains, with muffled sounds of revelry spilling from within.

We mounted the three steps and Mr. Franklin rapped the brass knocker.

After a moment the door opened a crack, Mrs. Couch's sly eyes peering at us in the streaming dark.

These eyes widened. "We want none of you here!" squealed she, attempting to close the door, but Mr. Franklin placed his stout boot in the way.

"You shall speak to me, ma'am—or to Mr. Principal Justice Fielding; it is all one in the end."

"The magistrate?" Her voice grew sly. "I have nothing to hide from the magistrate, let him come," said she with much show of indignation, "—yet you may speak to me if you must." She opened the door, flooding the street with light.

We were about to step in—when there came cries at our back, so faint amidst the hissing rain that they were at first barely heard. Yet Mr. Franklin and I turned as one. The sign INCH, PRINTER creaked on its chains. The light from Mrs. Couch's door illuminated the door of the print shop across the way, though nothing untoward was to be seen. Yet there came another cry, louder and more horrible in its tenor, unmistakably from Inch, Printer.

"Nick!" exclaimed Mr. Franklin, gesturing, and was across the lane in a flash, I on his heels.

Mrs. Couch's door slammed loudly behind me.

We found the print-shop door locked. Mr. Franklin thumped on it mightily but to no avail.

Another cry sounded, a shriek of despair.

"Fie upon it, Nick, how may we get in?"

"I do not know."

There came a commotion below us: footsteps, a scurrying, a rattle, the bang of wood.

"The tunnel beneath the road!" cried Mr. Franklin as he leapt from the stoop. Breathlessly I followed him to the wet cobbles and over the black iron rail, into the areaway by means of the rainbarrel, as we had done before. The lower door to the house hung open in the gloom. So too did that to Mrs. Inch's storage room. Someone had just made escape through it to Mrs. Couch's, it seemed, and I observed Mr. Franklin's dismay as he glanced from one door to the other. What to do? Pursue this unknown person or enter the house?

He chose the house.

Belowstairs it was dark, and I led the way up while the gentleman cursed at my heels. "Devil take it, I should have moved sooner," muttered he.

We emerged into more blackness, the printing room itself, with its familiar inky smell. I wondered how we should discover anything in such blindness—when a wavering light appeared upon the stairs above. "Mama?" came Tilda Inch's quavering voice.

"It is I, Mr. Franklin," called the gentleman, "with Nick Handy."

"I want Mama!" wailed Tilda.

She came into sight, eyes rolling, clutching a long robe at her throat and carrying a lamp, her straw-colored hair sticking out wildly. Mr. Franklin took the lamp from her. "Whose cries were those?" asked he.

"M-mama?" was all Tilda would respond.

"Poor girl," said Mr. Franklin, glancing gravely at me. "Yet another victim? O, I fear . . ." He led her to the shop in front of the house. "Wait here, child. Do not despair; we shall find your mama."

Upstairs our lamp pressed back the darkness. I wondered that Buck Duffin had not been roused by the cries, but he was nowhere to be seen. Long shadows parted before us. I showed Mr. Franklin the door to the Inch bedroom. It was ajar.

We entered into disarray: pulled drawers, scattered clothes, books torn and flung about—and Mrs. Inch sprawled dead and staring upon bloodstained sheets, with an ebon-handled knife plunged into her breast.

❧ 13 ❧

*IN WHICH a murderer is murdered and truth
laid bare . . .*

I felt sick at the scene in the lamp's rays. I wished to cry, No!, to
run, to hide, to bury my face in Mr. Franklin's side and sob
forever. I had sometimes hated Mrs. Inch, but I did not hate
her now. All my spite sank from me, and I knew only a wrenching
pity. I did not feel sad as I had at my master's murder, but I felt
what pained me more: guilt for ever wishing this or any person
harm.

Mr. Franklin murmured a soft oath. "Too late," said he. Turning
me away from the awful sight, he searched my face. "Nick, should
you like to sit down?"

"N-no, sir," said I, struggling to be brave, to keep my knees
from buckling.

"You must help me, then. The boy next door—rouse him and
send him for Constable Nittle, as you did before. The man is a
fool, but officialdom must be bowed to. Meanwhile, I shall . . ."
He gestured toward Mrs. Inch, and I left him bent over her body,
to see what he might discover.

Downstairs Tilda sat stony and whimpering in the shop as I
passed under the clinking bell. Outside, the chill and rain cleared
my brain. Mrs. Couch's door was closed, two or three drunken
gentlemen weaving away from it along the dark, glistening lane.
Might one be a murderer? Quimp's name floated to my mind like

174

something terrible bobbing up in the Thames, and I scurried next door quickly to rouse Jimmy to his errand.

When I returned, Mr. Franklin was with Tilda in the shop. He had placed the lamp on the counter, which made our black shadows hover about us. "Tilda," said he, taking her hands and chafing them, "this is Nick, whom you know. And I am Mr. Franklin. We have met before. I mean you no harm; further, I shall see that none comes to you. Will you speak to me?"

"M-mama?" stammered she plaintively, as if she heard not a word.

"You know your mama is dead, do you not? Come, you must face it, child. You saw her on her bed. It is a horrible act, yet we must find who did it. I wish only that, to bring the murderer to justice. You want that too, I am sure."

At these honest, sympathetic words, tears burst from Tilda's eyes, and she quaked with wracking sobs for full five minutes, Mr. Franklin stroking her shoulders and murmuring, "There, child; poor child," until at last she was dried of her tears—if not her sorrow—and could look at us and see us and speak with some sense amidst sniffles.

"Now. Did you see who did it?" asked Mr. Franklin.

"No-o," quavered she.

"Tell us what you know."

"M-Mama and I were b-both abed before nine. I was awakened by voices, angry voices. Then cries, my mama's cries. I h-hid under my sheets—but then I thought I must h-help her if she was being h-harmed, so I p-pulled on my nightrobe and opened my door. Someone bumped into me as I stepped into the dark hall; I was near struck down. Yet I called my mama, and called again and again with no answer. And then I lit a lamp and went to her room, and there . . . and th-there . . ." Tilda's little eyes grew wide, as if she saw again what I had seen, all the horror, and she began to gasp.

Mr. Franklin tugged hard at her hands. "Did you hear distinct words?"

"N-no."

"Did you see who ran into you?"

"It was dark, yet I th-thought . . . thought there were two."

"Two people?"

"Y-yes."

Mr. Franklin glanced at me. "Has anyone threatened your mother of late?" asked he. "Did she speak to you of any fears?"

"She was afraid. I knew she was afraid. Of what, I know not."

"She gave no names?"

"Names?" Tilda's lips seemed to form a word.

"Quimp," said I softly, hardly knowing I spoke.

Tilda blinked and looked at me. "Quimp?" said she. "No, indeed, the name was . . . Franklin." She blinked again, in startlement. "But you are Mr. Franklin, sir. You are kind, you would not frighten my mama."

"I would frighten no one willingly. She spoke my name, you say? In fear?"

Tilda seemed unable to answer.

"Do you know any reason why someone should wish your mother harm?"

She made tight fists. "O, how could anyone? She was the gentlest, most loving mother." Her pleading gaze found me. "You know that, do you not, Nicolas? Was she not gentle?"

At this I could only hang my head. In Tilda's vain plea I saw that she believed what she said, that she was blind and always had been, to the torments I had suffered from a most ungentle woman. Yet I could pity Tilda. Mrs. Inch had spoiled her daughter. Bereft of her mother, how would the girl make her way in the world? Had not I myself borne the selfsame burden since I was three?

Orphans—the world seemed made up of 'em.

"Tilda, who delivered Nicolas to live here? Do you remember?" asked Mr. Franklin.

"It w-was so very long ago, I do not recall."

"Did your mother or father ever say anything of the circumstances?"

"N-no," she sniffed. "Why should they? We always had boys of work. Does not everyone have a boy of work? They are not to be thought on."

Strong feeling informed Mr. Franklin's words: "I think on *this* one, child. Come, he arrived here at the age of three. Boys of work can give no help at three."

"Yet my mama had him at chores soon enough."

"More's the pity," said Mr. Franklin. "Nonetheless she could have got better work from an older boy, so why . . . ?" He rubbed his brow. "You must trust me to tell me more. The night your father was murdered—where had you gone?"

Tilda's round face twisted into anguish once more. "My father, my mother . . . is't true then, both dead? O, Mr. Franklin," she wailed, "I was with Bertie Hexham, who promised to marry me, and I am carrying his child!"

At this Mr. Franklin blanched.

"What will become of me now?"

Tilda sobbed anew. When her cries died down, Mr. Franklin asked, "Did your mother know that you snuck out to meet Bertie?"

"N-no. Yet I thought in the end it would make no matter, that was what Bertie said. Too, Mama seemed to have an understanding with his father that he and I . . . that we . . . O, but those hopes are all dashed! Mama told me that Mr. Hexham refuses everything, and Bertie has not met me or sent a note since that night, and . . . and . . ."

"Did your mother know you are with child?"

"I feared to tell her, though I must soon have done so. And n-now . . . now she is no longer here to tell anything." Tilda crumpled into soft moans.

I looked at Mr. Franklin. His face bore an air both of tragedy and anger, his lips tight compressed.

"Wot's this?" came a suspicious cry, and we turned to see Buck Duffin swagger in from the print shop, fists on hips. He wore his good suit of clothes, though his ribbon tie was undone and his black hair was tousled. He peered from face to face.

"Welcome, sir," pronounced Mr. Franklin. "You have been asleep, have you? In your very own bed?"

Buck's eyes narrowed. "I have. Where else should I be?"

"Asleep in those clothes?"

"I sleep as I chooses."

177

"And you rested well, with nothing to rouse you?"

"I always rests well. Ask Nick Handy. Aw, leave off your wailin', can't you, Tilda? Wot's it for? Has this gen'leman bin botherin' you agin?"

"Follow me, boy," said Mr. Franklin sternly, taking up the lantern and brushing past Buck into the print shop. Buck looked like arguing, but Mr. Franklin's grim gaze shut his mouth, and I heard their steps mount the stairs. A moment later a sharp cry floated down, and in another moment the two rejoined us, Buck as white as flour, with a cold sweat on his upper lip and his Adam's apple bobbing in his throat, his hands fidgeting at his sides. "Dear Lord, dear Lord," mumbled he.

"Now," Mr. Franklin thrust his bamboo against Buck's chest, "did *you* kill her, boy?"

"Me?" Buck recoiled as if the stick were iron hot from a forge. "I never! Never in the world! Why should I? I didn't hate her."

"Who did?"

"How should I know?"

"What was she about?"

"Wot's yer meanin'?"

"You spied for her. Why?"

"I did wot I wuz told, I didn't ask why. I wanted to get on. I wanted . . . I wanted . . ." Here he gazed at Tilda, pitiful, whimpering, and when his eyes returned to Mr. Franklin they appeared lost; I had never thought to see such a despairing look upon Buck's face.

"You wanted the print shop, did you?" pursued Mr. Franklin. "Ah, ambition! Further, you hoped to marry Tilda Inch. Yet you spent nights at Mrs. Couch's, enjoying the favors of her girls. Indeed you just returned here by way of the tunnel under the road, did you not? That is why Mr. Barking did not see you the morning Mr. Inch was horribly murdered. And tonight—on your return did you perhaps see two persons making their escape?"

"I never—"

"But you were at Mrs. Couch's."

"Wot of it?"

"And how did you pay for her girls' favors?"

"That's my business."

"Careful, boy," said Mr. Franklin. "Bloody murder may make it the law's business—and shall do so, if I do not hear the truth." But he had no chance to learn what this might wring from the apprentice, for at that moment there came a gruff, noisy clattering at the door, and Constable Nittle burst amongst us with his black, suspicious scowl and his pencil ready over his dog-eared book. "Murder again, is't?" demanded he, peering squint-eyed into each face and jabbing his pencil accusingly at Mr. Franklin. "What? How? Tell!"

"It may yet be here somewhere," murmured Mr. Franklin abstractedly upstairs at Inch, Printer, with the rain softly hissing at the panes.

"What, sir?"

"What Mrs. Inch was killed to obtain. Her murderer—or murderers—may not have got it, for her cries, or Tilda's calling of her name, or my pounding at the door may have affrighted them before they found it. I pray so, Nick."

It was an hour later, past midnight. We were in Mrs. Inch's bedroom, by the light of that same lamp which Tilda Inch had carried down. Her mother's pathetic body had been taken away by the undertakers. Only rumpled, bloodstained sheets remained to tell the awful story; I could hardly look at these. Constable Nittle had just thumped downstairs, having poked desultorily amongst the disarray but seen nothing beyond the end of his nose. "Housebreaking again. Woman caught 'em at it. Was killed. Miscreants fled. Shall track 'em down!" And he had stomped out, his duty done in making copious, brusque jottings. All the while Mr. Franklin merely stood rubbing his chin and nodding at the stout man's every word as if it were wisdom from Solomon, only adding, "I suggest you investigate the tunnel which you will discover in the areaway. Too, you may wish to apply to Mrs.

Couch across the lane, for the murderer—or murderers—fled to her establishment."

Now we were alone in the chill, bleak room. "And what did they seek, sir?" asked I.

"Papers of some sort, I believe. Documents, letters perhaps, and thus easily concealed. Dora Inch's murderers are unprincipled but shrewd; if they could not find what they sought, shall we? The papers may not be in this room; they may not be in the house— yet I believe the woman would keep 'em close. But where?"

Amidst the storm's soft moan we surveyed the violated room: the pulled drawers, the scattered clothing, the spilled books, the bed whose awful stain cried out the failure of all Dora Inch's ambition, which had delivered her but to death.

O, I should ever seek the honest way!

"Surely Dora Inch was no lover of reading, lad?" mused Mr. Franklin, eyeing the books on the polished wood floor, their pages ripped and crumpled, every one skinned for some secret.

"No, sir—except her own ledgers. The books were Mr. Inch's, to peruse at night. He loved books more than beer and gave me ones he thought should improve me."

"Aye, *Tom Jones* and the like." Mr. Franklin knelt with a grunt. "Here, even, is my own pamphlet on electrical matters." Shaking his head, he scooped up some torn pages. "They have done it especial violence, I see. Well, I am untouched; a man's words may be bruised, but that does not scathe him. And is this the family Bible? They have ripped that too; nothing sacred to 'em. And yet . . ." Mr. Franklin frowned. The sewn pages had been torn from the large, heavy binding and rudely flung aside. It was this binding which Mr. Franklin held, vellum-bound board that drooped dismally. His frown dissolved to a smile. "Many's the time have I bound books—yet not so odd a one as this." He laughed out loud. "O, knowledge of book-making may serve us well at this moment, Nick!" He handed me the binding. "See you what I mean?"

I examined it. "It is a poor binding indeed for such a book," said

I, "—crude and uneven. Here on the back it is very thick, and . . ." My eyes met his, glittering behind his little glasses. "Sir, you believe—?"

"I pray." Taking it from me, he began eagerly to peel the vellum from the board. It took several moments to effect this—yet before that time had passed it became clear there were papers hid inside both front and back covers.

At last we had them in our hands.

"Now—" said Mr. Franklin, carefully unfolding the sheets, which were old and yellowed. There were a dozen or so, and by the golden lamplight we stood perusing each one, I peering over the gentleman's arm. Eight proved to be letters, the other four, contracts of a rough sort, agreements to dispose of such and such items for certain sums. All were dated 1725, and all unmistakably implicated Gerrold Bixer in dealings in stolen goods. "The Woodford robbery," said Mr. Franklin, pointing to a scrawled line, "a famous theft of the time—a gentleman's house stripped of all its wealth and furnishings in the space of three hours. Sir Henry Woodford yet lives and would be happy, I am sure, to bring his influence to bear against the perpetrators of the crime, though it be thirty years over and done. It was an ingenious robbery, brilliant. Hexham has not the sort of mind to plan such a thing, though these make him a tool in it. The name Quimp does not appear on any paper, yet I'll wager my eyeglasses it was he who . . . but leave that. Here we have strong motive for murder. Eben Inch must have got these from Hexham when we all worked at Watts' Printing. Did he come upon 'em when Hexham forced him to participate in his sly schemes? However it happened, he knew to take 'em, to loose Hexham's hold on him. My sending him north saved him the trouble, but he kept 'em nonetheless and confided his secret to his new wife—or she wormed it out of him. In any case, she husbanded 'em against some hopeful future when they might prove useful—as indeed they did for a time, giving her proof against Jared Hexham, which she no doubt hoped to use to force his spoiled son to marry her Tilda. But Dora Inch played a dangerous game, which caught her in its trap. Unable to find what they sought, her murderers shut her mouth, in hopes the act might prevent the evidence ever coming to light."

"Was it Jared Hexham, then, who bumped into Tilda as he made his escape?"

"May be."

"And was my master murdered for the same reason?"

There was a ponderous silence. "No, lad," said Mr. Franklin, "that was not why he was killed."

A sudden wind made the old house creak. Mr. Franklin's grim certainty chilled me, but he would say no more on it. Turning away, he tucked the papers snugly in a coat pocket, and we went heavily downstairs.

There Tilda still sat in the front shop in her nightrobe, twisting her hands in her lap with a pale, stunned air. Nearby stood Buck. Having been questioned by Constable Nittle (he still insisted he had slept soundly in the attic and heard no cries), he scowled at us as if we were the root of all disaster. Had Mr. Franklin's investigations indeed precipitated Dora Inch's murder? Yet I could blame the gentleman for nothing; Mrs. Inch had set her own noose about her neck.

"The lawyers will be here soon enough, with their quirks and their quiddities," murmured he. "Have you any relations, child?" he asked Tilda gently.

"N-no, sir."

"And yet you do: an aunt, Mrs. Martha Clay, though you know her very little; she has not been welcomed here. Still, she may consent to take the part of guardian for a time—and you badly want a guardian, child, to teach you to make your way. 'Til then," he turned sternly to Buck, "you, boy, lock up and stand watch and see no one who is not sent by the magistrate crosses the threshold of Inch, Printer, hear?"

Buck grunted rude assent.

Family, thought I as we turned to the door—it was mixed up in this indeed. Tilda Inch's family had been destroyed bit by bit, 'til only the poor girl remained.

Buck's black eyes sent me daggers as Mr. Franklin and I departed into the glum, drenched night.

Yet our journeys were not done. "To Berkeley Square, Peter," commanded the gentleman as we climbed into our coach.

"We go to Mr. Hexham's house, sir?" asked I, blinking rain from my lashes.

"On a chance," said he, settling beside me. "It is some hours after the murder, but still it would be instructive if we should observe a rig returning to the place at this late hour. It may prove useless—yet, damn me, my fingers itch to close upon the villain who has spilt so much blood!"

The rain ceased. We rattled through the night, the buildings of London—the hovels and mansions and brick-terraced dwellings—looming darkly in the near-deserted streets through which the occasional lone traveler crept like something blind. A growing sense of peril made my hair prickle. Did the shabby black coach still follow?

Twenty minutes later we came in sight of Hexham's marble-porticoed mansion. At once it was clear something was amiss, for it was framed in lurid light. "Fire" breathed Mr. Franklin, "—but not the house, the stables in back. O, I pray . . . Go round, Peter!"

Peter sharply turned our coach, and shortly, after much swaying and jostling, we were at the narrow carriage lane behind the row of houses. The glow of the fire was visible here too, and shouts of alarm rose from neighboring dwellings. "Wait here," Mr. Franklin ordered Peter, clambering down. "Hurry, Nick!"

I followed his gouty trot. Fifty yards along the muddy lane we came to Hexham's stables and coach house, leaping with flames. A steaming crackle sounded from the rain-damp wood, but its wetness little hindered the flames, which sent up showers of sparks mixed in an oily smoke. Already parts of the walls were chewed through by gnashing yellow teeth, so that soon the building must crash in upon itself. The horses appeared to have been led out, for two stood skittishly blindfolded in the garden, one held by Bertie Hexham, who wore a look of petulant fury upon his fatuous face. The wall nearest us was least burnt, and to my horror I saw in its loft window a man illuminated by flickering light. It was the Indian brave. Slowly he raised his arms. In triumph? Terror? He held a flask. Liquor? Was that why he had not escaped with the horses?

And then the timbers gave way beneath his feet, and he vanished, amidst a hideous roar in which I imagined I heard his last anguished cry.

"Lord have mercy!" murmured Mr. Franklin at my side. Cries of horror went up all around us, for many neighbors had gathered, their anxious faces saying they hoped the flames would not spread. Yet the damp night seemed certain to prevent that. My eyes returned to Bertie Hexham. Near him stood his gruff father, one arm about the pinched Mrs. Hexham, the other holding his proud, beautiful daughter, all gazing into the hellish furnace of the stable, their faces gleaming redly by its light with a kind of unholy glow. This family lived and prospered, though others were pulled apart. How had the fire begun in their stables? Had a coach arrived there within the two hours? Had some lamp accidentally been overturned? Had the brave himself, in a reeling drunkenness, done it?

There came a groan of wood, a roar, and the roof tumbled amidst snapping beams in a fiery blast of wind.

"O, Mr. Franklin!" cried I, gripping his hand.

Chance, it seemed, had avenged my master's murder.

I spoke this idea to the gentleman some quarter of an hour later as we plodded back toward Craven Street, the lonely rattle of our wheels mingling with the hollow clip-clop of our mare's hooves.

"That fire was no chance," replied he. "It was designed to kill the Indian, so he could reveal to no one who sent him to Craven Street." Mr. Franklin turned towards me in the darkness of the carriage. "You must know more, Nicolas. Your master was never meant to be killed."

184

"Robbers really did him in?"

"No. Murder was planned that morning, an assassin dispatched, that assassin being the Indian who so pitifully died before our eyes. But it was *you*, Nick, who should have been stabbed."

"I?" The spark from his electrical apparatus had not given me so great a start.

❦ 14 ❦

*IN WHICH truth leads on to new questions,
we make many visits, and disaster befalls Nick
Handy . . .*

MR. Franklin and I sat in his room in low lamplight, he in
his fireside chair, I on the desk stool. The air was chill,
but we lit no tinder; I hardly knew I was cold. In my lap
I limply held the journal in which I had recorded every detail of
our pursuit. Why had it not let me see as Mr. Franklin had done?

With his forefinger the gentleman made slow traceries on his
chair arm. The soft drip of the eaves accompanied his words. "I
suspected the truth immediately; that was another reason I
returned that very evening, to spirit you away from that sad and
iniquitous house. Dora Inch gave me the first hint: 'Not him, not
my Eben!' wailed she, as if she cared for the poor man. Yet clearly
he was nothing to her—less than nothing. 'Not him'?—it
suggested at once that some other soul had been intended for
murder. Who? Eben Inch was small, your height and weight, with
your hair color. You recall I asked if he ever wore a wig. I wished
only to establish the possibility that my suspicion was true.
Further, Eben was where you ought to have been, in the back
yard." He heaved a grim sigh. "Indeed you would have been there,
Nick, brewing ink, had he not ordered you to remain abed 'til
seven because he was meeting some mysterious person. O, it

pains me to think that that person was I!" His eyes smoldered with a bleak fury. "For it was I, Nick, summoned by Eben to save you from some peril. Yet had Eben not appointed that hour for our meeting, thus keeping you asleep, you would be dead now, unknowing, he gave his life for yours." He drummed the chair arm. "It must be so. Paint in the dark hour, and all falls into place: persuaded by gin and oppression, the Indian came upon a lone boy where he had been instructed that boy would be. In the dark morn the boy appeared from behind as the Indian had been told he should appear, and so, stealthily creeping, the savage felled him. Eben must have flailed, tearing the seashell necklace and ripping a button in his hand—but those were his last acts. Swift murder was almost certainly all the Indian had been instructed to do, afterward some frail excuse of robbery would be made, which would easily be believed by our knothead constable. But the habit to take scalps was strong, to the Algonquian it is not a cruel or ignoble act. This call from the American forests sounded in our savage's gin-washed brain, and he began to saw with the black-handled knife at the root of Eben's hair. At this juncture some twist of Eben's head must have given him glimpse of the old face—he had murdered no boy! Did he cry out then? Was that what woke you? In any case, he dropped the knife and fled as he had come, through Inch, Printer, along the tunnel to Mrs. Couch's house and from thence, out the rear way, back to Jared Hexham's."

Belowstairs Mrs. Stevenson's grandfather clock softly bonged two. I was for a moment struck speechless, the journal slipped to the floor. "My poor master!" cried I, peering fiercely into Mr. Franklin's face and wringing my hands. "Did Mrs. Inch hate me so much?"

"She hated you, lad, though you must not take her feeling to heart. It was Dora Inch's nature to hate. Ah, may we not pity her, a little? Poor, twisted soul, she was victim too, in her way, forced to turn whore as are so many women in this imperfect world, learning lying ways to stay alive. Yet as to motive . . . hatred does not suffice, for if it were her only reason she would have better tossed you in the street rather than contrive a murder for which she might hang from Tyburn Tree. No, something more made her wish you dead."

"But, what?"

"Fear." The gentleman pulled at his lip. "How much did you know of her business? I mean not printing but . . . other matters?"

"Why . . . nothing."

"Yet you saw her speak to Jared Hexham more than once, heard his name."

"I made naught of it."

"Perhaps not, yet she may have thought you did. Further, you observed the traffic in girls."

"But little."

"Still, she may have believed you dangerous to her ambitions for her daughter."

"Enough to seek to murder me?"

"We deal with unscrupulous people, lad."

I took this in. "Mrs. Couch, sir—if the Indian came from her house, was she part of the plan?"

"She surely knew the Indian used the tunnel. Was she aware the purpose was murder? I know not."

"Yet if the Indian came from Mr. Hexham's, must not he have been in on the thing with Mrs. Inch?"

"Hexham? Aye, it seems so, does it not?" But Mr. Franklin's thoughts appeared elsewhere. Rising with a rheumy wheeze, he blew his nose. "We shall put it from us for now. The hour is late; soft beds await. Let us sleep." He clapped my shoulder. "Tomorrow we shall finish all, delivering our proof of Jared Hexham's rotten dealings to the good John Fielding; thus our hands will be clear of it."

Yet I could acquiesce with but ill ease, many questions seeming unanswered. These whined like gnats in my brain as I traversed the corridor of the dark, silent house to my little room, very cold, and slipped quick as I could beneath the comforter, curling to a ball. There I shivered long. Mrs. Inch had indeed been a woman corrupted by meanness; further, it was true she must have seen her low past as a danger to the respectability just within her grasp. But to murder a mere boy of work? And by such an elaborate plan? How could she think I would ever come before a magistrate to testify against her, or whisper truth among society? Why should Jared Hexham consent to let his Indian be used in the plan, when he himself might be implicated? True, the Indian was now dead, perhaps murdered—yet that seemed some vicious afterthought, not arrived at 'til late.

I flushed with shame—how dare I wonder at Mr. Franklin's wisdom? Yet wonder I did.

And what of my mother? Had he determined to let that mystery go?

My last thoughts before sinking into sleep were of her soft hands, caressing me, protecting me in Jared Hexham's big house, just as I had remembered her that morning near a fortnight past, when poor Mr. Inch was struck down in my place.

I had thought we would go direct to Mr. Fielding's office in Bow Street next morning—indeed in spite of my misgivings I should have been happy to do so, wishing that the danger we drew to ourselves, as one of Mr. Franklin's magnets drew iron shavings, might be deflected from us by that stronger force—but the gentleman announced that there were some few final matters to see to, "some sweeping up to be done," as he put it as we went down to breakfast at ten.

Clearly he was reluctant to leave off his investigations 'til he himself had seen their end.

The sun was out this late October morn, shining amidst shreds of cloud. Mrs. Stevenson's cozily crowded breakfast room had never seemed so comforting and cheery, with Polly and young William Franklin present, the white-damasked table smelling sweetly of porridge and boiled eggs and fresh hot bread and new-made jam. Mrs. Stevenson briefly touched her mole and sniffed at Mr. Franklin, no doubt knowing full well how late he and I had returned last night; yet she made no reprimands, only urging us all to eat heartily as she settled herself like a mother hen to oversee her chicks.

Mr. Franklin did eat well. He wore a kind of pleasant ease, as if double murder had not occurred last night—or if it had, as it must in a city blighted by poverty and lawlessness, it did not touch him. His son inquired after his business with the Penns, to which the father replied with an elaborate sigh. "I am an upstart American who must be taught humility by cooling his heels in the antechambers of power."

"And your business about town with Nick?" Polly pressed him. "How goes that?" She cocked her head shrewdly. "Indeed, what is't? You have never said."

"Business with Nick, my dear? Why, none. He merely accompanies me on my rounds, jotting notes to prod an old man's memory."

"Old?" She laughed gaily. "You are younger than many a boy."

At this Mr. Franklin smiled and burst into "The Old Man's Wish" in his warbling baritone:

> May I govern my passions with absolute sway,
> Grow wiser and better as my strength wears away,
> Without gout or stone by gentle decay . . .

"Fie, sir, leave off, if you please!" cried Mrs. Stevenson, her housewife's cap bobbing. "I love to hear you sing; yet, pray, do not speak of decay. We hope to have you amongst us many years."

All, including I, assented, to which Mr. Franklin modestly hung his balding head. Indeed I loved the man. I loved this house too, and all its occupants; at that moment I trembled with love. Here I had learned that kindness truly lived; here was the hub of the world, and though many spokes of the great wheel that radiated from it might be weak and rotted, yet I hoped the center was strong and would hold.

Fervently I hoped the center would hold.

An hour later Mr. Franklin directed Peter to deliver us to Bradford Street, near West Smithfield, some fifteen minutes away.

It proved a lane of shabby gentility, muddy from the night's rain. Half-way along hung a shop sign with a pair of scissors and JOHN CLAY, TAILOR in reddish letters almost scrubbed away by time. Getting down, we entered amidst bolts of cloth and pincushions and reels of thread. A pocked, shy-eyed seamstress busily sewed in a corner.

From a back room came Martha Clay to greet us. Yet she appeared distraught, hands wringing, eyes anxiously peering past us out her front window, as if some peril lurked there. "O, Mr. Franklin," cried she, near tears, "you should not have come!"

"Pray, why?"

She led us through a door to a small parlor. There we sat, she perched on the edge of her chair looking terrified and helpless. "I have been warned, sir, that I am to have nothing to do with you. I was seen twice in Craven Street, and I must never be seen there again, that is what I am told. I must not speak to you of my brother or any other matter."

"Who told you this?"

"A woman."

"When?"

"This morning. She came to my shop at seven, before my seamstress arrived."

"Her appearance?"

"She was tall and thin, an older woman, perhaps sixty, with iron-gray hair, and she was bundled up from toe to throat in some old velvet stuff, with a greasy hat across her brow. Yet her eyes . . ." Martha Clay shivered.

"Frightening?"

"I have never been so frightened."

"And her voice?"

"Rasping, wheedling."

"Deep?"

"For a woman, yes."

"And did she have a beaked nose?"

"Why . . . yes. You know her?"

"I am coming to know her—him, I should say, for I am near certain it was a man in disguise. Nick has met him, for he too was

191

threatened by the same sneaking fellow. Quimp, he's called, among other names."

"A man? Now you tell me, I . . . yet why does he threaten me?"

"He did not say?"

"No. Only that I must never see or speak to you again."

"I do not think my coming here puts you in danger, though in future I shall be circumspect. How I begin to despise this fellow, Quimp! He has something to do with your brother's death, though not directly, I believe. He acts after the fact, to protect his enterprises. We have made progress, Nick and I—yet there are terrible things to tell." Mr. Franklin described Dora Inch's murder, the death of the Indian, his beliefs about Mr. Inch's end.

The woman listened with wide eyes. When he was through, she exclaimed, "Then it was this boy who was meant to be slain, and not my brother?"

"I believe so. I ask you again, can you recall anything about Nick which your brother may have said?"

"Only that he was like a son to him, the son he never had."

"I see. And now I must raise a new subject. Tilda Inch is left an orphan—except you take her in. Will you, Mrs. Clay?"

The woman made violent protest.

Mr. Franklin merely nodded. "You are right, you are certainly right. Indeed, why should you take in the daughter of a woman who treated you so ill, no matter that the daughter never did you harm? True, though she is Dora Inch's daughter, she is your brother's child as well, your niece, your only niece, with nowhere else to turn, but that must make no matter. True, too, that you may be able to turn round the mother's ill influence and make something of the girl . . . but no, it is impossible. Tilda will only shame you with the illegitimate child she bears in her womb."

This roused Mrs. Clay. "Shame me? You go too far, Mr. Franklin. Think you I am proud? Not so. Many a good girl has found herself in the same place as Tilda, through a mistake of the heart. I see no shame in that." A dampness came into Martha Clay's eyes. "My niece," mused she, "—why, she might become the daughter I never had. And a baby too . . ." Her chin lifted. "I shall do't, Mr. Franklin!" Two spots of pink shone in her cheeks. "And I believe I shall come to be grateful to you for persuading me."

"I am much pleased to see we may bring some good out of this," said Mr. Franklin as we drove away. "Yet, Quimp . . ." He thumped the carriage top as signal. "Peter, take us to Lord Bottom's!"

"May I speak to one of your servants, milord?" asked Mr. Franklin less than an hour later in Lord Bottom's book-lined study. "The Algonquian Indian woman?"

Lord Bottom lifted one of his porcupine brows. "Indeed, yes. May I inquire why?"

"I have sad news to impart to her: her son's demise."

"How dreadful!"

"Dreadful indeed. He burned to death in a fire in Jared Hexham's stables last night. May I ask . . . did you know this Indian brave, who sometimes drove Hexham's coach, was her son?"

"I did. He was used to visiting his mother here. They spoke in the Algonquian tongue; these moments were little enough consolation to 'em."

"You felt for their circumstance?"

Some strong emotion shook the peer. "Uprooted from their land? Torn apart from one another? How could I not feel for 'em?"

"Yet you kept one of 'em a servant."

Lord Bottom's brown eyes flashed. "Do you suggest I added to their misery? Sir, I alleviated it. All unknowing they had contracted themselves to Hexham; he had their marks on paper as indentures. Thus they were his to do with as he wished, with English law to take his part if anyone challenged his mastery. If the woman were not servant here, she would be elsewhere—or Hexham might turn her whore; he had it in his power. Yet I persuaded him to let me keep her. I treat her with all the kindness I may, and let her son see her whenever Hexham looses his leash."

His fine hands trembled as he spoke. "The poor creature will be crushed to know those visits may no longer be. O, slavery of any sort is an abomination, Mr. Franklin!"

Mr. Franklin bowed his head. "I had no intention of accusing you of any cruelty, milord. And yet . . . I must inquire about some other matters. Your coach is embellished with a B, is't not?"

A wary look flickered in Lord Bottom's eyes. "It is."

"And was early Monday morning last week in Fish Lane, Moorfields?"

The peer had turned to gaze gloomily out the window at his garden. Now his head swiveled slowly, glancing first at me, then Mr. Franklin. He gave a weary smile. "So. Observed, was I?"

"Not you, your conveyance. But you were in it?"

"I was."

"Alone?"

A hesitation. "When I departed."

"You came with someone? To Mrs. Couch's?"

"A young woman." The gentleman's shoulders drew back. "A woman I love."

"Ah . . ." said Mr. Franklin feelingly. "She works for Mrs. Couch, does she?"

"Would that she did not! Would that she had a heart! Would that she loved me too!"

Mr. Franklin pursed his lips at this outburst. "I see. You take her from that establishment of an evening? And return her next morn?"

"That is our arrangement, for which I pay dearly." Lord Bottom began to pace. "Since my wife died I have been very alone— except for my Anne, who is my one joy. Yet a man needs . . . you understand. I dabbled in erotica; I spent myself in a succession of wasteful dalliances. Panders offered me women. I took to frequenting low dives and keeping vile company." He halted. "Then one evening Jared Hexham took me to Mrs. Couch's. Already he had a chronicle of my despicable alliances and was beginning to pressure me in the direction you know, to engage my Anne to his son. At Mrs. Couch's I met the young woman of whom I spoke. Camilla is her name—dark-haired, dark-eyed, with skin that smells of some exotic isle—and she bewitched me. She leads me by the nose; she is like opium: I wish to rid myself of her yet cannot. Hexham threatens to expose this mad affair to my daughter; worse, he will destroy my place in society—and my Anne's—if I do not do his bidding."

"Might not society overlook or forgive?"

"Dare I take the chance? It is not I alone who would fall, but Anne too, to double ignominy: the spurning by her peers, and the pain of discovering her father's feet of clay."

"You are not the first man to fall in love with a whore."

Lord Bottom wrung his hands. "The shame of it! Not the loving, but knowing it is hopeless yet going on with it."

"I believe I have it in my power to free you, at least from Hexham's coils."

"Tell me how, sir, I beg you!" Hope burned in the peer's eyes as Mr. Franklin summarized all we had learned of Jared Hexham's felonious dealings, including our proofs: the letters and contracts from Mrs. Inch's Bible and the secret room in the warehouse.

"Yet these can do no good," said my lord bitterly when Mr. Franklin was done. "If Hexham is thrown in Newgate he may still—nay, shall, out of vicious spite—expose me."

"But what if he is not taken? What if I keep the letters and contracts as surety that he will leave off his importunings, indeed cease all his underhanded work?"

"You would do this?"

It was Mr. Franklin's turn to gaze somberly out the window. "Is justice better served by punishing past wrongs or by preventing future ones? It is not an easy question." His eyes came back. "One thing I know: I heartily wish to save your daughter." He offered his hands, palms out. "I do not say I can do what I suggest; I say only that there is some hope."

I observed Mr. Franklin's conversation with the Indian woman some ten minutes later. They stood close in the redolent kitchen, Mr. Franklin having chosen not to have her called up but to deliver his message to her in her domain below. He spoke softly, gently in the Algonquian tongue. The woman took it stoically, it seemed, with only the slightest start and shudder of her strong body, and a faint movement of her thick fingers at her sides. Her sturdy frame looked as if it could absorb much punishment without flinching, as if she could wait and wait 'til the time should come for . . . I knew not what, though the sense of pent fury that radiated from her like cold fire made me quake.

Her son had murdered my master, in place of me.

I could envy the dead brave: he had been a son who knew his mother.

Past noon the morning sunlight was effaced by a chill gray gloom, into which London's chimneypots spewed their gritty smoke. We returned to Craven Street near two, having first stopped for some brief time at Mrs. Mountjoy's pleasure barge on the Thames, where Mr. Franklin imparted our sad news to the Indian girl. I did not observe this interview, but settling himself once more gravely in our coach, the gentleman said she took it with less restraint than her mother, crying out and tearing at her long black hair.

"I must see if I may reunite mother and daughter," said he as we drove along Fleet Street. He slapped his knee. "Indeed I shall do't!" His deep voice trembled. "O, 'tis a crime 'gainst Nature to rip children from their parents."

"Sir," put in I, "would not Lord Bottom be thought an excellent match by many women of quality?"

"Surely," replied he.

"Strange, then, that at the death of his wife so fine a gentleman should choose to spend himself in wasteful dalliance."

Mr. Franklin sighed. "The human heart is full of mystery, Nick, and no man is without his failings. Remember this should you ever be prompted to judge too harshly."

At Craven Street Mrs. Stevenson brewed tea, which she served with honeyed seedcakes. Mr. Franklin was rheumy-eyed and said he wanted rest. Truly his distemper had not let up since he took me from Inch, Printer, he ever wheezing and sniffling. Watching him growl and cough in the front pàrlor, rattling his cup on its saucer deep in thought, I wondered what so impelled him to press on in spite of illness.

Love of justice?

Love of me?

I hardly dared hope he might stand in for the father I had lost.

But what of my dear mother? The question still harried me as I went to my little room, Mr. Franklin wishing an hour of rest before he took some final decision. He was much agitated climbing the stairs. "Broach what we know to Mr. Fielding, and let law take its course? Or keep it against Jared Hexham, twist the knife in him as he has done to others, and save Lord Bottom and his daughter? It is a great dilemma, Nick."

I shut my door and gazed out the casement window. Below, humming dirgelike, the somber negro King turned earth in the muddy yard for winter vegetables. Further back I glimpsed by the door of the small stables Peter combing the mare who pulled our hired coach. I turned my gaze to the Thames. If Mr. Franklin delivered Hexham to Mr. Fielding's men, would we ever have opportunity to ask him of my mother? Would he tell us aught? How had she come to his house? And who was my father? I faced the dark possibility that he might be Hexham himself. Indeed the son, Bertie, was old enough for it to have been he. Lord Bottom? Could that be? Preferable, I thought, and yet . . . I even wondered if I might be related to the Indians. Yet again, there was Eben Inch, who had treated me like a son. My mother herself was as much as ever a wraith in my mind. If I should meet her after nine years, with only the memories of a three-year-old, would I know her?

Was it possible I had met her since, within the fortnight past?

This led me to reflect on the women I had glimpsed at Mrs. Couch's and Mrs. Mountjoy's. Did my mother continue life in such a place?

Had she ended it there?

I trembled. And then another thought struck me cold: what if the cherished woman of whom I had dreamed all these years had not been my mother but only a woman I knew as such, a nursemaid, taking the place of my true mother?

This thought made me blanch, and I shut my eyes tight, wishing to think no more, to have all resolved: Mr. Franklin's explanation of Mrs. Inch's fear of me still seemed wrong. And what of her fear of him, which he had never touched on? Did he not see it? I recalled what he had said of the gnawed, dusty ledger of payments in her storage room: that it figured in the murder of my master. Had he meant that it figured in my intended murder? As for the actual slayings, what of the bent bell? Was Buck Duffin innocent of all? Had Mrs. Couch played a part? Why had Mr. Franklin seemed reluctant to say it was Jared Hexham who, fleeing in the dark, had bumped into Tilda Inch? Tilda had thought two people fled. Which two?

In a fog of confusion I flung myself onto my bed as Mrs. Stevenson's grandfather clock struck three.

"We go to Bow Street, Nick," said Mr. Franklin, shrugging into his plain brown coat an hour later and striding from his room to call Peter to bring round the coach. "Damn me," he muttered from the hall, "I have forgot the proofs against Hexham." He poked his head back in the room. "Fetch 'em from my desk, there's a good lad."

His heavy steps descended the stairs. I went to the desk in whose bottom left-hand drawer I had seen Mr. Franklin drop the damning documents we had found in Mrs. Inch's Bible. Customarily this drawer was locked, but it now stood part open, and I imagined the gentleman perusing its contents as he made his decision. I tugged the drawer, but it stuck, and in yanking hard I tumbled it from its niche, myself slipping, overturning the drawer and spilling all within. Hastily I sifted through a jumble of papers, searching for those I was to fetch. My eyes lit upon a bundle of letters, tied with string. The top one of these was brief:

Respected Sir [it began],

The boy does well at school, being apt at Latin and ciphering. He proceeds healthy and cheerful. All is well.

Ever your Humble Servant,
Agnes Foote

Some familiarity about the handwriting had drawn me to read what I had no business reading, but I dismissed this familiarity, being stung with jealousy of William Franklin, who had had such advantages of schooling and care that this old report to his father could testify to his cheerfulness. At once I was shamed by this petty thought. Burning red, I found what I had been asked for, returned the rest to the drawer, and hurried to join Mr. Franklin in Craven Street.

Shortly we rattled northeast toward John Fielding's office.

The morning sun had been but a hiatus. The afternoon was murky, dun-colored, and acrid. Nonetheless the streets were thronged with a kind of dark bustle, as of figures moving in some dim reach of hell. Draymen heaved bundles from carts, costers pushed barrows, beggars stretched out hands like claws. And everywhere were shouts and cries, of a mercantile buying and selling. Human souls too were bought and sold in the city. Seeing all about me, close-packed and seething, shifting, joining or tearing off and breaking away, currents in a great stream, I was reminded again how vulnerable we were, a floating leaf which might at any moment be spilled and drowned. I remembered the black coach. Did Peter still keep sharp lookout? Yet how could he amidst this surge?

We were abruptly halted by some commotion in a narrow way ahead. I turned to Mr. Franklin, good, kind Mr. Franklin, so solid in his beaver hat and little glasses. He seemed a rock amidst the river of life. I opened my mouth to speak, to say again my gratitude—when hands tore open the door at my side, and hands reached in, and hands dragged me from the coach, and a smothering cloth was pulled over my eyes, and then I was struck on the head so that sparks, as from an electrical battery, flashed in my brain before all plunged into blackness.

❧ 15 ❧

IN WHICH I meet some murderers and learn some secrets which I am unlikely ever to have opportunity to reveal . . .

THERE came a sound out of the blackness, a licking, a lapping; then the distant creak and soft thump of hulls; then a muffled screaming of birds, and I knew I must be near the Thames. It was cold. Under my prostrate body I felt rough wood planks. I did not open my eyes; that seemed impossible, for after the sounds, which brought me to consciousness, came a wave of pain that made me moan, turn on my side, and vomit the seedcakes which I had eaten at Craven Street.

Craven Street. Should I ever see it again? And Mr. Franklin? And good Mrs. Stevenson and her Polly?

"He's wakenin'," came a gruff male voice.

"I see," said a woman.

I fluttered my lids. Even this caused pain, but I wished to put faces to these unfriendly voices and to know where I was. A light near blinded me. Squinting, I made out a single oil lamp hung from an angled beam above my head. Moaning, lifting a hand against this light, I turned to see more. A place I knew took shape out of a blur: the low-ceilinged, slope-roofed loft of Jared Hexham's dockside warehouse. Temples throbbing, I lifted upon one elbow.

Two black-booted feet stood six feet away, up which I raised my aching eyes. Clenched fists rested on hips, then Buck Duffin's squarish face came into view, glaring in haughty triumph. "Not so high and mighty now, eh?"

My mouth was dry as dust; I knew not what to say. There was but one stick of furniture in the long, frigid room, a rickety wooden chair. Perched on this, as elegant as if she waited to be admired in some lord's parlor, sat Lydia Hexham in dark-red velvet, a small peaked hat on her powdered curls. "The boy smells," said she, holding a lace handkerchief to her nose. "Pray, clean him up, Mr. Duffin."

"I'll never!" exclaimed Buck.

"O, you shall." Her lashes sweetly fluttered—yet there was a tinct of venom in her voice. "For me."

"Awright," grumbled Buck, bending and swiping roughly at my face with a cloth, then swabbing at my vomit. "There," said he, tossing the rag into the room below. "A pretty sight, ain't he?"

"Not very pretty," said the dark-haired young woman. "O, where is Mama?"

"Never fear, she'll be here." Buck prodded me with his boot. "Git up, you."

Head swimming, I groaned to my feet, placing a hand on one of the beams to steady myself. "Wh-where is Mr. Franklin?" I asked.

"Gaddin' about, pokin' his nose where it ain't wanted, I s'pect," said Buck. "But yer here, and that's wot counts."

I was about to reveal that I knew this was the Hexham warehouse—but a strong desire to live told me to pretend ignorance. "Where am I?" asked I.

"Never you mind."

"Is't night?"

"Th' time o' day ain't none o' yer business, I say."

"But, why . . . ?"

Buck jabbed my shoulder. "We'll ask th' questions! Shut up and save yer breath."

I was glad to sink into silence. I raised my fingers to my

201

throbbing head, they came away sticky with blood from a matted spot in my hair.

How . . . ?

And then I remembered traveling toward Bow Street with Mr. Franklin and the commotion in the road and being dragged from our coach and smothered by black cloth and struck a ringing blow. In the milling throng it must have been easy to spirit me away down some alley, to a waiting coach. Who had struck me? Buck? Why? His gruff stare and Lydia Hexham's cool, veiled gaze of revulsion said I would get no answers from them. Were they the two who had murdered Mrs. Inch? Did they mean to murder me? Yet if so, why had they not done it when I was unconscious? Though I felt imperiled—Mr. Franklin's words rang in my brain: "We deal with unscrupulous people"—I struggled to keep my head, to make the gentleman proud of me by acting bravely and sensibly, even if it should not save me.

A quarter of an hour passed, during which I fought pain and sickness and struggled to find some hope in my plight. Buck seemed content to pick at his blackened nails, Miss Hexham to sit as still as a portrait. No rattle of iron wheels, no cries of dockmen or sailors rose from Thames-side; I concluded it was night.

Did Mr. Franklin search for me? Might he discover I was here?

At last came a clanking from below: the great lock. Next the creak of the door and faint footsteps. Lydia Hexham's small pale chin lifted in alertness, and Buck Duffin grew stiff as a stick.

"Mama?" breathed Lydia.

"Who else would it be, child?" came Mrs. Prudence Hexham's desiccated voice from below.

A moment later the woman's wrinkled face poked up into the loft.

In an instant the rest of her was in view, in a brown traveling coat. She trotted at once to me. Small, barely my height, she thrust her crabapple face in mine. Her breath smelled like brine. "So, awake, are we?" said she. "And asking questions, is my guess. You were ever asking questions when we suffered you under our roof."

"You knew my mother. You *must*," said I breathlessly. "Who was she?"

The woman cackled. "Did I not say he asked too much? Rose Handy was your mother, from America, who else would't be?"

I took this in. "Handy? She, whose father was a printer in Boston?"

"The same. Your snooping Mr. Franklin surmised that, did he?"

"And she named me Nicolas Handy?"

"She did."

"Yet why do I have her last name and not that of my father?"

Prudence Hexham laughed. "Because the slut was never married."

"Do not call her that!" cried I. "Who was my father? Tell me."

At this the woman's glinting eyes clouded, her small fists clenched, and she shuddered all over. "I hate to speak of it, I loathe to speak of it!" she near screeched. "But to you I shall—in the certainty," she shot a fierce look at Buck and Lydia, "that not one of my words will leave this room. Your father was—is," her shoulders drew back, "—Mr. Jared Hexham, my husband."

I felt a dismal sinking.

Mrs. Hexham grasped my collar. "You dare to shrink at the news? Stand proud, boy! To be the son, even though a bastard, of so fine a man! For he *is* fine! And he chose me, and I have ever been loyal to him, prodding him when he was slow, taking affairs in my hands if need be, and keeping him ignorant of what he need not know. Your mother, for one. I despised having her in our house, so I found means to see she left it."

"Where did she go?"

"To hell, I pray. She died by my hand—and died slowly, I am pleased to say."

I stared in horror.

"Sweet thing, pretty thing—but she must die," Prudence Hexham went on, "as must you, bastard—though not until you have acted as bait for Mr. Benjamin Franklin."

Buck clumped to her side. "Here, now, wot's this about murder? I want no part o' murder."

203

Mrs. Hexham twisted upon him. "Be quiet, you! You shall have a part of whatever I say!"

Buck fell back under her threatening gaze.

"You . . . you *poisoned* my mother?" said I, all atremble.

"O, it was taken as a putrid fever; no one will ever prove poison. Jared wished to keep her about, a favored thing. He had got her with child in Boston. He brought her to London to save her shame—so he told her gullible parents. 'I know a fine gentleman who'll have her, baby and all,' said he. Ha, there was never a fine gentleman, only himself. He took her because he wished to try if he might make her come round to him once more, though there was nothing between 'em in my house, I saw to that; not that she, with her fine airs, would have had anything to do with him. I am a good wife! I love my husband so far even to forgive his straying! Did he not see something in me and choose me and keep me all these years? But I could not abide that young woman. How the servants and everyone took to her! Thank God I have good children; they hated her as much as I."

"Indeed, I despised her," put in Lydia languidly, as if she spoke of despising bad weather.

"Dear daughter," cooed Mrs. Hexham. Her eyes flicked back to me. "So your mother wasted away, and when the baggage was dead and buried in a pauper's grave, my husband, to whom you were never more than a spoiled, troublesome brat, passed you on to Mrs. Inch to use as she saw fit. She was glad to take you, I never knew why, for she always hated you as much as I."

Hexham my father? My mother slowly poisoned? No greater blows seemed possible. "And . . . and you lent your Indian to Mrs. Inch, to rid her of me?"

"Your Mr. Franklin surmised that too, did he?"

"And then you killed Mrs. Inch when she would not deliver her proofs against your husband?"

Pride shone like a beacon in the shriveled woman's eyes. "I serve my family how I must!"

"But . . . Tilda Inch said there were two people that night.

And Buck was at Mrs. Couch's. So—" My eyes flew to Lydia Hexham's cold beauty: her pale, powdered face and bosom, her hard mouth, her slender hands perfectly arranged in her lap as they had been since I woke. Her porcelain face turned to me; she arched one painted brow, as if to say, "Am I to be blamed for doing what I must?" and, chilled, I wondered which of the two women, mother or daughter, had plunged the ebon-handled knife in Mrs. Inch's breast? Certainly both had equal motive: reputation; and Lydia surely would want no soiled past to stand in the way of marrying well.

I shuddered—the daughter had learned much from her mother—and I thanked my stars that, though my life seemed sure to prove short, no taint of this family, to which I belonged by blood, had seeped into my veins.

Yet I wished to know all. "Did you set fire to your stables?" asked I.

"Yes, though everyone believes the drunken Indian did it."

"To seal his mouth?"

She snatched at my sleeve. "As I will *yours*, boy, if your Mr. Franklin does not do as I wish."

"And what is that?"

"Give to me what you found in Dora Inch's bedroom."

"We found nothing."

She shook me. "Do not lie. You found papers injurious to my husband, and thus to me and my children. Buck Duffin discovered the Bible skinned of its binding and reported the news to me. Buck has been an excellent agent, Dora Inch never guessing he served me; through my arranging he has had much pleasant reward at Mrs. Couch's. Clever Dora Inch, to hide her wicked secret in a Bible!—though not clever enough to speak up to save her life."

Pure wickedness gleamed in Mrs. Hexham's squinted agate eyes, and I doubted if speaking would have saved Mrs. Inch. Indeed in Mrs. Hexham's strong grasp I mistrusted being delivered safe to Mr. Franklin, whether or no he did her bidding.

205

I began to pray to heaven he would defy her, for I fervently wished the Hexham family damned to ignominy for their outrages against my mother.

"I do not like this cold, dirty place, Mama," broke in Lydia. "Did you send the message?"

Mrs. Hexham released me. "To Craven Street, but an hour past, my dear. Mr. Franklin may ponder it this very moment. Soon we must return home to unburden him of his hard-won proofs, little good they will do him."

During this exchange I glanced at Buck. His face was pale beneath his shock of black hair, his Adam's apple bobbing, and he stared at mother and daughter as if they were devils. Clearly he had not known they murdered Mrs. Inch. He saw how deep in he was: he too might dangle at Tyburn Tree.

Was there hope for me in Buck's fear?

"Then your husband does not know what you do?" stammered I to Mrs. Hexham.

"I take it all in my hands," pronounced she.

"And do you know a man named Quimp?"

She started as if I had struck her. "How do you know of Quimp?"

I saw I had said too much and determined on silence, bracing myself for punishment, which came at once, viciously. "Saucy boy!" She slapped my face. "So, Quimp has been at you, has he?" Her lined features worked. "Well, he need not, for I shall see to you—and to snooping Benjamin Franklin as well. Now, you must tell me all he knows."

What could I say, even if I wished? Had the gentleman guessed it was Mrs. Hexham and her daughter who had slain Mrs. Inch? Did he know my mother was dead? Had he guessed my father was Jared Hexham? I gave Mrs. Hexham more silence, while my head rang and my stomach heaved with nausea.

"O, brave," said she, scraping my cheek with her nails, "though not for long." She turned brusquely to her daughter. "Come, my dear. We do not wish to keep Mr. Franklin waiting. Bind the boy tight, Mr. Duffin." She laughed. "Make him suffer."

Amidst a rustling of skirts mother and daughter descended the ladder. A moment later the great lock snapped below and Buck Duffin and I were alone in the long, chill room.

Buck glared meanly—but there seemed some uncertainty in his look, some darting desperation, as if behind his black brows and black eyes his mind raced amidst a maze, seeking escape. Scooping up a length of cord, he came at me, and I shrank away, remembering Mr. Franklin's advice from that first morn when he said how I should defend myself. But I was weak and staggering, no match for Buck now. Grasping me easily, he flung me down and knelt hard on my chest. "Tight, is't? Tight it shall be." And, turning me, he proceeded to loop the cord about my wrists behind my waist. These he tied to my ankles, drawn back, and then pulled the cord fast so that I was bent in a steady, unremitting anguish.

Trussed for sacrifice, thought I. Yet I would not give up. "They shall hang you, Buck," I got out between my teeth as he went to the chair Lydia Hexham had sat in and flung himself down, folding his arms.

"They shan't."

"You are an agent of murderers. Who is to say Mrs. Hexham may not blame the murdering on you?"

"Shut up, you! She'll never!"

"She may. She is not to be trusted. The Indian helped her and was burnt to death for what he knew; you may go his way. Yet if you save me, if you let me go, I shall say you did so and testify to all I heard here, that you did not know their plans or act in any murder."

He leapt up. "You shall have no breath to testify to anything, boy!" And he kicked me so hard my breath was torn from me. Stomping back to his chair, he sank down heavily and laughed, though he remained uneasy, fidgeting and turning this way and that and staring broodingly in the jagged lamplight.

For my part I was flooded with despair.

Thus I sank into painful waiting, praying Mr. Franklin would find a way to thwart Prudence Hexham and her corrupted daughter. The whistling cry of river birds had stilled, it must have been dusk, perhaps six P.M. when I had first wakened from being struck, so that all that remained in the lengthening night was the steady slosh of water and the muffled creak and thud of hulls and an occasional scurrying of rats. The throbbing of my head sank to a dull ache, though I shivered where I lay on the rough planks and grew stiff in my pulled-back shape and was swept with waves of sickness.

I cursed my helpless state!

Hours passed. My pain lengthened each minute in anguish. Buck sprawled back, legs out, snoring. I too fell into fitful, nightmarish sleep, marked by startled cries in black dreams.

And then there came sound once more.

Both Buck and I heard it at the same instant: the clank of the lock.

Mr. Franklin, here to rescue me?

Buck took no chances. Lifting a cudgel of thick gnarled oak from beside the chair, he crept to the opening in the floor.

But it was Mrs. Hexham who came up into the room a moment later, her round, wrinkled face quivering with fury.

"He did not come, damn him. Benjamin Franklin did not come." She scurried to me. "He must care nothing for you, boy," she quavered, staring down in a fury, "for he leaves you to me. Well, he shall never see you again. Nor shall anyone. Weighted with stone, you shall sink in the Thames to be eaten by fish. Afterward I will with my own hands see to your Mr. Franklin, for he shall not deliver his proofs if I may prevent it."

I gave thanks that the woman had been foiled—yet I felt deeply hurt: had Mr. Franklin abandoned me?

"Help me drag him, Buck," snapped Mrs. Hexham, grasping my arms. "We shall fling him to the floor below and break his neck, then it will be easy to sink him." She thrust her face into mine. "How glad I shall be to see the end of Rose Handy's brat!"

My heart pounded with fear. I glanced at Buck. He hesitated

but a moment, then flung his cudgel aside and came quickly and grasped me too, and they began to drag me towards the hole in the floor. A twelve-foot drop, head first; I had no doubt it should snap my neck. I wriggled and squirmed and cursed, but to no avail; I was firmly trussed, they moved me inexorably. Splinters cut me. Mrs. Hexham struck out to silence me. The hole drew near.

Mr. Franklin's head rose through the opening. "Leave the boy be!" cried he.

My heart leapt in my breast.

Buck stared, released me, scrambled back like a dog from an angry master. His face swarmed with alarm, and he scooped up his cudgel and stood ready to strike.

Mrs. Hexham too was quick. With a little, hissing cry, like a cat's, she was in an instant at her bag where she had left it a dozen feet away. From it she snatched out a large hunting pistol, which she pointed with both hands, quite steady, at Mr. Franklin's breast. "O, you are here, sir, you are here," she gloated, "and I am glad. Just in time for your boy." Her wreathed smile so wrinkled her cheeks that I thought her face should crack. "And have you brought what I demand, or must more blood be shed?"

Mr. Franklin looked only at me. "Are you well, Nick?" asked he.

"As well as tying and beating may leave me, sir," gasped I. "O, thank you for coming!"

"Did you think I would not?" The gentleman's shoulders rose into the room. His pale jowls shook, and behind his little glasses his brown eyes clouded. Yet he gave a small, glinting smile. "Well, Mrs. Hexham, indeed I have brought what you wished." Lifting a leather satchel into view, he placed it carefully on the planks. "Yet the boy must be untied before I shall give it over."

"It is a large satchel," said Mrs. Hexham with squinting eyes.

"And must be, to hold all which must be delivered—many papers—for it is not only what I found in Mrs. Inch's Bible which damns your husband. No, there is more, much more." One brow lifted inquiringly. "Surely you wish it all?"

"All?" said she suspiciously.

"All. Release the boy."

Mrs. Hexham's gaze darted to me. Her tongue flicked over her thin, pinched lips. "Untie him," said she to Buck.

Buck scowled at this order but obeyed, kneeling by my side while he kept his cudgel near. In a moment my bonds were loose, though I could barely stand for the stiffness in my limbs.

Scurrying back, Buck lifted his stick once more and stood, stout legs apart.

"Excellent," pronounced Mr. Franklin. "And now . . . ah!" he cried, "damned gout!" Pulling himself full into the room, he stood wheezing and leaning heavily on his bamboo, wiping his bald head with a cloth. He grimaced with pain. "The disease rebels against the damp night air and punishes me for venturing out."

Mrs. Hexham raised her pistol higher. "Perhaps this may cure you."

"I sincerely hope such desperate physic may not be called for. Have I not kept my side of the bargain, dear lady?"

All this I watched and heard with alarm. Surely Mrs. Hexham had no intention of letting Mr. Franklin live. Why had he placed himself in this trap? Rubbing chafed wrists, I made to go to him, but he sharply raised a hand to stop me.

"Why did not you meet me at my home, as I required in my message?" demanded Mrs. Hexham.

"Because I knew the boy was not there. A servant of mine named King has watched your house several days; he saw you return with no prisoner."

"Clever. And how came you here?"

"I followed you. Your daughter remains at home?"

"She does."

"And takes care of herself, I am sure; she has had a fine tutor in self-interest. Ah, my leg!" He rubbed his thigh. "Were't not for my bamboo I could not stand. Shall we attend to business, ma'am? The sooner done, the sooner I may rest abed."

"Take care you do not rest sooner than that."

Mr. Franklin picked up the satchel. "If you are not true to your word, you shall never have this."

She aimed the pistol between his eyes. "I shall have what I please."

Mr. Franklin gazed at her almost sadly. "I see you mean it. Then take this," said he with a shrug, setting down the satchel and pushing it towards her with the point of his bamboo.

"You had best try no tricks," warned the woman, eagerly bending, reaching out with one hand while gripping the pistol with the other—yet her fingers never touched the satchel's handle.

From it leapt a crackling spark, which made her start and shriek.

Her whole body shuddered. Her pistol fired, but her sudden puppetlike twitching caused the ball to strike the ceiling harmlessly.

With a withering sigh Mrs. Prudence Hexham fell—unconscious or dead, I knew not—to the rough plank floor.

"Wot's this?" cried Buck, rushing at Mr. Franklin with his cudgel.

Mr. Franklin calmly raised his bamboo. From its tip leapt another spark, striking Buck's white knuckles.

"Ow!" cried he, dropping the weapon and leaping back.

His head thudded against one of the low, angled beams, and he too fell in a heap.

"Demonstrating," said Mr. Franklin, smiling at me with no sign of pain from the gout, "that the electrical flux may serve the cause of justice. Nay, do not approach me yet, for I must first . . ." He brought the point of his bamboo near an iron bolt in the floor. There was but a small spark, then none. "I am free of an excess of electricity." He embraced me, tousling my hair. "I am very glad to find you safe, lad!" He searched my face. "I feared they might have killed you. Your bewilderment asks how I have effected these fine results. There is a battery hid in that satchel, with which I charged my bamboo. A wire—you see?—runs down my stick. It delivered the spark to Buck. As for Mrs. Hexham, when I lifted the satchel before giving it to her I released a mechanism—a small invention of mine—which allowed electricity to flow direct to the handle. Mrs. Hexham's greed effected the rest." He regarded her crumpled form. "Her chest moves; she is alive, and strong enough, I hope, to stand before a magistrate. O, the reputation of women as the softer sex misleads men; the creatures may prove dangerous. Come, lad, let me help you below. Peter waits with our carriage. We must complete our interrupted journey to Mr. Fielding."

Truly I needed aid, for I ached from my struggles and from the blows rained upon me. With some grunting and wheezing Mr. Franklin got me down the steep ladder. Outside, supported by his arm, I shivered in the frosty night. Great ships loomed and creaked in the Thames. Somewhere a clock struck five. Five it had been, thought I in a haze, when I had waked that last morning at Inch, Printer. How much had passed since then! And was it over? All resolved at last?

I chanced to glance back as we reached the corner of the shed from which we had first spied on Hexham's warehouse. "Mr. Franklin!" cried I, pointing. A small figure had just slipped from the warehouse to scuttle out of sight in deep shadow.

"Aye, lad, Mrs. Hexham. The woman is determined. And sly. Yet I do not believe she will 'scape punishment. Come. Peter is some distance away. I wish as soon as possible to place you under Mrs. Stevenson's healing ministrations."

"Sir," said I as we reached the coach under a black overhang, "I know the truth about my parents at last—and it is terrible." It was as if the knowledge which Prudence Hexham had imparted only now brought home its full meaning, and I burst into sobs.

Mr. Franklin held me. "There, Nick. You have endured much."

"B-but, my mother is dead, poisoned in Hexham's house!"

I felt him flinch. "Is she, lad? Poor Rose, I feared some such end. If only I could have prevented it."

I lifted my wet eyes. "But how could you? You were in America. Further, Jared Hexham is my father. I do not want it to be so! A father who would be happy to find me dead? And after you deliver your proofs to Mr. Fielding must I watch my own father hang?"

"I heartily hope not!" He held me at arm's length. "Mrs. Hexham told you Jared Hexham was your father? No doubt she believes it, though it is not so. You must face more truth, lad. I hope it may not displease you. I am your father, Nick Handy. Benjamin Franklin is your father."

❧ 16 ❧

*IN WHICH death finds a final victim, and
Mr. Franklin tells all . . .*

"TRULY you must be my son, Nicolas," said Mr. Franklin
as Peter drove us through the black London streets, I
sitting stunned with the gentleman's arm about my
shoulders. "All evidence points to this truth, which I long
suspected but had no surety of. O, I am proud to acknowledge it!
Think," his arm gently shook me, "—there can be no Hexham
blood in your veins." He laughed. "There is printer's ink, is there
not? And clear common sense in your head? And goodness in
your heart? You are surely my son and ever were, and I shall tell all
the circumstances which make it so when we are warm and safe at
Craven Street, with time and comfort to answer every question.
Meantime," his voice grew grim, "we must finish this. A creature
as dangerous as Mrs. Prudence Hexham must not be let roam free.
Her plans are spoiled, but spite may make her seek revenge. Mr.
Fielding's men must take her; we must be made safe."

Our mare's hooves clopped briskly. Our carriage swayed.
Occasional lamplight pierced the inky night, gliding over Mr.
Franklin's round, bespectacled face as he leaned forward to urge
Peter quicker to Bow Street. My father's face? My heart beat fast.
How could it be?

And then I felt a rush of joy. Mr. Franklin did not lie. Good Mr.
Franklin! Kind Mr. Franklin! I was certain of his honesty, and tears

streamed down my cheeks once again, and I leaned in silent, gulping happiness against my father, who had saved me twice.

We reached Bow Street shortly. Mr. Franklin strenuously mounted the steps and banged the great knocker. "I hope this may not ruin Lord Bottom," said he, "but all must be delivered. English law must take its course."

Not more than five minutes later Mr. John Fielding, wrapped in a great shaggy robe, was listening in his office with his large curled ears while his sightless eyes hid in fat folds of flesh. "So, stolen goods cached in a warehouse? Double murder? You have 'em indeed, Mr. Franklin, not only Jared Hexham but mother and daughter as well, and it is time to lay hands on 'em, I see." His ample lips spread in a smile. "Brogden!" he rumbled, and wiry Mr. Joshua Brogden scurried in, rubbing sleepy eyes, "—fetch three stout men to go with Mr. Benjamin Franklin!"

Shortly a large carriage, like a traveling coach, was drawn up in front, which we mounted, all five: Mr. Croft, Mr. Brattle, and Mr. Noone, sturdy, big fellows, and Mr. Franklin and I. These gentlemen wore no uniforms but plain workmen's clothes. "The better to pass among men unnoticed as agents of the law," Mr. Franklin murmured softly. We set out, springs creaking. Two strong horses drew us, and in less than a quarter of an hour we neared Berkeley Square, where dawn light was just pushing back the night, setting off the sharp outlines of Jared Hexham's looming house.

I shivered at sight of this edifice, which had once been my home. Here a sly, conniving woman had poisoned my mother; further, this same heartless woman had meant to kill me too. I pictured Prudence Hexham—slitted eyes in a pinched, crabapple face—devilish! Her vicious jealousy had killed my mother.

As we got down I thanked God I was no Hexham.

Immediately our feet touched the cobbles it became plain that something was amiss. A woman's cries rang from the house, from some upper window, slicing across the morning, shrieks of despair that sent goosebumps up my spine: "O, no . . . O, no, no, no . . . !"

Mr. Fielding's men were quick. Scrambling to the broad white door, they pounded hard, shouting. A manservant in half-buttoned livery opened. To their brusque queries he quavered, "I know not . . . the mistress . . . upstairs," and with an expression of confusion and dread he pointed a trembling finger into unlit shadows.

Brushing past, the men thudded up the curving stairs, Mr. Franklin and I close on their heels.

We were brought short at the door of Jared Hexham's study, where a new horror greeted my eyes. Mrs. Hexham was there, huddled on her knees beside her husband's body, shrieking and swaying and flailing her arms. As for the merchant, who had made such threats, who had climbed towards his goal over human lives, he lay on his back by his big desk, staring with eyes as sightless as John Fielding's—but not from blindness.

An ebon-handled knife protruded from his chest, and his scalp was gone, his skull hairless and bloody, while Mrs. Hexham's laments shook the very walls.

I buried my face in Mr. Franklin's side.

I awoke next day to sunlight and birdsong, sparrows fluttered outside my bedroom window. Slipping from the covers, I peered into the back yard. Crooning his dirge, King was crouched over turnip rows gently turning earth, and I silently thanked him for watching Jared Hexham's house so well. To the right, past some dozen other back gardens, barges plied the Thames as if this day were no different from any other. The slant of light told me noon had come and gone.

Dressing quickly, I stepped into the hall. With much fussing Mrs. Stevenson had seen me to bed at six this morning. Thus I had had no chance to hear Mr. Franklin's explanations. Indeed he had looked much done in after the dreadful scene in Hexham's study and with excessive wheezing and sniffling had himself hurried to bed, though not before affectionate assurances that tomorrow should answer all questions.

Aching still from bruises and long hours trussed, I came to the gentleman's door. He was awake, for from his room violin music flowed, as it had that morning, which seemed so long ago, when, bewildered but hopeful, I first woke in this loving house. Stirred by the sweet tune, I remembered that hour: the bustle of Mrs. Stevenson, which I heard again below; Mr. Franklin taking his air bath; my first curious glance round his room at the feather bed, the high desk, the comfortable chair by the fire, and on his dresser the little paintings of his daughter and his long-dead son, Francis.

And I too was Mr. Franklin's son?

I knocked. The gentleman briskly called to enter, and I found him standing in his maroon dressing gown by the front window, violin in hand. Turning, he cocked a brow. "Time, Nick? For all to be made clear?"

"I pray so, sir," said I.

He sneezed, loudly.

"O, sir, take your ease in bed."

With a wheezing laugh he set aside his violin. "A boy after Mrs. Stevenson's heart!" Waving a handkerchief like a flag, he thumped in bare feet to the bedside. "She should be happy if I were her constant invalid, to coddle with brews and poultices." He blew his nose. "Well, I shall never satisfy her in that. Come, Nick, sit you down." He gestured at his chair. "I shall slip under the covers, so that if our good landlady should discover us she may have no cause to chide."

Settling himself against fat pillows, the gentleman drew the white coverlet to his waist. I sat in the chair by the grate, where coals softly glowed. The dying fire told that he had been up some time. Setting his thoughts in order?

The warm, yeasty smell of baking bread crept under the closed door.

"Now, Nick . . . my son," added he, "—for so you are, I believe, though I cannot prove it to a surety—you must be told a history. You may find me blameful in some of it. If so I beg forgiveness, though I have never forgiven myself. It began long ago, when first I came to England. That part you know: my employment at Watts' Printing, with Eben Inch and Gerrold Bixer, whom I shall hereafter call Hexham; how I helped Eben work free

217

of Hexham's coils; how I returned to America; and how not long after that Hexham came there too, to 'scape prosecution in crimes devised by the man we know as Quimp. In America he rose by crooked ways to money and position, along the way taking a wife and fathering two children. Two only, I say, Nicolas: Bertram and Lydia.

"That is Jared Hexham's story. Mine is far different, one of honest diligence and hard work, both in business and public affairs, wherein I prospered. I too took a wife, my guileless Deborah, and with her steady help made a success in printing. Along the way I helped to found a library, a fire company, and a college, and became clerk of the Pennsylvania Assembly and postmaster of Philadelphia. At the age of forty-two I retired to study Nature, but public affairs would not let me be, concluding in my being chosen agent for Pennsylvania on these shores.

"I thank God I was called to London.

"Now I must tell you that of which I am ashamed. In my prosperity I was sometimes in a place to help other men. Such a one was Arthur Handy. Older than I, he had fallen on hard times through no fault of his own. He had a wife and six children. Further, he was an excellent printer. So, wishing to help him and his family, never doubting my investment should prove a sound one, I loaned him money to establish himself in Boston."

"Sir, there is no shame in this," said I.

"Yet in what follows . . ." the gentleman's features showed pain at his remembrances, "—for you see, Nick, in those days before the Handys left Philadelphia for Boston I was much in the company of Arthur's eldest daughter, Rose. He used sometimes to send her to purchase some small items at our shop, but she took to visiting it of her own accord, oftener and oftener, with some small excuse or other, usually that she wished to browse the books we sold or to borrow some volume of mine. Yet her eye followed me. We talked often of books, and I found her as intelligent as any man, with a lively mind that saw deep into the heart of matters. She was twenty, I thirty-seven. There came a spring eve when my soul felt a pang that she had not come that day, and I saw how it was with me. O, she was pretty, with blooms in her cheeks and

218

sweet-smelling auburn hair and a way about her that was earnest and straightforward and captivating! She provoked my mind, she engaged my heart!

"In short, I was in love.

"But, what of my wife, Deborah? I never wished her harm. Truly to this day I feel for her an unremitting affection. She has been devoted to me from the first—but she has no mind for anything save household matters. Why did I marry her? Because at a certain stage in life a man wants a wife. I chose a good, steady companion, no doubt of it—yet I could never speak to Deborah of ideas.

"Imagine, Nick, my joy at discovering a woman to whom I could speak my mind, fully, and who understood and was as eager to know the world as I. I was smitten; I felt the girl was too.

"Yet all remained chaste between us. I had no intention ever of touching her. Soon she would go with her family to Boston; all would be finished between us, save for some exchange of letters. Then one day I would hear that she had wed.

"Yet our passion, our love, overcame us."

Mr. Franklin's brown eyes found me. "You, Nicolas, are the issue."

The bustle of Craven Street sounded through the front window. I sat on the edge of my chair.

The gentleman adjusted his little glasses on his nose. "At first I knew nothing of the result of our indiscretion," continued he softly. "She went with her family to Boston, where Arthur Handy had bought an old fellow's print shop."

"Then some three months later I received a letter from Rose declaring that she would shortly set sail for London.

"There were no reasons why. This and the sorrowful tone of her words alarmed me, and under some pretext of visiting my brother in Boston I took coach to the town of my birth. The roads were muddy from heavy summer storms; the journey took five days.

"When I arrived my dear Rose had gone.

"Arthur Handy told me the truth of it. 'O, the shame,' lamented he—his daughter had got in the family way. Who was the man? She would not say.

"Yet Arthur had no suspicion of me; his blind trust made me chide myself all the more. He had hopes for Rose's fortunes, he said. A wealthy merchant, a Mr. Hexham, was just removing with his family to England and, knowing of Rose's condition, had volunteered to take her with him. Hexham knew a generous gentleman in London who looked for just such a wife; her being with child would make no matter. This story of a gentleman who would take a wife without first meeting her sounded a lie, Nick, but I did not say so to poor Arthur, who, ever trusting, and finding himself in difficult straits, clearly wished to believe his daughter saved. Who was this merchant, Hexham, of whom I knew nothing? Inquiring about town, I soon learned disquieting news: he was disliked, a thoroughly unprincipled rascal, yet clever enough to make a fortune.

"What could I do? Confess to the father? That would accomplish nothing. All that remained was to return to Philadelphia, brood upon my error, and pray dear Rose would fare well.

"This I did. The year fled to winter. I wrote to Arthur Handy often, always asking of news of his daughter. She had not married after all, he said in some discouragement. She had been delivered of a son. She lived in the Hexham household in London. Was she happy? I knew not. I did not attempt to write England for fear of wounding the girl I had wronged. Always I cursed myself for lack of forebearance!

"Three years passed. Then one day came news from Arthur that his dear daughter had died. It was a staggering blow. How? Why? A slow wasting away, he said—the cause of which we now know: Prudence Hexham's envy. Here we must speculate. Attracted by the girl, hoping to take advantage of her vulnerable state, Hexham had lied both to Arthur Handy and to his own wife, telling her he had got Rose with child as an excuse to carry her off. A selfish, unprincipled streak runs in the family, Nicolas. Once the girl was in his house, far from her family and dependent on him, he sought to have his way with her; but—we have Prudence Hexham's testimony to it—he never succeeded. Your mother raised you well, Nick, loving you, teaching you to read, protecting you from the spite that must have raged about that house."

"At last she died, and Jared Hexham sent you to Dora Inch."

"But, why should Mrs. Inch agree to take me?"

"Because there was profit to be made, from me."

"You, sir?"

Mr. Franklin's feet stirred beneath the bedclothes. "In 1748 I received a letter from Mrs. Agnes Foote of Fenchurch Street saying she had the care of Rose Handy's son. She understood that, though Miss Handy had never married, I was the father, and asked: did I wish to pay for my son's good upbringing? A great weight was lifted from my heart! She sounded a kind, sensible woman; all should be managed discreetly. I agreed at once, and from that time until only months ago I sent quarter-yearly stipends—generous sums, nothing too good for my son—to the address she gave, receiving from her in turn reports on Nicolas Handy's progress: well-fed, well-clothed, well-schooled, cheerful."

"The ledgers in Mrs. Inch's storeroom!" exclaimed I.

"Aye, Nick. Agnes Foote was Dora Inch. The address in Fenchurch Street belonged only to a conniving friend, who denied any knowledge of Agnes Foote and Nicolas Handy when, hoping to see my son, I applied to her shortly after arriving on these shores. Those ledgers recorded my payments to her."

With burning cheeks I recalled the letter I had chanced to read, signed "Agnes Foote." I had assumed it referred to William Franklin; now I saw it spoke of me, clever lies to lead Mr. Franklin on. I was stirred to know he had kept the letters nine years, even carrying them to England, yet I was still puzzled.

"How did Mrs. Inch discover you were my father?" asked I.

"In his letter informing Arthur of his daughter's death, Jared Hexham said he would keep care of her son. I mistrusted this and wrote to him under pretext of a friend of the family, inquiring about the boy. Hexham must have learned my name from Rose. We may guess the rest: he saw through my pretext at once. I was no mere family friend, but Nicolas Handy's true father, deeply concerned for his son's welfare. Hexham owed Dora Inch much; besides, he knew by then that she possessed damning evidence against him. So, as a sop, he tossed you to her to be used to milk me. O, she readily agreed!—a boy of work, who would be her slave, and fine profit to boot! As for Hexham, a chance to get back at Benjamin Franklin, who had crossed him long ago, had fallen in his lap; he snatched it eagerly.

"Neither ever dreamed I should come to England, nor that my doing so would endanger their plans.

"But I did arrive and applied at once to Fenchurch Street, where I was rudely turned away. Much shaken, at wit's end, I contemplated inquiring of the merchant Hexham (whom I did not yet know was Gerrold Bixer)—when came that note from Eben, which I showed you, Nick, and which drew me to Fish Lane the very morning your master died."

"You, then, were the reason Mrs. Inch wished to murder me?" asked I.

He nodded grimly. "Her friend in Fenchurch Street had told her I was arrived and nosing about. If I discovered her wickedness I might call her before a magistrate. This would at the very least besmirch her reputation; it might result in prison. Tilda could never marry well. Then she learned her husband meant to apply to me. It is my belief that Eben knew from some slip of his wife's tongue that I was your father, though we may never be certain of that. At any rate he wrote to the old friend who had once saved him, knowing I should come. This set Dora Inch in a panic. Her remedy?—Jared Hexham's Indian, corrupted by drink. But the brave spilt the wrong blood, with results we know."

The coals had crumbled to ash in the grate. Questions crowded one another in my mind. "Sir," said I, "did you know from the first that I was your son?"

"I suspected. Something about you, lad, the moment I saw you . . . I cannot say what . . . but I was moved. A resemblance to your dear mother perhaps, for you have her lineaments. And then, when I heard your name . . . that is why I inquired so closely into how you came by it. I could not leave my son at Inch,

222

Printer, so I returned that night determined you should depart under my protection."

"And when did you know for certain?"

"When I saw the silhouette you carry about your neck. I carry it too, Nick—her brow, her nose, her sweet mouth—engraved upon my heart."

Tears filled my eyes.

"I knew then that you must be my boy," said Mr. Franklin, leaning forward, with half-held-out arms. "Can you forgive me?"

"I, forgive you? For what, sir?" cried I. "For loving my mother? For doing all in your power for your son?"

Rushing to him, I flung myself against his breast.

"So you *shall* remain with us, Nicolas," cooed Mrs. Stevenson at breakfast some days later, when my bruises (which Mr. Franklin and I ascribed to a rough encounter with some street ruffians) had begun to fade. "I am very happy to hear it." She turned her kindly gaze upon the gentleman. "But was there ever any doubt?"

"Tut, there may have lain some small hurdles in our path," said he airily, "but we have o'erleapt them."

"By means of mysterious traveling about at all hours?" inquired Polly with a glint in her eye.

Mr. Franklin blinked. "'Mysterious,' child? I do not catch your drift. You know I have much business in London."

Polly only said, "Hmm."

Silently I ate my porridge. I understood now why Mr. Franklin had kept much of our particular business secret; further, why he had appeared reluctant to talk of my history with William. We had discussed the issue, I readily—and with no regret—agreeing that I should not publicly be acknowledged the gentleman's son. There was no doubt in his mind, or mine, that I was—but neither he nor I had any wish to injure his wife's feelings, or those of his daughter or William. "Yet you shall have every attention of a father, Nick," assured he with his honest, deep gaze. "You have Ben Franklin's true word on it."

I heartily believed him.

By that morning, cozy within but blustering outside, much else had been resolved. Mrs. Hexham was clapped into Newgate Prison for the murder of my mother and Dora Inch. Her daughter Lydia was with her, for her part in Mrs. Inch's stabbing. It was a gloomy path they now trod. At Fish Lane I had heard much of Newgate, Mrs. Inch often terrorizing me with threats of plunging me into one of its rat-infested cells if I was wicked. I shuddered to picture the Hexham women in such a hole, Mrs. Hexham spitting and cursing fate while her daughter perched on a dirty straw pallet as prim as you please, as if some lord must come to rescue her. Yet there was little chance they would 'scape hanging.

Did remorse stir these women's hearts? I did not think so. As for Bertie Hexham—he being innocent of any crime save cruel bullying, which might not be prosecuted—he roamed free, but unhappily, for he was stripped of all means. The whole of the Hexham lands and property had been impounded, pending investigation into the origin of the moneys which had bought 'em, which seemed pretty clear to prove thievery. Mr. Franklin informed me that the young man could now be seen wandering like a ghost about Pall Mall, ragged of collar and dingy of cuff, his once-gleaming boots quite dull, begging loans of former friends who would not vouchsafe him twopence.

"I believe I shall set him up in America," pronounced the gentleman. "He is a coxcomb, yet I pity him. One ought never to allow a human soul to go to waste—or two strong arms. He should do well clearing lands in some backwoods forest, and I am certain I can find him passage, which he may work off in four or five years." Mr. Franklin smiled at this. "I shall surely see to't!"

Jared Hexham was buried. As for his murderer—or murderers, "The Indian woman, sir?" I had asked in a trembling voice as we rode away from the cursed Hexham house for the last time.

"So it must be, and so I shall tell Mr. Fielding," Mr. Franklin had replied gloomily, "though I do not wish to do it. Yet the law must know all." He sighed. "When at Lord Bottom's I informed the Indian woman of her son's fate, I said I felt sure it had been no accident. Was that error, Nick? I saw a dark flame leap in her eye;

a tremor shook her. I named no names—I could not—but clearly she drew conclusion that it must be Jared Hexham who had killed her son. It was the last straw for her, and so she laid plans and carried them out." The gentleman grew pale. "Did I suspect what she planned? Did I half hope . . .? O, Nick, at times I may be as wicked as any man!"

We were both unhappy to think of this bereaved woman imprisoned—but that did not come to be, for when Mr. Fielding's men applied at Lord Bottom's they found her gone.

Her daughter too had vanished from the *Folly*.

"They are together, Nick, somewhere, making their way," said Mr. Franklin. "I fear for 'em—yet they took their revenge, they righted the balance." He stared off as was his wont, with wrinkled brow and thoughtful eyes. "Think of it: two mothers and two daughters with hands steeped in blood . . ."

As for Lord Bottom, he was so overjoyed to know his daughter was free that he regaled Mr. Franklin at a fine dinner, to which I too was invited, being placed next the pretty Miss Bottom, who treated me so civilly my cheeks burned red.

Tilda Inch had gone as planned to her aunt, Martha Clay, in Bradford Street. Visiting there, we observed Miss Inch prick her finger seven times at sewing. We heard her wail too, often, but Mrs. Clay was patient, and I believed if anyone could tame the girl's spoiled nature it was she, who applied equal measures of strictness and love. Indeed Mrs. Clay already looked upon her niece as her daughter.

A baby was on its way. Their circumstances would be much alleviated by the selling of Inch, Printer, shop and goods, all profits going to Mrs. Clay as Tilda's guardian and Eben Inch's sister.

As for Mrs. Inch's papers and ledgers in her storeroom and the wicked books we had set and printed, they were offered by Mrs. Clay to the Fish Lane neighbors as fodder for their fires.

In twenty minutes they were gone and in days up in smoke, proving some good after all, to warm men's bones.

Buck Duffin had disappeared, no doubt fearing Mr. Fielding's strong arm, Newgate, and Tyburn Tree. Where had he gone?

"He is a sturdy young lad," said Mr. Franklin, "—foolish, but not stupid. He too will make his way."

Some questions remained, for one: who had bent the bell at Inch, Printer?

"It was Tilda, lad, surely," surmised Mr. Franklin, "—it being only she who left and entered by the front way on her secret visits to Bertie Hexham."

"And how did the Indian girl recognize me on board the *Folly*?"

"No doubt her brother described you to her when he confided what Mrs. Inch had hired him to do."

A more disturbing question was Quimp, about whom I still had nightmares. He had sent threats, which Mr. Franklin had ignored. Were we thus in danger? Truth to tell, we had a dire hint of him the very day after Jared Hexham was murdered, Mr. Joshua Brogden arriving hat in hand at Craven Street to inform Mr. Franklin that Mr. Fielding's men had hurried to Jared Hexham's dockside warehouse to retrieve the stolen goods which Mr. Franklin said might be found in the hidden room.

"But we came upon the building in flames, sir; it burnt right to the ground. Further, we discovered no jewels or melted gold amongst the ashes." Mr. Brogden twisted his hat awkwardly. "Mr. Fielding said you would understand the significance of this."

Mr. Franklin gazed somberly. "Quimp," pronounced he.

Yet this was not all. A fortnight after this disturbing news, as Mr. Franklin and I were departing Bibb's in Bond Street near St. George's, where the gentleman was buying me a second pair of boots, a bent old woman jostled him in the road.

"O, I beg pardon," said he.

From under the dirty hood of her long brown cloak the woman twisted her sallow face up to him. She had a long, beaked nose. Her yellowish eyes glittered. "Mr. Franklin, is't?" said she in a deep, rasping voice, smiling. "Well, sir, you did for Jared Hexham nicely, and I can admire a clever fellow, though I cannot like him. You have caused me some small pains, yet in the main I thank you. Hexham was a fool, and I am well rid of him, though I shall miss his shrewd wife." The voice hardened. "Yet do not cross me again, sir, or you shall have great cause for regret." She peered at him a moment longer before stepping into the street. A shabby black coach appeared as if from nowhere, hiding her from view. When it had passed, she was gone as if taken by the wind.

I trembled from toe to crown. Mr. Franklin's eye met mine. Neither of us had need to pronounce the name of him who had accosted us in new disguise.

I continued to act as Mr. Franklin's secretary, keeping careful records in my ledgers, from which this account has been drawn—and from which there are many further stories to be told. Of these I may say now that it was not the last we heard of Quimp.

Mr. Franklin kindly presented me with a new set of *Tom Jones*, the volume which Buck had torn to shreds having proved irreparable. This was the first of many gifts of books.

At last Mr. Franklin's distemper ended, and he resumed his air baths and his pursuit of justice for Philadelphia.

Then one raw November day, 1757, he caused me to bundle up warmly, and we again took coach with the faithful Peter as our steersman. I sensed some strong emotion about the gentleman; tight-lipped, he seemed reluctant to speak of our destination.

In an hour we arrived at a small churchyard in Finsbury, north of Moorfields, with misty countryside and a few cottages visible in the distance, and the clanking of cowbells. Windmill arms creaked. A chill wind whispered amongst long grass and time-worn gravestones.

Mr. Franklin led me to a small mound marked only by a rude wooden cross. "Your mother's grave, lad," said he. "I was at some pains to discover it, but a servant of the Hexhams knew where they buried her, hoping she might be forgot. I have ordered a stone made, to dignify her final rest." He placed his arm about my shoulders and we stood there long, the wind moving about us.

Often since then have I brought flowers to this spot—but no visit meant more than the first, when, standing next the best and wisest man I have known, I felt at last that I was home.